BADASS

Book One in the Bombshell Series

CARLA R.

CONTENTS

Chapter 1	1
Chapter 2	6
Chapter 3	12
Chapter 4	17
Chapter 5	20
Chapter 6	27
Chapter 7	35
Chapter 8	46
Chapter 9	56
Chapter 10	67
Chapter 11	72
Chapter 12	83
Chapter 13	89
Chapter 14	94
Chapter 15	107
Chapter 16	115
Chapter 17	122
Chapter 18	128
Chapter 19	137
Chapter 20	150
Chapter 21	159
Chapter 22	168
Chapter 23	182
Chapter 24	195
Chapter 25	207
Chapter 26	216
Chapter 27	226
Chapter 28	239
Chapter 29	248
Chapter 30	257
Acknowledgments	269
About the Author	271

CHAPTER ONE

March

Molly

*S*tomping down the sidewalk toward the end of the block where I parked my car, I pull my phone out of my purse and call my best friend Sammy.

"Yo, Batch! How was your date? I'm assuming it didn't go well since you're calling me at 8:58," she answers — using our standard greeting. It became a thing on a drunken evening out in our early twenties.

"Yeah, you could say that. Remember the pic of the bearded hottie I sent you yesterday? We decided to meet at McMurphy's." I don't wait for her to answer. I just keep ranting. "Well, that must've been an old picture because he certainly didn't look like *that* anymore." His profile picture on the dating website I found him on had shown a fit, well groomed, late twenty-something man straddling a motorcycle. "First off, he was about twenty-five minutes late. Or, at least, I *thought* he was late. I got there and asked if anyone was waiting for me. No big deal that I got there first. I sat down, ordered a Woodchuck and people watched. I texted him after eight o' clock came and went. It took him a while to text back. And when he did, he said he'd be there in a minute." I pause to unlock my car and slide in.

"So, I'm watching the people at the pub and realize that this older guy, who had been standing at the bar when I came in, was walking toward me. It took me a minute to realize it was him. He's obviously using an old picture on his profile and lying about his age. I asked him how old he was — his profile said 30 — he's actually 47! He's put on a good 120 pounds too, I'd say. You know I don't have a problem with heavier guys. I mean Hank was a big guy." I cringe mentioning my ex's name.

"So, he admitted he was older? Did he think you wouldn't notice? He had a six pack in that picture!" she whisper shouts into the phone. I have to assume she's trying to be quiet because her 2-year-old twins are sleeping.

"I don't know *what* he was thinking, to be honest. Anyway, he sat down, and his beard was not well kept at all. I noticed he had something in it, and I mentioned it to him. I shit you not, Sammy, he pulled out about half of a french fry, sniffed it, then popped it into his mouth!" I hear Sammy making gagging noises on the other end of the line.

"OMG!!!! That is disgusting." I hear her repeating what I just told her to her husband Jared. "Jared said, 'At least it's not as bad as Sir Farts-a-Lot.'"

Sir Farts-a-Lot was a guy named Greg I went out on about a quarter of a date with a month ago. He picked me up at work in an Uber and proceeded to fart loud and long. He thought it was hilarious and kept trying to blame the driver for it — like I couldn't feel it vibrating the seat. It stunk so badly, and when I tried to roll down the window for some air, I realized the window was locked. The driver said it was a fairly new car, and he couldn't find the button to unlock it. We were gagging by the time he found it. When we pulled up to the restaurant, I jumped out as fast as I could. My date didn't see the issue and proceeded to laugh like it was the funniest thing ever. He told me I didn't have a sense of humor and I needed to pull the stick out of my ass. I told him that he should probably see a gastroenterologist because that was not normal. Then I took another Uber back to the salon and picked up take out on my way home.

"I don't know if it was as bad as Sir Farts-a-Lot smelled, but I'm definitely not done. In hindsight, I should have left then, but while I was waiting for him to text back, I had ordered the corned beef nachos." Those nachos are my all-time favorite food, and I go to McMurphy's often. Mmmmmmm. Nachos. "So I was going to ask Sasha to just bag it up, but while I was trying to get her attention, he started badgering me to take a shot with him. I told him I was good; I already drank a cider. I finally signaled to Sasha to the table and asked her to get it to go. Mr. Frybeard stopped her and said he wants two Redheaded Slut shots. Then he looked at me and waggled his eyebrows."

"What the actual fuck?!" she whispers into the phone. "What a fucking asshole!" she then shouts. I hear a "Shhhhhhh!" in the background from Jared. "You, shhhhh." she says back at him. "What did you do?"

"I excused myself to the bathroom! Then I met Sasha at the bar, where she gave me the nachos. I told her to put my nachos on his tab, and she helped me sneak out. Now I'm going home to eat my nachos and watch This is Us, since I DVR'd it to meet Mr. Frybeard tonight."

"Mr Frybeard," she chuckles, "that's perfect!" This is something we do. We nickname the guys we date, or I date, since she's a married woman now. Most of the names are descriptive of something that happened during the date or their appearance. There was "Mustachio" — a hipster guy with a handlebar mustache — who whipped out a tiny comb to comb his handlebar mustache while we were having coffee. Not just once, but for the entire two hours we were together, he sat there combing his mustache. I also dated a guy we dubbed "Dick Pic". He seemed like a really nice guy. We went on two very nice dates and shared one sweet kiss at the end of date number two. The day after date number two? I received a dick pic. I assumed he sent it by mistake, which made me think maybe it was supposed to go to someone else. I called him to ask what the fuck, and he said he wanted to show me what I'd be getting on date number three. He was a firm believer in third date sex. I told him there would be no third date and to lose my number ASAP thank-you-very-much.

"I gotta go, Molls. Jared is giving me baby making eyes." I think she's crazy to be ready for another baby so soon. Her twins keep her so busy. They are the most awesome kids ever and they love their "Aunt Moll-wee." Somehow, they are the sweetest little angels, and at the same time, tiny terrorists.

"Ok my love, go make more nieces and nephews for me. Talk to you tomorrow."

I'm so happy for Sammy, but also so jealous at the same time. I thought I had what she has with Jared. I ended things with my ex-boyfriend, Hank, about a year ago. We had been living together for about two years and dating for two years before that. I thought we were on the same page. I was ready to get married and have kids. We were renting an apartment that was having lots of issues, and I was ready to start looking for a home to buy.

I came home early one day to meet the maintenance guy and show him what problems we were having. Instead I found

Hank with another woman in my bed. Lots of thoughts ran through my mind — most of them included busting in there and throwing shit. Somehow, I found it in myself to remain calm. I took a nice little video of them instead. You couldn't see anything too revealing, but you could tell it was Hank, and you could definitely tell it wasn't me. She was platinum blonde, and I'm a natural redhead. I left the apartment and met the maintenance guy downstairs and informed him that Hank was upstairs and could show him the issues. Then I texted the video to Hank, telling him we were over, and posted it to his social media pages — making sure to tag him in it. Apparently, he didn't see the text or the video since the maintenance guy showed up. I feel a little bad because his mom was the first person to see it and called him to find out what was going on. I loved his mom (even if she was overbearing and always told me not to be so sassy). I have since apologized for making her see that. For a while after we split up, she called me frequently and ask me to take him back. She said she didn't understand why we couldn't work it out and why I couldn't forgive him. She literally said, "The other girl was for fun, but you are forever." I stopped taking her calls after that.

If there's one thing I've learned over the past eight months or so of dating, it's that I am a bad date magnet. It doesn't matter where I meet these guys: online, blind dates, in the produce department of my local supermarket — all these dates turn out bad. It's getting pretty discouraging, but I keep trying because I believe in love. And I plan on finding it even if it kills me.

CHAPTER TWO

Molly

The alarm goes off early the next morning, but I have a busy day ahead at the salon. I'm part owner in a co-op salon and spa called Bombshells. We have five hairstylists, two estheticians, one massage therapist, and two nail techs. We've been open for almost three years now and its hard work, but I love it. There are four of us that own the business, and we each cover our own area of expertise. I'm the hair salon manager, Sammy runs the nail area, Anna runs the estheticians, and Emily is our massage therapist.

Sammy and I have been best friends for more than twenty years and we went to cosmetology school together. She gravitated toward nails and I toward hair. She can do hair, and she has a small list of loyal clients that come to her for cuts and color, but she prefers and primarily does nails. I, on the other hand, do not do nails. It ain't pretty to see what kind of mess I can make with acrylic and polish.

Sammy and I met Anna at a salon we worked at straight out of school. She's amazing with skin and makeup. When

Sammy and I decided we wanted to open our own full-service salon and spa, we called Anna to see if she was interested in working with us. She said her sister Emily had just moved back to the area and would be interested as well. I love our salon and our employees. It's like hanging out with your best friends all day.

Since this weekend is St. Patrick's Day and Rockplaines has a big Irish community, we're running a special for putting green streaks in hair. There's a big parade on Saturday morning; and on Saturday night, McMurphy's is hosting a Miss Shamrock pageant. I've avoided entering it for years, but the girls at the salon talked me into it using the excuse that it would be great advertisement for the salon. Besides, they promised to help me with my talent. How can I argue with that?

I drag myself out of bed and head into the bathroom to take a quick shower. Once done, I style my hair in loose curls and wear my regular daily makeup. I pull out my favorite black skinny leg pants and a green v-neck sweater. Tan low-heeled boots and my black pea coat finish the look. I drive to the salon and park down the street. I've got about forty-five minutes before we open, just enough time to stop for coffee and a muffin at Common Grounds. It's an awesome coffee shop and bakery next door. I love their blueberry muffins. When I get to the door, it swings open, and I see a couple of guys from the local firehouse coming out. Jared, Sammy's husband, holds the door open for me and gives me a one-armed hug. "Sorry about your date last night," he says smirking.

"Ugh, don't remind me." I say as I roll my eyes. "You guys coming to McMurphy's on Saturday night? I could really use your yells." They let the crowd judge the competition by loudest cheers. I'm going to be singing. I have a decent voice. I'm not going to win American Idol, but I can carry a tune, and I could really, really use the cheers.

"Me and Sammy will be there, of course. Some of these guys have to work, but I know some of the other guys will be there. I already told them they have to cheer for you," Jared glares at the other guys. A couple of the guys say they'll be there, and two of them promise to call the salon today to get a haircut appointment.

Heading in to the coffee shop, I order a large caramel iced coffee and a blueberry muffin. I shove a large bite of muffin into my mouth, and I'm looking at my text messages when I feel a tap on my shoulder.

"Hey Molly, how ya been?" It's John Palmer, one of the local police officers and we went to high school together.

I hate when people ask me questions when I've got food in my mouth. I hold up one finger while I try to quickly swallow the bite. "Hey, John. I'm doing well. Just grabbing coffee before I start my day at work."

John used to come in for haircuts, but right after Hank and I broke up, he asked me out. I wasn't quite ready to date then, and I declined. I haven't seen him around much since, and then he stopped coming into the shop all together. He's a nice-looking guy, but I'm really just not interested in him that way.

He nods, "How's business been?"

"We're doing really well, actually. You should come in and get a cut soon," I say. The barista calls my name, and I grab my coffee.

"I just might," John says with a smile.

"I gotta get to work. I'll see you later," I head out of the coffee shop with a wave.

When I get to the salon to unlock the door, Gracie, our

receptionist follows me in. "Good morning, Boss Lady! How was your date?"

I immediately hear a snort. "Yeah, ask her about Grandpa Frybeard, " Sammy says snorting uncontrollably as she walks in the door.

"Grandpa Frybeard?!" Gracie asks, confused. "You dating old guys now?"

"His name was actually Mike. He wasn't *that* old, but he was older than his profile claimed. He was late for our date because he was drinking at the bar and when he sat down, I noticed he had something in his beard. It was a french fry that he proceeded to sniff — and then eat. I bailed fairly quickly after that." I rattle off quickly to Gracie's horrified face. "Please don't make me repeat this all day long."

"It could have been worse. Remember the guy that kept calling you his little kitten and wanted you to pretend to be a kitty?" Gracie says with a shudder.

"Meow Mix! Hey, I looked that up after the fact, and just because I didn't want to play kitty with him, doesn't mean I wouldn't play kitty with the right guy. If Jason Momoa walked in right now, I'd crawl on my knees and meow for him, tail and all." I laugh and turn around to see possibly the sexiest guy I've ever seen in my life standing there with a curious smirk on his handsome face. I open my mouth to say something. Anything. I stutter out a, "hi," and feel my cheeks flame.

"Are you guys open yet? Some of the guys down at the station said you could probably fit me in this morning." the hot man says.

Sammy leans over and whispers, "That's what she said." I close my eyes to try and contain myself.

When I open my eyes, I lock onto his blue, blue eyes. They're so blue that it makes me want to sing Blue like LeeAnn Rhimes. Dark, long-as-fuck lashes frame his gorgeous blue eyes. He's got a short, shaped beard on his face and a smile that will haunt my daydreams for the rest of my life. I pull myself together and speak, "Gracie should be able to tell you if anyone is available. I have to run to the back. I'll be back in a moment." I turn and hightail it to the office feeling Sammy hot on my heels.

"Holy fuckballs! That is one good looking man," she whistles while fanning herself.

For some reason, a spark of jealousy hits me, and I'm angry that she even noticed he's attractive. I clinch my teeth while I hang up my coat and purse. Sammy knows me too well to be able to play it off like I didn't practically swallow my tongue looking at him. "I am so fucking embarrassed that I said that in front of him. He said station. Does he work with Jared?"

"Jared said they hired two new guys, Brenden and Tyler, I think. I have no idea which one he is. I think I'll just refer to him as Blue Eyes." That ping of jealousy hits me again, and I frown. "Ooooooh, I fucking know *that* look. It's the same one you got when Kevin Green asked me to the Valentine's dance in 8th grade instead of you. Have you forgotten I'm married with children, Batch?!"

"You fucking Batch. I knew you would bring that up. And if I remember correctly, you got the same look when Brock James asked *me* to see the Scream marathon at the drive-in senior year—" I throw back at her. Neither of us went out with these guys. We had a strict rule for our friendship. No dating guys that the other of us had a crush on. If one of us did want to break that rule, we had to have a serious discussion about it. We have never had that discussion because, as Leslie Knope says, we were always Hos before Bros, Uteruses before Duderuses, Ovaries before Broveries.

Gracie pops her head in the doorway. "Sorry to interrupt! That guy needs a cut. Kelli has Mrs. Lonstein coming in about ten minutes, and Jessica and Caitlyn aren't in until one today. Can you fit him in, Molly?"

"Yeah, Molls, can you fit him in?" Sammy gives me a shit eating grin and waggles her eyebrows at me.

"Don't you have work to do?" I shoot a glare at Sammy. "Yes, Gracie, I'll get him. Tell him I'll be right up." She turns to head out the door and I remember to ask, "Gracie," I whisper shout, "what's his name?"

"Brenden......Brenden Clarke, I think he said. But I think I'll call him Blue Eyes," she says dreamily as she heads out of the office.

"You little shit." I whisper under my breath.

"You better get out there and meet your future husband." Sammy says, giving me her smartass smile.

"Fuck off." I mutter as I head down the hall to the main salon.

CHAPTER THREE

Molly

I quickly walk to my station and get my stuff set up. Really, I should have done this when I got in instead of hiding in the back. I give myself a once over and smear on some Dr. Pepper flavored lip gloss before I walk to the front to greet him.

"Brenden?" I say. He's looking at his phone, but he looks up

He moves his gaze over me slowly. I feel very exposed, though I'm fully dressed. I'm pretty confident in my appearance most days, but the way he's looking at me makes me feel like I'm trapped in that dream where you're naked at school and can't find anywhere to hide.

"Yeah," he says as he stands. I think I can see a tinge of pink on his cheeks like he knows I caught him checking me out.

"I'm Molly, I'll be taking care of you today," I say as I reach out my hand. When I feel his massive hand wrap around mine, I think about what it might feel like to feel one on each of my ass cheeks. Wowzah! Calm yourself, Molly, before you climb into his lap at your chair. I clear my throat and drop his hand. "Follow me," I catch Sammy's smirk, and it takes everything I've got not to flip her the bird as I walk by.

"So, what are we doing today?" I ask as I run my fingers through his hair.

"Mostly I just need the back and sides cleaned up. Can you fade me up from a zero?" he asks.

"Sure can. Do you want anything off the top?" I ask as I keep running my fingers through his hair.

I look up at him in the mirror and see those blue eyes staring back at me. "You can take off whatever you think I need cut. I like a little length up there, the guys said you do a nice job, so I trust you."

I smile at him in the mirror and then pull the drawer open where I keep my clippers and get to work. We chat a little about how long I've been doing hair and how long he's been a fireman. I fade him up, and when I get to the top, I like the way it looks long with the short sides.

I'm just starting to dust the ends when Emily walks up and says, "Sammy texted this morning and told me to ask you about your date with Grandpa Frybeard? I can't wait to hear about this one. Does this one measure up to the Italian Job?" My eyes bug out at her and I nod my head in Brenden's direction, as if to say, not in front of the client. "We'll talk later," she whispers, seeming properly chastised as she makes her way down the hall to her massage room.

"Grandpa Frybeard? Italian Job? I feel like I need some explanation," he flashes me that curious smirk again.

I smile awkwardly, "Yeah, I definitely don't know you well

enough to tell you about my awful string of terrible and embarrassing dates. How's that length on top?" I say trying to change the subject.

"Looks good," he says running his fingers through it and turning his head side to side to get a better angle.

"Ok then, let's go back and shampoo you." he stands and follows me back to the shampoo area. I have him lean back and start rinsing his hair. I glance down and realize he's staring right at me. I'm really kicking myself for not putting a hot towel on his face when we started. His eyes are burning little holes into me, so I finally say, "Ok, fine. I'll tell you about Grandpa Frybeard."

He gets a big smile on his perfect face, and I can't help but to smile back. I launch into the story about my ridiculous date from last night. He's laughing as I'm telling it. When I get to the part where the guy ordered the shots, his smile falls. He actually looks almost angry and is clinching his jaw. "He called you a slut? What's his name? I'm gonna go kick his ass," he grits out.

"What? No. I mean. Not really." Now I wonder if that's what he thought of me. Not that I care what a man who lies about everything on his profile and eats beard fries thinks of me. "Hey, it's ok, I'm ok. I think its par for the course in today's dating world. You can't just go around kicking asses all the time."

He seems slightly less agitated and even gives me half a smile. I begin running the conditioner through his hair. I generally give a nice scalp massage while the conditioner sits on the hair. Most of my male clients love it. So, I give him the same massage I always do. I get to the spot at the temples and rub right behind the ears, and I hear him let out a low growl. That one little noise he made sent a zing right to my lady bits. I think I'm soaking my panties just from that one little sound.

I finish rinsing him out and instruct him to sit up while I dry his hair with a towel. I feel his hand touch my wrist and I stop to look at him. "So, do I get to hear about Italian Job now?" he asks with a laugh.

"NO!!" I say laughing. "You definitely do not get to hear that story. Not ever if I can help it." We head back to my station, and I style his hair. I know our time is coming to an end — especially when I look at the clock and see that it's three minutes past my next clients start time. Mrs. Milton is a sweet old lady, but she will not be kept waiting. Once I ran over with a color client by ten minutes, and I got quite a lecture about wasting her time. I try to always be available to her the second she comes in. I walk him to the front. "Gracie can get you checked out. It was so nice to meet you, Brenden. Gracie, be sure to give Brenden one of my cards, so he knows who to ask for next time. Mrs. Milton, so sorry you had to wait! Let's get you started." I smile at Brenden as I walk with Mrs. Milton to my station.

"It's ok honey, I'd lose track of time too if he was sitting in front of me," she says with a wink.

Two hours later, Mrs. Milton's little granny curls are perfectly styled and have been toned to the perfect shade of almost blue that she likes.

"Gracie, can get you checked out and booked for next week. Thanks for coming in today, Mrs. Milton." I start to walk back toward my station to get set up for my next client when Gracie stops me.

"Brenden left you a note." She hands it to me with a smirk on her face.

I hope to see you on Saturday. Don't worry, I'll cheer loudly for you.
- Brenden

I walk away from the front with a smile on my face and a little pep in my step.

CHAPTER FOUR

Brenden

*W*ell that went better than expected. I've been trying to figure out how to meet her for three weeks. On my first day at Station 4, Jared was showing me around. We walked past a wall that had some big bulletin boards with different articles and pictures tacked up.

"Some of the wives put this up and keep it up. They post pictures and articles from some of the fundraisers and events we help with." Jared points to the board.

I notice a picture of Jared and two women. He's standing between them with his arms around each of them. I immediately zero in on the redhead in the picture. She's wearing some short as fuck denim shorts and a t-shirt, I assume for whatever charity they were supporting. Her hair looks long and bright coppery red. She's got a curvy little body that I want to run my hands over, a bright smile that makes you want to smile back, and the most mesmerizing eyes I've ever seen. I point to the picture, "Is this your wife?" hoping like hell he says it's not the redhead.

"Yeah, the blonde is my wife Sammy. The redhead is her best friend Molly. Sammy stops by a lot. I'm sure you'll meet her. They own a shop in town, if you ever need your haircut. There're my twins with Sammy and me." He points to another picture, but I merely glance at that one because I can't keep my eyes off the redhead.

Later that evening, after lights out, I sneak down to look at the picture again. I notice she's in a couple of other photos too — always with that same bright smile. When I look at the picture of her and Jared, it pisses me off. I know his wife is in the picture, but I fucking hate that he's touching her. I wanted to rip the picture down and cut her out of it. I didn't want anyone else looking at her. Fuck, I sound like a psycho. I pull out my phone and take a picture of the picture and do same with every one that I can find of her on the bulletin board.

When I walked into the salon this morning and heard her talking about playing kitty with someone... I don't know what that means exactly, but I don't want to think about her playing anything with anyone else. She was so fucking cute when she noticed I was standing there. Watching the skin on her chest, neck and face turn pink in embarrassment gave me a warm feeling in my chest. I got a little worried when she ran to the back. I specifically went in there to have her cut my hair. I wanted to feel her hands on me. Lucky for me, the receptionist said she was the only one open, but she had to check to see if she could squeeze me in before her first client arrived.

When I heard her call my name, I swear it was the sweetest sound I've ever heard. I was worried about standing up with the erection I could feel starting to push against my zipper. Her curvy hips and that sweater showing just a tiny bit of cleavage had my mouth watering. When she placed her tiny hand in mine to greet me, I envisioned seeing it wrapped around other parts of my body. I'm glad she put a cape over me in the chair, so I didn't embarrass myself. The last thing I need to do is look like a fucking pervert to this girl.

Between the conversation I heard when I walked in and her friend asking about her date last night, I gathered she was, indeed single. I wanted so badly to ask one of the guys at the station, but I didn't want to get shit about it if she wasn't.

Every time she touched me; it took all my self-control to not pull her into my lap. Having her cut my hair was torture. When she said she was going to shampoo me, I didn't know if I'd be able to handle it. Her hands felt so nice rubbing my head. Her sweater was just low enough to see her cleavage as she leaned over me. I knew she caught me looking when I saw that same pink rise from her chest to her cheeks.

When she started telling me about her date from the night before, I got a kick out of the way she told it. She's so animated. I couldn't help but think how cute she was. When she said how the fucker called her a redheaded slut, I nearly lost it. I was about to charge out of there and find him. He better hope I never run into him. She played it off like it didn't bother her, but I could tell it did. I had to lighten the mood. I asked her about the one she called Italian Job, and she let out the biggest laugh that lit up her whole face. She said she'd never tell me that one, and I'm taking that as a challenge. I for sure don't plan on my girl keeping secrets from me. Yeah, my girl...that has a nice ring to it.

CHAPTER FIVE

Molly

*a*s is our Thursday night tradition, because Jared almost always works Thursday nights, I pull up to Sammy's house around 6:30. On Thursday nights, we usually eat dinner, I help her get her kiddos in the tub and to bed, then we drink some Moscato, eat something chocolatey, and watch Grey's Anatomy. She typically cooks dinner, and I bring the wine and dessert. Tonight, I brought the triple chocolate cheesecake from the bakery next door to the shop. It's ahhhmazing and happens to be Sammy's favorite.

"Hey, Samsonite!!" I bellow out one of the many nicknames for her. I hear the sound of pounding little feet heading in my direction. I set my bags down and squat down with open arms. Around the doorway comes a blur of blonde curls, capes, and tutus. Joey hits me first and nearly knocks me on my ass. Aubrie is close behind him. She jumps into me before I catch my balance, so I do, in fact, hit the floor. You'd think I'd learn to just sit on the floor. Joey's in his typical superhero garb, wearing a Batman mask with a Superman cape, and extra-large Hulk hands covering his little fists. Aubrie is a mix of extra girly and superhero. She's wearing a pink batman cape, a rainbow tutu, and what I believe to be a pair of welding goggles.

"How are my favorite twins in the whole world today?" They both ramble gibberish. I only understand a few words here and there, and they always talk at the same time. What I can clearly make out is "Moll-wee," which is what they call me. I look up when I see Sammy come out of the kitchen holding a dish towel.

"Hey, guys, let's let Aunt Molly up. I'm making spaghetti." Sammy says. The twins hop up and run down the hallway toward their room shouting.

"Sweet! I'm starving. That color correction I had to do today made me miss lunch. I was about to eat this entire cheesecake on my drive over." I say handing her the bag. I head over and open the refrigerator and pull out a bottle of water.

"So, I stopped by the station today to bring Jared his new phone charger. I saw your future husband," she says in a sing-song voice.

"Oh, did you?" I try to sound nonchalant.

"Yeah, I introduced myself to him officially. You're never going to believe what he asked me," she says giddily.

I get excited, expecting her to say he wanted my number or something. "What did he say?"

"He asked me if I knew what Italian Job was." she says laughing. I'm sure my face is white as a ghost.

"Did you tell him?" Italian Job is the nickname for a guy I dated. It was not good. I will not speak about this subject. The end. Goodbye. End of Story.

"Of course, I didn't tell him! We agreed to never speak about him again. Apparently, he asked Jared too, but he knows better than to ever repeat that one. How does he even know about it?" she asks.

"UGH! Emily! Damn her! When I was cutting his hair the other day, she came over and said you told her to ask me about Grandpa Frybeard. Then she asked if it was as bad as Italian Job! I gave her a look, and she rushed into the back. I was so nervous being so close to him that I told him about Frybeard. He got kinda pissed too." I've been thinking about his reaction since yesterday.

"He got pissed? Pissed about what?" she asks as she drains the noodles. "Aubrie! Joey! Come eat, babies! Will you strap them into their highchairs for me?"

I hear the pounding sound of the twins' feet running toward the kitchen. I scoop Joey up and kiss his chubby little neck while he laughs and squirms. "Excuse me, Batman, have you seen Joey?" He squeals and rips off his mask.

"Moll-wee!!!! I Joey!!" I kiss his cheeks again and put him in his highchair.

"There you are! Have you seen Aubrie?" I look around like I don't see her. She stands there bouncing with her arms up.

"Moll-wee! Moll-wee! I Aub-wee!!!" I scoop her up and smooch her little cheeks too.

"I didn't see you there!" I put her in her highchair too. I turn to Sammy and answer her. "He was laughing one second about Frybeard, and then I told him about how he ordered the shots and looked at me. He got seriously mad. He wanted his name and said he was going to 'kick his ass.' I thought he was joking at first, but he was dead serious."

"Hmmmmm. That's interesting. I'd say he sounds a little

protective of you already." She raises her eyebrows and cocks her head to the side.

"We barely know each other. Though he did leave me a note that said he would be there Saturday night. Speaking of, do you have time tomorrow after two to run through it one more time?" I ask, referring to the "help" the girls are giving me for my talent in the pageant.

"I still can't f....fudging believe you talked all of us into this," she says looking at the twins. She's been trying to not swear around them. I don't know if it's working though. "You're lucky a few of us took lessons as kids. I'm just hoping I don't get up there and bust my ass. I'm already having nightmares about someone recording it when I fall off the stage."

"You're not going to fall off. If anyone fell, it would be me. I'm more concerned with flashing everyone my goodies" I say, referring to the short dress I'll have on.

"I think I should be done by two. Want me to send out a text to all the ladies to see if they are available?" she asks while putting cut up spaghetti noodles on the twins' trays.

"I just did." I walk over to the counter and load up a plate with spaghetti, salad, and bread. "This looks so good. I'm starving."

Over the next thirty minutes, we eat and chit chat about the shop and the parade on Saturday. Typically, on Saturdays, we open at nine in the morning, but the St. Patrick's Day parade starts at ten, so we aren't opening until the afternoon. Our first year in business, we tried to remain open during the parade. But since our shop is located on the parade route, no one could get to the shop. Besides that, most people were watching the parade. So, now we take it as an opportunity to advertise the salon. Jared has a big truck he's letting us decorate, and we're riding in the back. Most of the girls from the shop will be there. We'll be throwing green beads and some candy for the kids. We'll all be wearing our costumes for the talent portion of the pageant.

We also discuss the birthday party we're planning to throw for our receptionist Gracie. She's turning twenty-one and is the baby of the salon crew. The plan is for dinner with the girls at Rare, the fanciest steakhouse in town, before heading to McMurphy's to get her hammered and make her do karaoke. She's like all a little sister to all of us, and she grew up in foster care, so she doesn't have a lot of people on her side in Rockplaines. She's been taking business classes at the local community college, and I'm hoping she'll consider cosmetology school when she's finished and join us.

By the time we're done eating, I get a text back from most of the girls saying that they can be at the shop by two to practice if they aren't already working. If we can squeeze another practice in on Saturday afternoon, we will. To say I'm nervous is an understatement. Plenty of people at McMurphy's have heard me sing. They host a karaoke night twice a month, and I try to make it to at least one…sometimes both. But they've never seen me do what we're doing for the show.

After dinner, we put the twins in the tub, and then its pajama time. I give them Moll-wee snuggles and leave Sammy to rock them. I head into the kitchen to put the leftovers away and clean the dishes. I try to help Sammy out when I'm here. She's got her hands full with those little monkeys. She's a rockstar though and still works four to five days a week — even if the hours aren't long. We've been thinking about hiring another nail tech to pick up the slack because Sammy and Taylor are both incredibly busy. They typically have fully booked schedules, and we end up turning away walk-in customers. I've tried to fill in and help before when I could, but either Sammy or Taylor had to fix my mistake, so it's really more work for them in the long run.

I pour the wine into our glasses and cut us each a generous slice of cheesecake. Then I head into the living room with our goodies and find Grey's Anatomy on the TV. We usually watch it live but with a few minutes' lag.

Sammy plops down on the couch beside me. She's lucky that her mom and dad live just around the corner from her. They watch her kiddos so she can still put in time at work. I worry about her wearing herself out — especially since she's working on getting pregnant again. "I'm so tired." she says with a yawn. "Let's watch this so I can get to bed."

"We don't have to watch it tonight. We can wait until next week and have a double feature. You look exhausted," I say shoving a large bite of cheesecake into my mouth.

"No, I want to watch it tonight. You know Kelli and Jess will be talking about it tomorrow, and I'll end up hearing the spoilers from those batches. Play it, and give me my cheesecake!" She grabs for my piece.

"Hey, Batch! That's my piece! Yours is over there. Hands off, you cheesecake whore!" I say jerking my plate away from her. Yes, this is the way we talk to each other. We've been best friends since kindergarten. She's like the sister I never had. We swear at each other and call each other horrible names. It's like an Olympic sport to us to come up with the snarkiest comebacks and nicknames. We also say fuck. A lot.

I start the show, and we both swoon over how hot DeLuca is. I can certainly appreciate a good head of hair. "He's so hot. I think he's way too young for Meredith," Sammy says, finishing off her wine.

"I'd let him take my temperature for sure." I nod in agreement. When the show ends, I collect our plates and glasses and put them in the dishwasher and start it. I come back into the living room, and Sammy is sleeping on the couch. I've made the mistake of trying to wake her up to go lay in her bed before. I paid for it with a split lip when she sat up quickly and head-butted me in the mouth. So, I just take the blanket off the back of the couch and cover her up. I go to her room and get her phone charger and plug in her phone. Then I set the alarm on her phone for tomorrow morning, in case she sleeps out here all night. I turn off the tv and the lights, except the one above the stove. Then I set the alarm and lock the door on my way out.

CHAPTER SIX

Molly

$\mathcal{I}$ remember on my drive home that I need body wash, so I swing by the supermarket. I grab a basket because it never fails, I'll see about ten other things I want and will need to balance all of it in my arms. When I finally make my way to the checkout, I have a bouquet of flowers for the reception desk at work, a package of shamrock shaped sugar cookies, a six pack of cider, a six pack of Diet Mt. Dew, light bulbs, a loaf of bread, and a can of cream of mushroom soup. I get in line and wait behind a little old lady buying her weekly groceries. Seems a bit late for her to be out shopping, but maybe it's because its not a busy time in the store. The cashier is taking her time, so I grab a magazine to look through while I wait. I notice an ad for body wash which makes me look in my basket and realize I forgot the damn body wash. "Fuck." I say under my breath.

Turning around to go get it, I run smack into a wall of muscle. Strong hands reach out and grab me so that I don't fall on my ass. I slowly raise my eyes to meet the eyes I've been thinking about for the last thirty-six hours. I can feel the goofy grin on my face as I say, "Well hello there."

I'm rewarded with a blinding smile, and I notice that he has a little dimple on the right side when he smiles. Is it weird I want to put my tongue in it?

When he says, "Put your tongue in what?" I realize I just said that out loud. Well, fuck. I stand there with my mouth hanging open completely flabbergasted.

I shake my head, reach out to the side, and grab a candy bar off the shelf. "This, I have a sweet tooth and love chocolate," I say in a tone that can only be described as shrill. Brenden stands there looking at me with a knowing smile. Could I be any more of a dork?

I think he takes pity on me because he changes the subject, "Where were you going in such a hurry? Forget something?"

"Yeah," I realize he's still holding me close, and we're actually standing chest to chest. I take a step back, but he keeps holding on to me. "I... uh... Forgot body wash, which is what I actually came in here to get."

"I'll walk with you to get it," he says, grabbing my hand and leading me in the direction of the toiletries. I notice he doesn't have a basket or cart and nothing in his hands.

"Uh, do you make it habit to just walk around the store at night? Don't you need anything?" I question as he practically drags me toward the soap.

"I just picked up a prescription from the pharmacy. It's in the pocket of my jacket already. I just happened to see you standing there as I was walking to the exit," he says looking over his shoulder at me.

"Are you sick? Sorry, I'm nosy," I say sheepishly.

"No, it's for my grandpa. I live with him. I actually moved here to help take care of him. He's getting older and had a bad fall a few weeks ago. I'm helping him out while he recovers. I have to go to work tomorrow morning, so I wanted to make sure he had what he needed," he says with a shrug.

The fact that this big, sexy man moved here to help care for his grandpa has my heart warming. "That's really sweet that you take care of him."

"He's a pretty special guy; he helped raise me. When my dad passed, he came to live with me and mom for a while. It's the least I can do." He does that shrug again.

We stand in the aisle with body wash, and I reach for the one I usually buy. I realize I don't have my basket, but then I realize that he's carrying it. How did that happen?

"Is there anything else you need?" he asks.

"Nope, I think that's it," I say, but then the toothbrushes catch my eye, and I grab a three pack and toss it in the basket "Sorry, I just remembered that I need a new one."

We walk in a somewhat comfortable silence back to the cashier, me periodically picking up random items and tossing them in the basket as we go. "Uh....do you just want me to get you a cart? I don't think you can fit much more in this basket."

"No, I'm done." I look around to make sure I don't see anything else. "I promise I'm done."

I expect he'll hand me the basket and head out once we make it back to the cashier. Instead he stands in line with me and even puts my stuff on the conveyor belt when it's my turn. The cashier tells me my total, and I start to hand her my card — but Brenden shoves his card in front of mine.

"Uhhhh....what are you doing?" I question. "I can pay for my own stuff."

"I'm sure you can, but I got it." he shoots me his dazzling smile, which would usually make my lady parts tingle, but right now it's making my blood boil.

"Yeah, no. You're not paying for my stuff. Ma'am, please use this card." I say with an edge to my voice. The cashier takes my card and swipes it. I say thank you and grab my bags, stomping off toward the door.

"Molly, wait. Hey! Please talk to me," he begs. I stop abruptly, right outside the exit and whip around to face him.

"I'm not sure what the fuck you thought you were doing, but let me make one thing perfectly clear. I am not some helpless little girl that can't afford a few things at the grocery store. I happen to have a pretty successful business, you know. I own my own car and house — all of which I bought by myself. If you were trying to impress me, it didn't work. Have a good night, Brenden." I spin around and start to stomp off in the direction of my car when I suddenly feel a strong arm wrap around my waist, and I'm pulled against his warm body.

"Babe, could you just calm down for a second and let me explain?" he says against my ear.

"Don't call me babe, and you have ten seconds before I break your foot and knee you in the balls." I say calmly.

"Yes. Ok, I was trying to impress you. I just wanted to do something nice, and I like you. Am I fucking this up already?" he says sounding a little defeated.

"You could just ask me out, if that's what you want." Relaxing against him, I turn my head to look at him. "Or I guess I could ask you out."

Brenden gets a big smile on his face. "I'd really like to take you out. Would you have dinner with me Saturday?"

"No," I say. Then I rush to correct myself. "It's St. Patrick's Day. I've got the Miss Shamrock Pageant. But we can hang out together afterward."

His face goes from disappointment to that gorgeous smile in about half a second. "Yeah, I forgot. I was planning on coming to cheer you on." He loosens his arm around me. "Can I carry your bags to your car?"

"Yeah, I'm just over here. " Hey, I might be an independent woman, but I'll always allow someone else to carry my stuff. Independent, yes. Lazy, yes.

We walk over to my convertible VW Beetle. It's gecko green with a black top and tan interior. It was my dream car even before I could drive. I look at Brenden, and he's eyeballing my car. "Why am I not surprised this is your car? Are those eye lashes on the headlights?" After a long pause, he says, "It fits you."

"I'm gonna take that as a compliment," I say smiling.

"Look, I'm excited to see you Saturday night, but can we plan to have a proper date soon?" he asks, and I feel a flutter in my tummy.

"Yes. Sunday night?" I suggest quickly.

"Perfect. Can I get your number, and I'll call you about the details?" he asks holding out his phone to me to put my number in his phone. I type my number in and hand it back.

Brenden opens my car door and before I get in, I reach up and touch his cheek. "See you later, Blue Eyes."

I sit down in the car, and before he shuts my door he says, "Soon, Red." He stands there while I back out, so I decide to blow him a little kiss. I drive off with a smile on my face.

Brenden

I stand there rooted to the cement until she drives out of the parking lot. When she started yelling at me, I just wanted to grab her and kiss her. I'll keep that in mind for the next time she yells at me. I'm sure this won't be the last time. I love how she felt in my arms. Her little hand fits so perfectly in mine. "Fuck me," I say under my breath. I've got it bad.

I walk over to my Jeep and get in. I pull up her number in my texts and set one of the pictures I found on the bulletin board to her number. I want to text her and tell her I miss her already. But I don't want to come off too .... crazy.

I decide to text her later. I've got to get home and get to bed. I've got a twenty-four hour shift at the station starting at seven tomorrow morning. I'm new to this station, so I'm pretty shocked I have Saturday night off — and on St. Patrick's Day? It's like a major holiday in this city.

I pull up to my Grandpa's house. He and my Grandma moved into this house when it was built in the 1960s. It still has all the original fixtures and wallpaper. At some point in the mid nineties, they did get new living room furniture. When my grandma died in 2005, it was really hard on Grandpa. Then, my dad passed the next year in a fire. I come from a long line of firemen. My Dad was, my grandpa was, and even my great grandpa was a fireman. Some people think losing my dad to the fire would make me run toward a different career. But I'm a Clarke. It's what we do.

Walking into the house, I see Grandpa sleeping in his recliner. We bought it for him last Christmas because his old one was nearly twenty-five years old. He didn't want the new one at first, but this one is electric and has power lift. When I showed him that, he was like kid in a candy store. I'd never seen an eighty-year-old man so giddy.

"Grandpa," I say shaking his shoulder. "Let's get you to bed." He opens his eyes and glares at me.

"How many times do I have to tell you? I'm fine right here," he says with a grunt.

"You're not fine here. Last time you slept in the chair, you could barely stand up straight for three days. Let's get you to bed." I help him put his legs down, and the power lifter helps stand him up.

When I moved in here, we moved him downstairs to the spare bedroom. It's easier for him to get to. He fell on the stairs about a month ago and ended up with a sprained wrist and a mild concussion. Grandpa's too stubborn to go live in an assisted living facility, so I came to help out. I get him into his room and help him settled on the bed before handing him his bi-pap mask. "Do you need anything?"

"I need you to turn off the GD light and shut the hell up so I can get back to sleep," he says with a huff.

I smile as I shut off the light and close the door. I make my way through the house turning off lights and locking doors. I wasn't completely gung-ho about uprooting my life and moving hundreds of miles away, but I'm glad I get this time with Grandpa. He's not always so grumpy. He's actually a pretty funny old guy. He just hates to have his sleep interrupted.

The room I sleep in used to be my dad's when he was growing up. I had planned on moving into the master bedroom, but to see the look on Grandpa's face when we talked about putting some of the furniture that wouldn't fit in the guest room downstairs into storage just about broke my heart. He never quite got over losing my grandma, and the master bedroom is like a shrine. Same furniture and bedding. My Grandma's clothes still hang on her side of the closet. We asked him a few years ago if he would be interested in meeting a lady friend. He said it would feel like he was cheating on Grandma.

I head upstairs to the hall bathroom to start the shower, stripping off my clothes as I go. I step into the stream of hot water. It feels good on my muscles. I feel the water run over me, and I think about Molly. I've been hard as a rock since I walked into that salon yesterday morning. I wrap my hand around my hard cock and stroke it. I tip my head back as I move my hand up and down the length of my shaft. Fuck, this is the third time today I've rubbed one out. You'd think it would go down at some point. Something tells me it won't until I come inside her. I fuck my fist, picturing Molly on her knees in front of me, naked, pulling on her nipples, her mouth open taking my cock as deep as she can. I can picture her looking up at me with those blue grey eyes. I feel the orgasm crawling up my spine. My balls draw up, and I come while groaning her name, splashing ropes of come all over the shower wall. I feel relief for a minute, but it doesn't last. I make quick work of washing my hair and body. Then I hop out, dry off, slide on a pair of boxer briefs and climb into bed. I used to sleep naked, but in the event that Grandpa needs me, I like to be somewhat decent. I lay in bed thinking about my date on Sunday evening with Molly. I grab my phone and text her:

"Good night, Red."

I set my phone on the nightstand and try to go to sleep. A minute later I get a text back.

"Good night, Blue Eyes."

CHAPTER SEVEN

Molly

*I*t's Friday around eleven in the salon, and we've been fairly busy already this morning. People are really taking advantage of our green highlight promotion. I have a few minutes before my next client, so I slip into the back office to sit for a minute and drink one of my sodas. I pop the top on the can and put my feet on the desk. These chunky boots look fabulous but are killing my feet. I pull out my phone to see if I have any new texts from Brenden. I was pleasantly surprised that he texted me good night last night. Then shortly after I got up this morning, I heard my phone ping. It was another text from him that simply said, "Good morning, Beautiful. Have a great day."

I eagerly texted back, "You too, Blue Eyes," with a heart emoji. I immediately regretted that damned heart emoji, but he sent a winky face back. So I'm calling that a win.

Sammy runs into the office and slams the door behind her. "Hank is out front." She says with wide eyes. I sit up quickly and drop my feet off the desk.

"What?!" I gasp in surprise. "Why is he here? What does he want?"

She shrugs and shakes her head, "I have no fucking idea. He just asked for you. I told him I'd let you know he was here. I don't want to send him back here. Why don't you come up front and step outside with him maybe?"

"Yeah, I suppose I could do that." I say biting my lip. Hank and I obviously didn't end on good terms. I've only seen him once face to face since I uploaded that video and ended things. It didn't go well. I had come to the apartment with the movers and brought along Sammy and Jared. I wanted things to go smoothly. They did not. He was angry that I had posted the video. I mean, his family and friends had seen it before he reported it to Facebook and had it taken down. A lot of them took my side on it — because he was the one in bed with another woman.

I had tried to call and text to let him know I was coming that day to get my things. He never responded. Hank was less than hospitable to say the least. He had boxed and bagged up some of my stuff, breaking a lot of my collectibles, and he'd poured bleach on quite a few items of clothing. When I saw that he had broken my music box, I fucking lost it. My grandma had given it to me when I turned thirteen. She had gotten it for her thirteenth birthday. It meant a lot to me, and he knew it. We yelled and screamed at one another, and I threw a lamp through the screen on his 55-inch flat screen. A neighbor heard the fight and ended up calling the cops. The cop that showed up was sympathetic to my situation and talked Hank into leaving for an hour so I could finish up promising to stay and watch to make sure I didn't cause any more damage.

"Molly?" Sammy says snapping her fingers in front of my

face. "Earth to Molly." Are you coming, or should I go throat punch him?"

I stand up and grab my cardigan off the coat rack and slip it on. I'm really not looking forward to talking to him. I walk toward the front desk and see that he's sitting in the chairs at reception flipping through an issue of Cosmo.

"Hank?" I ask cautiously. "What are you doing here?"

He stands up, I think not having seen him for almost a year made me forget how big he is. Hank is big, I mean BIG. He's about 6 foot 5 and easily 300 lbs. At one time, he was training for strong man competitions. He hurt his shoulder pretty badly a couple of years ago and gave it up. The sheer size of him makes me wonder if he's back at it.

"Molly," he says trailing his eyes up my body. I pull my cardigan closed and cross my arms. "Can I talk to you for a minute? Alone?" he says looking around the salon at all the eyes on us.

"Uh.... Yeah," I say hesitantly. "Let's step outside." I point toward the door.

He walks toward the door, and I turn and mouth to Sammy, "Call Jared." Jared isn't nearly as big as Hank, but he can hold his own. I would feel safer if he came up here in case there is trouble. She nods and pulls out her phone.

Hank holds the door open for me, and I walk through it. I wait until it closes behind us before I look over at him. He's sort of shifting from foot to foot. He seems nervous. "What's up Hank?" I'm not trying to prolong this, and I really want to know what the hell he could possibly want.

"You look good, Angel." He says running his eyes up my body again. Angel, the nickname he had always called me. I used to think it was sweet. Now it just pisses me the fuck off.

"Ok, I'm gonna stop you right there. Do *not* call me Angel. I'm not your fucking Angel. Why. Are. You. Here. Hank?" I'm done playing nice. I've got a short temper, and he's already used up what calmness I had. I could have been somewhat cordial if he hadn't called me Angel.

"C'mon Molly, can't we just talk and be friendly? I miss you. I miss us. I thought maybe you missed me too," he says trying to give me his saddest puppy dog eyes.

"Well Hank, you thought wrong," I say with a little venom in my voice. "I think too much has happened for you and me to be friends. I'm not ready to forgive you, let alone be friends."

"Forgive me?" he says incredulously. "Forgive me for what? You're the one that plastered my naked ass all over Facebook and threw a fucking lamp through my brand-new LED TV!" He starts to get loud. That escalated quickly.

"Forgive you for what?! Let's start with that fact that you cheated on me! You fucked some other woman IN OUR BED! You broke most of my shit and poured bleach on my clothes!" I yell back, ticking each of his crimes off on my fingers. "Did you forget you did all of those things?"

"Oh, please, Molly. We had an understanding about sleeping with other people," he says to me. I look at him in complete shock and confusion.

"WHAT?! No, we most certainly did not!" I'm screaming at this point. People on the sidewalk are starting to mill about for the show. "We never once talked about your being allowed to sleep with other women. I would *never* be ok with that. Are you fucking insane?"

Hank suddenly realizes we're drawing a crowd. I can visibly see him trying to calm himself. "Look Angel, I'd be willing to forget about what happened if you will. Let's give us another chance." He reaches out and tries to touch my face. I slap his hand away, and I see the calmness he's trying to pretend to have slip.

"Am I in the fucking Twilight Zone right now? You cannot be serious!!! I will never *ever* forget what happened. You CHEATED, Hank! You broke my fucking heart. Then you broke all my stuff. Please leave, and don't ever come back." I turn to start to walk back into the salon when I feel his huge hand grab my arm. He's strong, and it hurts. "Let go of me, Hank. You have got to be out of your fucking mind right now." I say through gritted teeth.

"Now, Angel, you're overreacting. I think we need to sit down and talk about this calmly." He says while squeezing my arm even tighter.

"Let go of my arm, Hank, before I break every fucking finger on your hand." He has the nerve to smirk at me. I lift my arm up and rotate it over his arm which breaks his hold on me. He's not expecting me to get loose at all, and it throws him off balance. I take the opportunity when he bends forward, and I hit him as hard as I can in his throat. He falls to the ground gasping with one hand on his throat, and when he uses the other hand to break his fall, I stomp on it with my boot. I hear at least a few fingers crack, and Hank cries out in pain as he falls to his side.

I hear Sammy behind me say, "Holy shit, Molly, you kicked his ass." I think the adrenaline spike, coupled with the fact that I just hurt Hank, hits me then, and I start to cry. I'm talking heaving, sobbing, ugly, snot running down my red face kind of cry. I started taking self-defense classes after Hank and I broke up. I never felt scared of him when we were together, but getting back in the dating pool made me nervous. It's a scary world out there. I figured taking the classes couldn't hurt. Obviously, I was right.

"What the fuck is going on here?" I hear Brenden over the

crowd that has gathered. I look up from Sammy's shoulder to see his confused, worried eyes taking in the scene. Hank rolling on the sidewalk coughing and sucking in breath while holding his hand. I think he might even be crying. Jared and couple of the other guys from the station look around in confusion.

"Hank showed up, and they got into a fight. He grabbed her arm, and Molly beat his ass." Sammy says matter-of-factly.

They all look at me in complete confusion. I suck in a breath and wipe the tears and snot with the back of my hand. I shrug and say, "I've been taking self-defense classes."

Someone must have called the cops because a cruiser pulls up, and John comes over to check things out. Some of the guys from station 4 help Hank up and tend to his injuries while John asks me and a few onlookers what happened. Several people from the crowd had whipped out their phones and recorded the altercation. Isn't technology grand? In this case, it only helped me out. John loaded Hank up and took him to the hospital for x-rays of his hand and then to the station to book him. I wasn't sure I wanted to press charges, but Jared and Sammy talked me into it. I also asked about getting a restraining order.

The entire time John asked me questions, I watch Brenden. He stands there listening to me recap what happened with his jaw clenched so hard that I'm surprised he doesn't grind his teeth down to nubs. Then he watches the video someone took on their phone. He looks irate. He looks like he is ready to kill. I think if John wasn't there, he might have done something stupid.

After they take Hank away and the crowd clears, we go back into the salon. The client I was supposed to do next ended up seeing part of my fight with Hank. She rescheduled her appt for the next week. Kelli covered for me with my last client so I could sit in the back and gather myself. Sammy, Jared, and Brenden followed me inside.

I plop down in the chair and catch my reflection in the full-length mirror we have on the wall. I wheel myself over to the mirror. "Fuck me. I look like I fell out of the ugly tree and hit every branch on the way down." I've got mascara running down my face, and the winged liner I did this morning is completely smeared.

"You do not look ugly." I hear Brenden mutter.

"She definitely looks like the conductor of the Hot Mess Express," chimes in Sammy Without looking at her, I hold up my middle finger. "Why don't we give you a minute to get yourself together." She suggests while dragging Jared from the office.

"Brenden, you coming? We gotta get the truck back to the station," Jared calls.

"Yeah, give me a few. I gotta talk to Molly," he says without ever taking his eyes off me.

I hear Jared ask Sammy, "How long has this been going on?" as they walk out the door.

It's silent for a good thirty seconds while I'm cleaning the makeup off my face. "Damn, baby." Brenden says sounding pained. I look over at him. He's sitting in the chair on the other side of the desk with his head in his hands. "When Jared said you were in trouble, I was so fucking scared." He looks up at me. "Come here, Red." I look at him for a second. "Please," he pleads, and I give in. I stand up and walk over to him. He reaches for me and pulls me down onto his lap. He cups my face with his hands and looks at me like he's trying to see inside of me. "Has he ever put his hands on you like that before? Has he hurt you?" He says with concern written on his face.

"He really hasn't. I'm not sure what came over him today. I hadn't talked to or seen him in almost a year. He showed up here today and said he wanted me back." I feel Brenden tense under me. "Don't worry, I pretty much told him to go fuck himself. When I tried to walk away, he grabbed my arm. I told him twice to let go. He didn't listen, so I punched him in the throat and broke his hand."

He looks at me with wide eyes. "So last night when you said you would break my foot and knee me in the balls, you were serious, weren't you?"

I nod my head. "Yeah. I took karate when I was a kid, and we did a self defense class as a team builder here at the salon. When I decided to start dating again, I thought it might be a good idea to take classes regularly. It's a fucked up world. A girl's gotta protect herself, ya know?"

"I'm so fucking glad you took those classes," he says with a little smile on his face. "I am slightly scared for my balls, if I'm being honest."

I throw my head back and laugh. "I promise your balls are safe … for now."

"God, you're beautiful," he says seriously. I get a warm feeling in my chest. I want to lean forward to put my lips on his. I'm already sitting in his lap. I start to lean forward, when he grabs my face and places his lips on mine. It's a sweet kiss that ends far too quickly. But it's perfect. When he pulls back and looks at me, I practically whimper.

"Wow," I whisper. I'm rewarded with one of his blindingly beautiful smiles. He leans forward again, and I wait with my eyes closed in anticipation of his lips on mine. Instead, he tips my head down and kisses my forehead.

"I gotta get back to the station, Red. I'd love to sit here with you in my lap all day, but if I walk out there this hard, the guy's will never let me live it down." It's then that I realize I can feel his hardness pressing against my ass. I jump up quickly.

"We definitely don't want that." I say trying to look anywhere but at the five person tent he's got pitched in his pants. My eyes, of course, shift so that I'm staring right at it.

"Red, baby, please stop looking at me like that. I'm only so strong," he says, and I realize I'm staring directly at the bulge in his pants and biting on my lip. "I gotta go baby." he says adjusting himself. "I'll call you tonight before lights out. Walk me to the front?"

I do my best to compose myself as he takes my hand, and we leave the office. When we get to the front, I see the fire truck they must have taken over here parked on the street in front of the salon. Sammy is standing out front with Jared. We walk outside to join them. I notice Jared's eyes go to Brenden's and my linked hands. He looks up at me. "You doin' ok, Molls?" I smile and nod. "I'm proud as fuck of you right now. I want you to give Sammy the information for those classes, ok?"

"I will," I promise.

Jared looks at Sammy. "We gotta go, baby. I'll be home later." Jared turns his attention back to me." Molls , you want to stay with us tonight?"

"I'll think about it. Thanks," I say watching Jared pull Sammy into his arms and lay a kiss on her that could melt the paint off the building.

I look over at Brenden, and his attention is on me. "You better get going, Blue Eyes. I'll talk to you later," I say in a whisper.

Brenden leans down and places another soft kiss on my lips "Soon, Red," he whispers back before he walks to the truck.

"Red and Blue Eyes sitting in a tree." I turn to look at Sammy singing with a stupid smile on her face.

"Fuck off," I say as I open the door to the salon. "C'mon. We gotta go practice."

Brenden

I watch Molly and Sammy walk back into the salon out the window of the fire truck. "Hey, Clarke." I look over at Jared. He's got a concerned look on his face. "What's going on with you and Molly?

I'm not really interested in getting into this with him right now, but I'd rather not have him giving me shit either. "We're dating." I say gruffly.

"Since fucking when?" he asks.

"Since last night. We talked about hanging out after the Pageant on Saturday, and we have a date Sunday," I say, annoyed that I have to explain anything to anyone.

"Well let me make one thing clear to you, Clarke. That girl is like family to me. If you're just looking to fuck her, you better end it now. She's not some piece of ass," he warns in a threatening tone.

"Not that I need to explain anything to you, Parker. But she's not just some fuck. She's mine. I better never hear you call her a piece of ass again," I say practically seeing red. I could knock his fucking head in for just insinuating I'd think of her that way.

"As long as we're on the same page," he says with a pointed look. Then I see his mood shift and a smile tip up his lips. "Your girl's a fucking badass," he says with a chuckle.

"Yeah, she fucking is," I say looking out the back window at the salon as we drive away.

CHAPTER EIGHT

Molly

$\mathcal{W}$e pull up to the area where we're supposed line up for the parade. Sammy and I hop out of Jared's truck, and I'm immediately regretting my decision to wear this little dress. Since our salon is called Bombshell's we often dress up like Pinup girls when we are promoting the salon or going to networking events. My dress has a halter neck with a full skirt; it's black with a shamrock print. The other ladies are wearing the same dress but with a white background to the shamrock print. They were all past our knees when we ordered them online. Anna is a fantastic seamstress, and she cut all of them shorter and added a petticoat to make them puff out. They hit above our knees now. Caitlyn had the good idea for us all to wear green cardigans for the parade, so maybe we won't all freeze our asses off. March is still a pretty chilly time in these parts. I've got my hair down with a deep side part and a shamrock hair piece on the side.

I ended up taking Jared up on his offer to stay at their house last night. After the day I had, I went home and showered. I was just sitting down to eat a grilled cheese and watch TV when I got a call from John, the officer from today. He wanted to let me know that the judge released Hank without bail. Since this was the first time Hank ever had any kind of run-in with law enforcement, besides our fight when I moved out. The judge said that since I didn't sustain any injuries, they were treating it as more of a public disturbance. Hank had to pay a $50 fine and was released. The judge also denied my order of protection, stating I had done more damage to Hank, and he probably needed protecting from me. I had, after all, broken three of his fingers.

I don't think Hank would come here to confront me about today, but I also never expected him to fight with me on the street or to grab me and refuse to let go. Yes, Hank cheated, but he had never so much as given me a noogie when we were together. He was a different person today, and that's what scared me.

After I hung up the phone, I called Sammy and told her what John had just told me and that I'd get my stuff together and head over after I finished my dinner. Then I looked up at the tv, which I had muted while I was on the phone, and I recognized the video playing while the newscaster talked. The ticker at the bottom of the screen read, "Local salon owner brawls with Strongman." Well, hell...that wasn't going to make anything better.

While I pack up clothes for work tomorrow and everything I needed for the parade and pageant, my phone rings again. I answer without checking, and I get another shock. It's Hank's mom, Betsy. She launched into it immediately, yelling and screaming about me embarrassing her son and injuring him and how I must be insane. I've had enough.

"BETSY!!!" I yell, and she finally goes silent. "Hank grabbed me and wouldn't let go. I asked twice. It hurt, and he bruised my arm. I did what I had to do to protect myself. They're playing the video someone took on the news. You can see for yourself."

"I can't believe I ever thought you were good enough for my baby boy." I roll my eyes at this. Baby boy my ass.

"I hope he can find someone that makes both of you very happy," I snark back at her.

"One of theses days your smart mouth is going to get you in trouble, Molly. You just don't know when to stop. I know what you've been up to young lady. I get reports from people every day about what a little harlot you turned out to be."

"I'm all done with this conversation, Betsy. Please don't call me again, or I'll report you for harassment." I hear her starting another tirade as I hang up the phone. I then block her number so I don't have to deal with her anymore.

I shake off the memories of the night before as the girls and I get to work decorating Jared's truck with green streamers and shamrock garland. We also have some magnetic decals we stick on each side. It's not much, but it'll have to do.

The parade gets started, and we ride along throwing candy and beads to the people in the crowd. It's a fun time. We all laugh and wave, and generally have a good time. I even caught Brenden's handsome face in the crowd. When we make it to the end of the parade route, we're all freezing and ready to get into some warmer clothes. Looks like we need to make a coffee run to Common Grounds once we get to the salon.

Jared drops Sammy and me off at the salon and runs to the coffee shop to get coffee for all the ladies. He's such a good guy. Sammy's a lucky lady. We all take turns in the dressing rooms putting warmer clothes on. We're only open until six on Saturdays, so it'll be a short day for all of us. We all get to sit around and chit chat for a few minutes, sipping coffee and catch up on each other's lives.

Emily had a date last night with a new lady named Heather. She said it went well, and Heather is supposed to come to McMurphy's tonight. Anna has been talking to a new fella also, but he's out of town right now and won't be there tonight. Kelli and her husband are officially trying to make a baby. Taylor just got engaged recently and complains about the cost of venues in the area. Gracie doesn't have any dating news, but she says she signed up online to try and find some family members. She hasn't found any yet but says the website takes a while sometimes. The rest of us ladies are single, and besides my string of ridiculously bad dates, we're also boring.

I've only got one client scheduled for today, and she's actually my competition for tonight. Emma has been one of my regular client since I worked at my very first salon. Today, we are putting a few green streaks in her hair, trimming it, and styling it for tonight. Emma works as an insurance agent and was basically voted to represent her company much in the same way I was put up for the salon. While I'm trimming her hair, I ask, "So what is your talent for tonight?"

"Oh, gosh. It's so stupid. I really only have one thing I'm good at as a hobby, and I didn't think it would be a good idea to do it on stage." That sure made me curious. "It's nothing too crazy. I do archery and have since I was a kid. I almost never miss the bull's-eye, but I had this image in my head of missing and shooting someone, so I decided against it. I'm doing the Napoleon Dynamite Dance," she admits with a laugh.

"That will be hilarious! I can't wait to see it." She asks about my talent, and I explain what we're doing and that the girls are helping me out.

"Dang! I didn't know we could have helpers on stage. Maybe I would have stuck with archery and shot an apple off Bonnie's head," she says in a whisper. I throw my head back and laugh. Bonnie is her boss and has got to be a hard woman to work for. She's been in here multiple times for services and is never completely satisfied. She always has a complaint or is trying to get us to take coupons from competitors.

I walk Emma to the front. "Ok, lady! I can't wait to see your moves tonight. I'll cheer for you if you cheer for me." Gracie get's her checked out so I can get my station cleaned up.

As I'm cleaning the hair out of my brush, I feel warmth at my back. Arms wrap around my waist and a sweet kiss is planted on my cheek. I look up in the mirror to see those blue eyes and the smile I'm becoming quite fond of. "Hey, Blue Eyes," I say with a smile. "Whatcha up to?"

"I was wondering if you had time for a quick bite to eat before you had to get over to McMurphy's?" he says planting a little kiss on my neck. Holy hell, did I bring an extra pair of panties for tonight?

I look at the clock on the wall. It's only 5:45. I don't have to be at McMurphy's until 7:30. "Yeah." I sound breathy when it comes out. "I can grab something quick. I just need to get back here by 6:50 to get ready.

"What's quick around here?" he asks placing another light kiss on my neck.

"Ummmm..." I hum out losing my train of thought. "You gotta stop that. I can't concentrate." I suddenly remember we're in the salon, and I look around. Every pair of eyes is looking in our direction. "We have an audience," I whisper. I can see Sammy thrusting her pelvis like she's humping the air.

"Why don't you finish up, and I'll wait for you in reception," he says a little sheepishly. I nod in agreement.

I quickly finish up and walk to the back to grab my purse and jacket. Sammy pops her head in and just looks at me with the biggest smile on her face. "Shut up," I say trying to hold back my own smile.

"I didn't say anything." She says holding up her hands in defense. I roll my eyes and shake my head at her.

"We're going to grab a bite. I should be back by 6:50. Do you want anything?"

"Nah. Jared's coming by in a few. We might go grab something too," she says leaning against the desk.

"Ok, I'll be back soon," I throw over my shoulder as I walk down the hall toward the front.

Brenden's standing up front talking to Jared. "Hey, Sammy said you were coming by and might grab a bite too. Do you guys want to go with us?" I see Brenden shaking his head at Jared.

"That's ok." he smirks. "You guys go ahead. We'll see you in a bit."

Brenden takes my hand and leads me toward the door. He holds it open for me and says, "Ladies first, Red. Where should we go?"

"Within walking distance, we can do burgers, burritos, or pizza. I could go for any of those, so you choose."

"Burger sounds good. Which way?" he asks while taking my hand again.

"Down this way," I point to the left of the salon. I'm taking him to a diner down and around the corner. It's called

Maybell's. It's been in this location since before I was born. The original owner has since passed, but her son and granddaughter run it now. The food is just as good as when I was growing up.

When we get into the diner, it's starting to get busy. I think we're just hitting the beginning of their dinner rush. Being that it's St. Patty's Day and everyone is probably going out to the many bars in the downtown area, it's crazier than usual. One of the servers sees us by the door and takes down our info. She assures us it's only a ten minute wait, so we decide to wait.

"I've never been here before, " Brenden says. "Good burgers huh?"

"Yes, I think everything here is good. We'll have to come for breakfast sometime. They have the most amazing waffles." I say thinking about the waffles.

Brenden gets a big smile on his face. "Sure. We can come here for breakfast anytime you want, Red."

Before we know it, we're being seated. Our server takes our drink order right away and gives us a few minutes to look at the menu. I don't really need to look because I rarely deviate from my regular order. For dinner, I almost always get a double bacon burger with their shoestring fries and cheese sauce. The server comes back quickly, and I order first.

"That sounds good. I'll have the same." He smiles at me.

"Did you enjoy the parade this morning?" I ask, trying to make small talk.

"Yeah, it was a much bigger parade than the one back in Springfield. I know it's a big deal here. You grew up here right?" he asks taking a drink of his soda.

"Yup, born and raised." I say nodding.

"What do your folks do?" he asks.

"My dad was a cop, and my mom was a schoolteacher. They both retired in the last few years. They still have their house here, but they bought this huge RV, and they drive it around the country. I talked to my mom yesterday, and she said they were staying outside of Yellowstone right now." I rattle off.

"Any siblings?" he asks.

"No, my parents tried for a while after me, but it never happened."

"Do you have any siblings?"

"No, I always wanted a brother or sister. My mom used to tell me I was like having ten kids, so why would she need more? I guess I was a handful," he chuckles.

We talk about our plans for tomorrow night. I offer to cook dinner and watch a movie at my place. I need to remember to pull some meat out of the freezer when I get home tonight.

Our food arrives, and we both eat quickly, only stopping to say mmmm and yum. I've only got about eight minutes to get back to the salon by the time we finish. He pays the bill, claiming he has the right since I'm taking care of dinner tomorrow night.

"I hate to eat and run, but I've gotta go get ready," I say standing up.

"I'll walk you back, Red," he says standing up and taking my hand. Then he guides us through the swarm of people that arrived after we got seated.

"So, what happens in this pageant tonight? I've heard a couple of people talking about it. It sounds like a big deal," he says glancing over at me.

"Well, I'd say it's almost more of a talent show. Women over the age of twenty-one can enter. Mostly we dress up in our most festive St. Patty's Day garb and perform. There isn't an interview section or swimsuit competition. Most people have an Irish or St. Patrick's Day theme to their talent. I'm not really sure why they don't call it a talent show and open it up to everyone. Probably just because it's tradition. My mom and my Aunt Renee both entered at one time. My mom got second place, but my aunt didn't place. She says it's because she got so drunk beforehand. She was so nervous to be on stage in front of everyone, she fell up the stairs and got a gash in her shin. She had to get eight stiches," I say giggling.

"So what's your talent gonna be? You gonna kick someone's ass on stage?" he asks in a teasing tone.

"I'm gonna sing, among other things," I answer with a little smile in my voice.

"What does 'among other things' mean?" he questions.

"You'll have to wait and see, but the girls in the shop are helping me out with my talent tonight. I'm just hoping I don't flash everyone in the crowd. I feel like my dress is really short." I say looking over at him. I see he's frowning. "What's with the frown, Blue Eyes?"

"I don't like the idea of you flashing anyone." he mutters.

I giggle. "It will be truly by accident if it happens."

We walk up to the front of salon. "Do you want to come in and wait while I get ready? You can walk down to McMurphy's with us."

"No, baby. I gotta run an errand real quick and call my Grandpa. His nurse only stays until six. I'll meet you there?" I feel a little disappointed that he's not going to come back and walk with us, but I know I'll see him there. He brushes hair back off my forehead. I brace for impact, assuming he'll kiss me good and hard. Instead, he leans forward and gives me another quick peck. "I'll see you in a bit, Red."

"Soon, Blue Eyes," I say watching him give me his gorgeous smile.

CHAPTER NINE

Molly

"Who's fucking bright idea was this?" I hear Anna say.

"Uh....Yours, I think. You're the one that signed me up for this and said, and I quote, 'Don't worry! We'll help you with your talent.' So it was your fucking bright idea, Batch." I shoot back.

"Why are you guys so nervous? We're gonna be awesome!" a more chipper than usual Caitlyn says. I have a feeling she's already had a few shots.

"The pageant starts any minute! You better go get lined up, Batch," I hear Sammy say over the crowd.

I nod my head and start making my way over to the side of the stage. I get a few "good lucks" from people who I know as I walk by. Most of the other ladies are already over here. Someone hands me a number to put on. There are ten contestants and I'm lucky number 6. I guess that's not a bad number to have. I've got my phone stuffed down the side of my bra, I pull it out and text Sammy that we're number 6. I notice my client, Emma, got number one. I can't wait to see her perform, but I feel bad she has to go first. Before the talent part starts, they introduce each of us and read a small bio. On top of being nervous, I'm wondering where Brenden is. Am I sounding too much like a clingy girlfriend? I don't want to be crazy. We only met on — holy fuck, was that only Wednesday? It seems like so much has happened since then. Tonight is the longest we've been in each other's company. I can't be thinking of myself as his girlfriend.

"Good evening, ladies and gentlemen." Martin, one of the owners of McMurphy's, says in his best Irish Brogue. "We hope you're all ready to see some talented, beautiful ladies tonight. Let's introduce you to the lasses."

We all walk up the stairs and stand in line across the stage. I try to hold my smile while my eyes search the crowd for the girls — and Brenden, if I'm being honest. I see the ladies. They're toward the left side of the stage, probably trying to stay close for when we perform. I still don't see Brenden, and I'm a little bit worried. What if he was in an accident or something happened to his Grandpa. Martin's making his way through the ladies, and it seems like he calls my name way too fast. I take a deep breath and step forward and do a little runway action.

"Molly O'Brien! You all know Molly. She's one of the owners of Bombshell's just down street. Molly is a talented singer too; she comes to our karaoke nights sometimes." I walk to the front of the stage and wave, blow some kisses to the crowd, do a little turn, and head back to stand next to Martin while he finishes up. "She's born and raised in our fair city, and from what I hear, can kick every one of your arses." The crowd cheers, and I feel the blush rise up my chest and heat my face. "Molly O'Brien, everybody." I take my place at the back of the stage and sort of tune out a lot of what Martin is saying about the other ladies. I'm still scanning the crowd for Brenden. It isn't until Martin calls contestant number ten that I snap back to reality.

"Mrs. Gladys Milton." Mrs. Milton? She's wearing a long, hunter green gown. It's reminiscent of something you might see a grandmother wear to her granddaughter's wedding. She looks very classy and sweet. She walks out there and does her little spin, waving to the crowd while Martin reminds us all that she's the former president of the Garden Club and has fourteen grandkids and two great-grandkids.

After the introductions it's time to get on to the talent show. Emma is first, and she runs back on stage wearing a bright green t-shirt that says "Vote for Emma" on it. The music starts, and she is moving. She has this routine down. It makes me wonder if she knew it before she signed up for the contest. Her music comes to an end and the crowd goes wild.

Last year's winner is standing on the left side of the stage in front of this big sign that looks like a gauge. She uses her arms like a needle to register the loudness of the crowd. Emma gets up to Super which is about third best.

The next few ladies are a cornucopia of strange. Monica Merano did a belly dance routine to a bagpipe rendition of an Eminem song. Courtney Smith does this bellybutton whistling thing to what I think was supposed to be My Bonnie. Jennifer Peterson did some yoga stretches that turned her into a contortionist. Who can bend like that? Sara Jordan sang Zombie by the Cranberries. Not a bad choice, but you could barely hear her.

Holy fuck. It's my turn. I come out to the center of the stage right in front of the microphone. I scan the crowd and finally see those blue eyes staring back at me. I feel a calm come over me. "How's everyone doing tonight?" I ask as the crowd cheers. "I've got some help tonight! Welcome the other

Bombshells to the stage please!" While the other girls line up behind me, I get my fiddle out of the case. I look at the girls, and they all give me nods. I look over at the guys in the house band and nod. I lift the fiddle up to my chin and start playing the first notes of Shipping up to Boston by The Dropkick Murphy's. The girls behind me start doing an Irish step dance. When the lyrics start, I kind of shout-sing into the microphone. The crowd is singing along with me. I continue to play the fiddle and sort of dance along with the other ladies as best I can. We must be doing pretty well because everyone is on their feet dancing and singing along. We end up scoring a Totally Awesome, which is second best. We all run off stage and hug each other. The other ladies all run into the crowd. I have to stay close because there are only a few other ladies before they announce the winner. I hate to sound cocky, but as it stands, I'm in the lead.

Nathalie Goodwin does fire batons while her dad and uncle play the bagpipes. It was pretty good, but one wouldn't stay lit. And when she threw the lit one in the air at the end, we all screamed thinking she might not catch it. She did catch it, thank goodness, and earned herself a Totally Awesome as well. Cierra Davis pulled an Aunt Renee. She, apparently, had one too many shots of liquid courage and couldn't quite find her way to the microphone. Her husband ended up hopping up on stage and helping her to safety. Kathy McMullins read a dirty limerick she wrote about a lephrechaun who pissed in a bucket. It was funny and got a little R-rated at the end, but she only got a Super.

I'm really expecting Nathalie and myself to have a shout off at the end to see who actually wins. But then, Mrs. Milton walks out on stage. She nods over to the band, and they begin to play Danny Boy. Mrs. Milton sings her heart out, and she has the most beautiful voice I've ever heard. It brings tears to my eyes, and I get goose bumps listening to her. When she finishes, it's literally silent in the place. I can see tears streaming down faces. Suddenly, the entire place goes up in cheers, and even I am screaming at the top of my lungs. Mrs. Milton gets a Soooo Wicked on the Cheer-o-meter.

Martin comes back out and announces, "Mrs. Gladys Milton is our winner!" Mrs. Milton stands in the middle of the stage while Erika Stanley, last years winner, puts a sash on her and a crown that has little rhinestone shamrocks on it. Mrs. Milton walks to the edge of the stage wearing the biggest smile. Martin starts singing, "There she is, Miss Shamrock." while Nathalie's dad plays the tune on his bagpipes. Mrs. Milton waves and blows kisses. I notice Mr. Milton standing down front, just beaming up at his wife. It makes me look over at Brenden. He's smiling at me. I have a sudden urge to run to him, and so I do.

Once I make my way through the crowd of everyone telling me good job and offering to buy me a drink, I finally come face to face with Brenden. He holds out his arms, and I jump into him. I wrap my arms around his neck and he catches me, holding my ass. "Hey, Blue Eyes. Glad you could make it."

"I know. Sorry I got held up with my errand," he says still smiling at me. He turns toward the pub table he's standing near, still holding on to me with one hand, and grabs a bouquet of flowers. Kermit mums, my favorite.

"How did you know these are my favorite?" I ask. I told Hank a million times they were my favorite. The few times he bought me flowers, he always got red roses. Don't get me wrong. Red roses are beautiful. They just aren't my favorite.

"That's my little secret, Red."

I look up at him, feeling a little emotional all of a sudden. "Thank you," I whisper.

"You're welcome, baby," he whispers back.

I realize he's still holding me. "You should probably put me down. I can feel your hand on my ass cheek, which means you might have my dress pulled up in the back. " He looks at me with wide eyes, and I slide down his body until my feet are on the floor.

"You want a drink?" he asks.

"I'd love one. Woodchuck, please," I say. He heads over to the bar. I look over and see Jared and Sammy looking in my direction. Both have big grins on their faces. "What?"

"Your boyfriend has it bad," Jared says taking a swig off his beer.

"Boyfriend?" Both Sammy and I say at the same time.

"That's what it looks like to me." He smiles and nods his head behind me.

Brenden walks back with my drink. I take it from him with a thank you and slam it back. I chug it. Then slam the glass down on the pub table. "I think I'm gonna need another," I say looking over at Sammy.

Brenden

Something's up. In the time I walked to the bar to get drinks and back, something happened. Molly was climbing me like a spider monkey before I left. In the last twenty minutes, she's chugged two pints of cider and some kind of green shot.

"Hey baby," I whisper in her ear. "Why don't you slow down? I want to spend some time with you without your head in the toilet." She stiffens next to me. "I'm sorry if I did something to upset you. I feel like you're upset with me. Did I do something?"

She looks up at me for a few moments. She closes her eyes and shakes her head. "You didn't do anything Brenden. I think I just freaked out a little bit because it feels like we're getting serious faster than I expected."

"I just want to get to know you, baby. We don't have to move fast. We don't have to do anything you don't want to do." I say — though it kills me to have to go slow.

"Did you tell Jared I was your girlfriend?" she asks in rush.

Fucking Jared. "No, I didn't. But I'd be lying if I said I didn't hope we get there. But, as I said, I promise we'll take it slow." I make a cross over my heart.

She smiles and leans into me a little. "I'll drink water for a while. I really do want to get to know you too."

After that, we dance and chit chat with the other ladies she works with and the guys that could make it from the station. I go to the restroom, and as I walk back to our table, I notice Tyler, the guy that started when I did. He's talking to Molly, and she's smiling her beautiful smile at him. I'd like to run up and clock him. I have a feeling Molly wouldn't be too happy if I did that. Instead, I walk up and wrap my arms around her waist. She turns her head and looks at me with a grin.

"Hey, Tyler, what's up?" I say, a little edge to my voice.

"I was just telling Molly how good she did in the show," he says looking down at my arms around her waist.

"Yeah, she did a great job. If that old lady hadn't made everyone cry, she'd have won," I say squeezing her around the middle and placing a kiss on her cheek.

"Jeez Brenden, why don't you pee on her," a tipsy Sammy shouts over the table. Everyone laughs, and I know I've been caught trying to stake my claim.

"I'm not into that sort of thing, Sammy. I'll leave that to you and Jared" I shout back at her. The whole group laughs again.

"Am I moving too fast?" I ask in her ear.

"No, this is perfect." She turns her head and looks at me. She licks her lips, and I take that as a sign she wants a kiss. I lean down and give her a soft, quick kiss. I need to get her alone so I can kiss her the way I want to.

The night goes on, and I try to stick close so I can fend off any guys that might think they have a chance with her still. I notice she's yawning. "You ready for me to take you home, Red?" I ask. We had agreed earlier that I'd drive her home tonight. Her car was still at Jared and Sammy's.

"Yeah, I'm ready," she says with another yawn. We say our goodbyes and a few people give us a hard time about leaving early. It's about eleven, so I think we've been here long enough.

I was lucky to get a parking spot on a side street only about three blocks from the pub, so we walk hand in hand to my jeep. I help her in and help her get buckled in. She gives me directions to her house, and I'm pleased to see she lives only about a mile and a half from my grandpa's place. We pull up in front of a little cottage type house. It's got a picket fence in front, and the house is white or light blue maybe. It's hard to see in the dark. There are red shutters and a red door and a one car detached garage set a little behind the house. It's adorable. It's cozy. It's Molly.

I walk her up to the door. Her porch light is on, but it's only just bright enough to see to put the key in the lock. She turns and looks at me. "Do you want to come in for a few?"

Fuck, yes, I do, but should I? We said slow. I just have to control myself and make sure I head home in just a few minutes. "Sure. I'd love to see your house. It's adorable, by the way. "

She beams. "I've only been here since last June. I really love it here." She unlocks the door, and I'm happy when I realize she's punching in a code for an alarm. She walks over to a small table and turns on a lamp. The light is low, but it's enough to take in the room. She's got little hooks on the wall where she hangs up her coat and purse. The small table with the lamp has big wicker baskets underneath. One has her shoes in it, and one has folded up blankets. She takes off the tall as fuck heels she's been wearing all night. She's so tiny now. I think I've only seen her in heels. How women wear those things, I'll never know.

"I'm gonna go get out of this dress. Make yourself at home. There's soda in the fridge or cider, if you want one," she says as she walks down a tiny hallway off the living room. I hang up my coat next to hers.

I walk into the open living room and kitchen area and look around. She's got a retro looking sofa that's a bright green. All of her furniture looks like it's from the 50s or 60s. It's all decorated in greens and blues with tons of throw pillows. Paintings of birds and flowers hang on the wall along with pictures of people — family and friends, I assume. Her kitchen is small — white cabinets and a bright green mixer on the counter with a little butcher block island and two stools. This whole place feels exactly like her. It's cozy and neat; I really like it here. I grab a soda from the fridge, which I realize looks like it's from the 1950s too, and then I notice the stove also looks retro. I walk into the living room and sit down on her couch. I can feel myself getting sleepy. I look around for the remote thinking maybe television will keep me awake. Where the hell is the tv? I'm looking around when Molly comes back into the room wearing some green and blue plaid pajama pants and a t-shirt that says Naughty Irish Girl on it.

She walks back over to the entry table and grabs the bouquet of flowers I got her. When I asked Jared if he happened to know what her favorite flowers were, I was surprised he knew. I was further surprised when he said kermit mums. I was expecting roses or tulips. I googled what they were and wasn't expecting these bright green little button flowers. He said she always puts them on the desk at the salon, and Sammy buys them for her on her birthday. She takes the bouquet into the kitchen, pulls a blue vase out from the cabinet under her sink, and fills it with water. Then she cuts the ends of the stems, arranges the flowers, and sets them in the middle of her little two-person table sitting between the living room and kitchen.

"Don't you have a television?" I say looking around.

She laughs. "Yes, I have a television." She walks over to this Armoire in the corner of the room and opens the doors. It's not huge, but it fits the room. "Do you want me to show you around?"

"Yeah, I'd love to see your place." I stand up.

"This is the living room and the kitchen...obviously." She points toward the kitchen. I follow her as she walks down the small hallway. I can see that there are four doors. The first door leads to a bedroom that is set up as a spare room and an office with a desk and a daybed. The next is a hall bath with a tub/shower combo. She shows me her bedroom. It's bigger than the first bedroom, but still kind of small. She has a white metal bed, white dresser, and a night stand. It reminds me of a bedroom you'd see in a seaside cottage with its sky-blue walls and fluffy white bedding. "This is my room," she says, "but this is the really cool part." She opens the fourth door in the hall, and I see stairs. She takes me by the hand and pulls me up the stairs. "It's still a work in progress." It's an attic space that is being refinished. Some of the walls are already framed out. It's the size of the entire downstairs with slanted walls from the roof pitch.

"Someday, this will be the master bedroom and bath and maybe one more small bedroom," she says looking down.

"Like a nursery?" I ask noticing a tinge of pink on her cheeks.

"That's a possibility," she smiles shyly. "C'mon, lets go back downstairs." She reaches for my hand. I take it and let her lead me back down.

"I know it's getting late, but do you want to hang out and watch TV for a bit?" she asks looking up at me hopefully.

"Absolutely." I say.

CHAPTER TEN

Molly

I know I probably should have him go home. It's late and he'll be here tomorrow night, but I'm not ready to be away from him. This might sound crazy, but I know this is going somewhere. I know he will be the one I spend forever with or the one that breaks my heart. He's not a fling, and as much as I want to jump into his lap right now, I also want to get to know him before we have sex.

"What should we watch?" I ask.

"Do you want to watch something, or would you rather talk?" he asks.

I smile, "We can talk." I'm kind of relieved. I feel so comfortable around him, but I feel like I barely know him.

"How long have you played the fiddle?" he asks, looking seriously interested in what I have to say.

"My mom made me start when I was five years old. When I was about fourteen, I stopped playing. I only picked it back up about three years ago. When I decided I wanted to play again, I thought it would be easy, like riding a bike. It's really not. It took me a while to get the basics down again. I've been practicing Shipping Up to Boston for at least two years. It's one of the only songs I can play somewhat decently." He's looking at me with is gorgeous blue eyes. I want to kiss him — really kiss him. No more pecks.

"Do you play any instruments?" I ask nervously, trying to keep my ass on the couch and out of his lap.

"We had a little piano when I was growing up. My mom would play once in a while, and I learned some easy songs when I was a kid, but I never went past what my mom showed me. When I was in high school, I tried to learn guitar, but I never really got the hang of it. I've been told I'm tone deaf, so I've come to the conclusion that music isn't in my wheelhouse. You, on the other hand, can sing, play fiddle, and dance. You're like a triple threat."

I laugh at that. "I wouldn't say I can dance. I can shake my ass when I get a few drinks in me, but I'm not much of a dancer, really."

"I bet you can slow dance." He stands up and hold his hand out to me. I put my hand in his. "Dance with me, Red." He pulls me up to standing.

"There's no music,.." He pulls out his phone, and I hear a familiar song. I cock my head to the side and look at him. "Are we listening to Celine Dion?"

"What? I love this song," he says seriously. I just smile and wrap my arms around his neck. We sway back and forth. I love the way he holds me close to his body. I lay my head on his chest. When the song comes to an end, he dips me backward. I'm ready for the kiss I just know is coming this time. And to my surprise, he touches my lips with a gentle kiss and pulls back before pulling me back up to standing.

My mouth starts talking before my brain can stop it. "Are you fucking kidding me?" He looks at me confused. "Are you EVER going to kiss me?"

He looks stunned, "I thought you wanted to take it slow."

"Slow, yes. I don't want to jump into bed yet. But…" Before I can finish the sentence, he's crushing his lips to mine. Fucking finally! He licks my lips, and I open my mouth for him. He slides his tongue inside my mouth, and I moan at the taste. My moan elicits a growl from him. I feel him walking backward a few steps, and when he sits on the couch, he brings me down to straddle his lap. I moan again when I feel his growing erection beneath me.

He digs his hand in my hair and grips it hard. He pulls his mouth away from mine. "Your lips are the sweetest thing I've ever tasted, Red." He kisses down the right side of my throat. "Are you sweet everywhere? I can't wait to find out."

He kisses my lips again. I feel one hand slide down my back and grip my ass. I'm rubbing myself against his hardness. It feels so good, I could almost come just from the friction. His hand slides up my side and slowly moves over my breast over my shirt.

"Fuck," he pulls his mouth away from mine and touches his forehead to mine. "We gotta stop, baby. If we don't, I'm gonna break my promise to go slow."

"Maybe we don't have to go slow." I say grinding against his hardness.

"Yes. We do. Please stop rocking like that, baby. You're gonna make me embarrass myself," he begs.

"Sorry," I pout.

"Red, don't look at me like that." He looks at the clock. "I should probably head home."

"You don't have to go. We can talk more or maybe watch a movie," I say. I'm not ready for him to leave.

"It's getting late, baby. I promised my grandpa we would go for coffee and donuts tomorrow morning. We have a date tomorrow night though, maybe we can pick up where we left off." He winks at me. I giggle. He's making me giggle.

"Ok, Blue Eyes, you better get going then," I say starting to get up. His hands hold my thighs. I look at him curiously. "I thought I was getting up."

"I just want to feel you in my lap for a couple more seconds." I lean forward and put my lips on his. This kiss is different. It's not the short, sweet one from before, and it's not the frantic kisses we were losing ourselves to minutes ago. It's slower. Lazy. Comfortable. I feel his tongue sweep into my mouth. I suck on it. I start to rock on him again. He stills under me. "Baby," he says against my lips. "if you don't stop, this is going to move faster than we want. And when we make love for the first time, I don't want to have to rush out afterward. I'll want to hold you all night."

I nod my head. "I know. You're right. We don't have to rush." I lay my head on his shoulder for a minute and feel his arms tighten around me. I'm so relaxed I think I doze off for a second. Did I just snore? Is that what woke me up? I feel his body shake beneath me.

I sit back. "Are you laughing at me?" I say with a smile on my face.

"Just a little, baby. C'mon, walk me to the door so you can set your alarm," he says nodding his head toward the door.

I climb off his lap and walk with him to the door. He slips on his coat and opens the front door. "What time do you want me to come over tonight?"

"Around 6:30 or 7?" I say, already wondering what I should make.

"Sounds good, baby," he says wrapping his arms around me and laying a kiss on me that could curl my toes. I'm starting to rethink this going slow idea. When he pulls away he whispers, "See you tonight, Red."

"Can't wait, Blue Eyes," I whisper back.

"Lock the door and set the alarm, baby." I nod and watch him walk to his jeep.

I close the door, lock it, and set the alarm. I miss him already. Would it be crazy to text him that? Only one way to find out.

CHAPTER ELEVEN

Brenden

As I'm driving home, I hear the ping of my text messages. I wait until I pull up to a stop light to look at my phone. I see there's a text from Molly that says, "I miss you already." I want to turn around and go back to her place and finish what we started. It was hard to walk away after that last kiss, both physically and mentally. I don't think I've ever been this hard in my life. I text back quickly, "Miss you too, baby."

Once I get home, I check in on Grandpa. One of his home health nurses was here this evening, and she left a note about his meds and what he ate for dinner. I peek in, and he's sleeping in his bed with his bi-pap machine on.

I head upstairs and strip off my pants. I leave my t-shirt on because it smells like her. I like having her scent on me. I crawl into bed and pass out as soon as my head hits the pillow.

Suddenly, I'm awakened. It takes me a few seconds to realize my phone's ringing. I grab for the pants I took off earlier and dig through the pockets until I find it. It stops ringing before I can answer it but immediately starts ringing again. It's Molly. "Baby? Is everything ok?" I ask feeling panicked.

"Brenden, someone tried to get in the house," she says sounding scared as fuck. Her voice is trembling. "My alarm went off a few minutes ago. The police are dispatching, but would it be too much to ask to have you come back?"

I look over at the clock. It's close to four in the morning. "I'm on my way, baby. Do you want me to stay on the line until I get there? Would that make you feel better?" I ask hoping I can calm her down.

"Could you, please?" she sounds terrified.

"Absolutely, baby. I'm here but I gotta get dressed. Give me just a minute," I say. I hurry and slide on some sweats and a hoodie. I pull on some socks and shoes. "Ok, baby, bear with me a minute, and I'll be on my way." I run down the stairs an peek in at Grandpa. He's sitting up in bed looking confused.

"Why the hell are you running around making so much racket?" he says groggily.

"Sorry, Grandpa, I gotta run out. My girl needs me. I'll be back later, and we'll get donuts." He waves his hand in my direction.

"Get the hell out of here then. Go take care of her," he says as he lays back down.

"Grandpa sounds sweet," I hear Molly say. "Have you told him about me?" she questions.

"Of course I have. I told him about you right after you cut my hair. He thinks you're beautiful," I tell her.

"How does he know what I look like?" she asks. Dammit.

"There's a bulletin board at work with pictures from different events. You're in a couple of them. I might have taken pictures of your pictures, and I might have shown them to him. "

"Oh... That's sweet in a slightly stalkery way, Blue Eyes," she says with a laugh. I'm just glad she doesn't sound terrified anymore. "Brenden, I think the cop is here. I can see red and blue lights outside the front window."

"I'm almost there, baby. You ok to let me go? " I ask.

"Yeah, I'll see you in a minute," she says before she hangs up.

When I pull up, I see the squad car. I park behind it and head up through the gate. I don't know if I should knock or not, but I feel like it's ok if I just go in. I decide to knock on the door before poking my head inside. "Molly?"

She pops around the corner wearing a robe over the pjs she had on when I left. "Brenden, come in here." she waves me in.

"Hey, baby, what happened?" I say taking her face in my hands. I look into her eyes and try to see if she's ok.

"Molly was just going over the details." The cop says. I recognize him. I think he was at a call we had earlier this week. I give him a head lift.

"Well, after you left earlier, I locked the door and set the alarm. I went into my room and read on my e-reader for a little while to wind down, and I ended up dozing off. I woke up to the alarm going off. I didn't know what it was at first, and then my phone started ringing. The alarm company was calling to see if I was ok or if it was an accident. When I hung up with them, I called you. I didn't even leave my room until he got here." She says, taking a deep breath gesturing toward the cop.

"What time did you leave?" he asks me.

"It was probably close to one. I live about a mile and half from here with my Grandpa," I say.

"Did either of you notice any cars parked out front that aren't usually there when you got home, or when you left?" he nods at me.

Molly answers with a simple no. The sliding door opens up, and another police officer steps through. It's the cop that was at the salon on Friday. John maybe? "Hey, Molly, did you notice when you came home last night that there was some graffiti on your garage door? And the side of your house?"

"No, what kind of graffiti? What does it say?" she says with wide eyes.

He looks uncomfortable, "It says WHORE across your garage and SLUT on the side of your house. Do you think Hank would have possibly done this?"

I feel my blood start boiling. That fucking overgrown prick. I'm going to beat the shit out of him. I feel her hand reach over and touch my arm. I look over at her. She's so little and sweet. She's trying to comfort *me* when her ex-boyfriend is terrorizing her.

"If you had asked me a week ago, I would have said no. But he was not himself when I saw him Friday. We were together for four years, and he barely ever argued with me, let alone tried to grab me. I have a doorbell cam," she says like she suddenly remembered. She pulls up the app on her phone. "I muted the alerts because it goes off when people drive by, and it drives me crazy all day at work."

You can only see the front yard from the angle of the door. The area that was defaced is out of view. We all gather around her to see. She watches it in fast forward until it get's close to the time her alarm went off. You don't see anyone, but you can hear the alarm on the video. You can't see anyone run away from the house. A few minutes later, an SUV drives by. It could be random though.

"Do you know what kind of vehicle Hank drives?" John asks.

"He used to have a red F150 pick up truck. I'm not sure if he still does. Before Friday, I hadn't seen him in almost a year," she shrugs.

"When did your relationship with Hank end?" the other cop asks.

"Last April...the 18th," she says.

"Can I ask why the relationship ended?" John asks, which definitely piques my attention.

"I caught him cheating," she states simply.

"Oh, right, you uploaded a video to Facebook didn't you?" John asks, smirking.

"Yup," she says, matter-of-factly.

"You had it on video?" I ask.

She kind of rolls her eyes and heaves a big sigh. "I came home in the middle of the day to meet the maintenance guy for the apartments we lived in. Hank was supposed to be working. I heard a noise and found him having sex with some other woman. I took a video, then I left and met the maintenance guy on my way out. I told him Hank was home. Then I texted the video to him saying we were over and posted it on Facebook. He didn't see either right away, but his mom called him to ask what was going on. It took Facebook several hours to take it down, and most of his friends and family saw it. A good number of them sided with me in our breakup."

Wow, this girl's savage. Is it weird that I like it?

"And you hadn't seen him since that day?" the other cop asked.

"No, I saw him one other time. The day I went to get my belongings. He had broken most of my stuff and poured bleach on my clothes. We got into an argument, and I broke his television set. The cops were called, but neither of us pressed charges," she says looking over at me nervously.

"Is there anyone else you can think of that would have wanted to break in or damage your property?" John asks.

"No, not at all." she says.

"We've still got a good hour to an hour and a half before the sun is up. Please stay away from the garage, the back door, and the side of the house. We're going to start filing the report. We'll be back to take photos and see if we can find any evidence of who might have done this." John says. They head out to their cruisers, and Molly closes the door behind them. She leans against the door with her eyes closed.

"Babe?" I say.

"Do you think I'm a crazy person?" Molly asks. "Are you feeling like you should run for the hills?" She laughs without humor.

I walk over to her, pinch her chin between my fingers, and tip her head back. "No, baby. If anything, I like you even more. You're fearless, and you stand up for yourself. I'll always worry about you, baby, but it eases my mind to know you can and do take care of yourself." I lean down and kiss her sweet lips. She wraps her arms around me, and I pick her up. I walk over to the couch and sit.

She pulls back. "This seems familiar," she says grinding her pussy against me again.

"Baby as much as I'd like to keep doing this, we have cops

outside the house. I don't want them coming back in and seeing you like this," I say trying to stop myself from grinding back into her.

"What would they see, Blue Eyes? I'm just sitting on your lap," she says moving against me.

"If you keep rocking like that, they'll see you come. I'm about five seconds away from laying you down and tasting your sweet pussy," I growl into her ear. "Is that what you want, baby? Say the word, and I'll take you into your bedroom and have you for breakfast."

"Yes," she says, so sure, not knowing she's unleashing the beast. Once I have her, there's no going back.

Molly

Brenden picks me up and starts to carry me into the bedroom. I know this isn't the best timing for this, but I can't seem to care right now. He pushes my back against the hallway wall. I feel his hard cock through his pants. He's grinding against me. I push him back, "Please, Brenden, take me to bed. I need you," I beg. I'm not ashamed to beg.

"Am I not moving fast enough, Red? I got you, baby." He starts to walk toward the bedroom. I trail kisses down his neck while he walks. He lays me down on the bed and stands back up. He walks back to the door and locks it. "Just in case they come in without knocking."

He comes back over and grabs my pj pants by the waist and pulls them down my legs. I forgot I'm not wearing any panties under my pajama pants.

"Fuck, baby. You have the prettiest pussy I've ever seen." He runs his finger down my slit. "Fucking soaked. I gotta taste you, baby." He gets down on his knees and puts both of my legs over his shoulders. "Push up on your elbows, baby. I want you to watch." He wastes no time either. He takes a big lick from my core to my clit. "Mmmmm. You taste sweet like a peach, baby."

I let out a shuddering moan. I'm gripping the sheets while he fucks me with his tongue. "Look at me, Red. Watch me make you come," he says, looking up at me.

It feels so good that it's hard to keep my eyes open. When I feel one of his fingers start to explore my opening, I fall back on the bed. "You better watch, baby, or I'll stop," he says pulling back a little.

I lean up on one elbow and grip the back of his head with the other. "Don't you dare stop. Ever!" I feel him push one finger into my pussy. "Fuck!" I nearly come just from that. He pushes another finger into me, and I nearly shoot off the bed. "Brenden, I'm gonna come," I practically scream.

"Come baby," he says before he attacks my clit.

I start grinding my pussy against his face. This orgasm rips through me like nothing I've ever felt before. I'm trying to hold back the scream that wants to erupt from my body. I think he's going to stop, but he doesn't. "Brenden, stop! It's too much!"

"No, come again baby. I want to taste one more." He's still fucking me with his fingers and sucking on my clit. I can't do it. I can't come again. "Give me one more!" he growls. And I do. I come so hard and so long that I think I've died, and this must be what heaven is — just one endless orgasm. And it's glorious.

He finally stops and pulls his fingers out of me. I open my eyes just in time to see him lick his fingers that were just inside of me. I swear I come again. Just seeing him do that sent another zing through me. He smiles at me like he knows.

He crawls up my body, kissing all along his way up. "If the cops weren't outside right now, I'd give you my cock, baby. But I need more time than they're gonna give us for that."

He wasn't wrong. We no sooner came out of the bedroom than they were knocking on the door. I slid on some socks and my sneakers. As soon as they say I can go out, I want to see what kind of damage was done outside.

I'm sure it should be able to be fixed by a coat of paint. If this really was Hank, he's in for another ass kicking. Probably not from me, I'm really not a violent person at all, but I couldn't be more thankful I've been taking those self-defense classes. I'm really hoping Sammy goes with me to class.

John and the other cop (Craig Voss is his name, I think?) go out and look around the house. They dust for fingerprints on the back door and the gate. After about forty-five minutes, they say I can come out and look around.

Standing in the driveway at six in the morning, staring at the word WHORE written in big black letters across the garage door was *not* my idea of a fun Sunday morning. I look at the side of the house and in even bigger letters is the word SLUT. I know the cops told me it was there, but seeing it with my own eyes really terrifies me. Who would do this? I can feel the tears welling up in my eyes. I don't want to cry. I don't want to give whoever did this the satisfaction of knowing they got to me. I suck in a breath, and I feel Brenden wrap his arm around me.

"Molly, we found something that might be disturbing to see. Let's go back into the house," Craig says.

A chill runs up my back. I have no idea what they might show me. We go in. Brenden and I sit on my couch. John pulls out a manila envelope that contains at least twenty black and white photos of me. They've been altered, but I know it's me by the clothes and the way I wear my hair. But my face — it's like they photoshopped a skull over my face. There's one of me walking down the sidewalk while talking on my phone after my date with Frybeard, me standing in the salon, and me on stage last night at McMurphy's. There are several from months ago on dates with various weirdos. There's another with me at my self-defense class. One looking into my living room window while I'm sitting on the couch reading. I pick one up and begin to sob. It's me, sleeping, in my bed. It was taken through my bedroom window. How long has this been going on?

"Oh my God. What is happening? Who is doing this?" I cry. There's another one of me with Sammy in the park with the twins. I'm going down the big slide with Aubrie. I am practically hyperventilating at this point.

"Breathe, baby. Put your head between your knees. Breathe, Molly. Breathe in, breathe out. Just listen to the sound of my voice, baby." Brenden is trying to calm me down. I feel like I'm having a fucking panic attack or something.

Once I can breathe without feeling like I'm going to pass out, John says," I didn't see this earlier when it was still dark. It was laying under the cushion on your patio furniture. I almost missed it. Just by looking at these, can you tell me when any of these were taken?"

"Yeah. This one was last night at McMurphy's. This one was Tuesday night. I think this one was taken last month on the 24th. This was two Sundays ago." I go over each picture and try to nail down the dates and times for them.

"It might be a good idea for you to stay somewhere else tonight," John says.

"Yeah, I can probably stay with Sammy tonight." I whisper. I'm trying to wrap my head around what's happening.

"You can stay with me." Brenden says.

"I can't ask you to do that. Especially since you live with your Grandpa. I haven't even met him yet." I know I'm looking at him like he's crazy.

"Well, once the officers are done, you can come with me to get coffee and donuts with him," Brenden says. No big deal. We haven't even had a real date yet, and I'm meeting his Grandpa. "It will be fine, Red."

"I'm having a hard time believing anything will be fine at the moment," I sigh and lean into his side.

"I think we have everything we need for now. Please call this number if you need anything, remember anything important, or come across anything strange," Craig hands me a card.

"Thanks, guys. I really appreciate your coming so quickly and being so thorough." I walk them to the door.

Before John steps out, he touches my shoulder, "Don't hesitate to call if you need anything Molly." I want to push his hand off my shoulder, but I think he's just trying to comfort me.

"I promise I will." With a nod, he heads out the door.

CHAPTER TWELVE

Molly

$\mathcal{I}$t's nearly 7:00 by the time the cops leave. Brenden won't let the idea of me staying at his place go.

"Brenden, don't you think it's too soon for me to come spend the night with you?" I ask.

"Fuck, no. I don't think that at all. I want you safe. You can go stay with Sammy tomorrow night. I still want to have our date tonight. It would be late by the time I was ready to let you go," he says. Like he's not asking me to spend the night on our first date.

"You're kind of a pain in the ass. Did you know that?" I sass at him.

"I've been told." he smirks.

"How about for now, you let me go take a shower, and I'll come have donuts with you and your Grandpa. Then we can see how he would feel about having me there tonight." I'm not completely opposed to spending the night with him. I haven't shared a bed with someone in a while, but I bet Brenden would be a good snuggler.

He gets a big smile on his face, "Do you need some help in the shower?"

"As much 'help' as I'm sure you'd be, I think its probably best if I go alone. Your grandpa would never get donuts." I smile as I sashay away. He doesn't let me get far before he grabs me around the waist and pulls me back to his chest.

"That's absolutely true, Red. I can't wait until I can eat you for breakfast again. Hurry in the shower, baby, or I'll come in after you." He purrs into my ear, then nips it with his teeth.

"I'll be quick, Blue Eyes." I head into my bedroom and grab clothes to put on after. Part of me thinks that maybe I should wrap myself in a towel and walk from the bathroom to bedroom when I'm done just to tease him. But I believe all plans for today would be canceled, and his grandpa would never get his donuts.

I make quick work in the shower. I decide not to shampoo my hair. I use dry shampoo and braid it to one side. I put on my favorite skinny jeans, a flowy cream-colored t-shirt, and my favorite Kelly-green cardigan. I put a smidge of concealer under my eyes, add some shimmery bronze eye shadow, and a couple of swipes of mascara. I run to my room and grab a chunky gold and black necklace, and I head out to my shoe basket to find my leopard print flats.

I realize that Brenden is stretched out on my couch with his arm thrown over his eyes. Is he sleeping? "Brenden," I whisper. I get a little closer to him and reach down to shake his shoulder. "Bren..." he grabs me and pulls me down on top of him.

"Ready to go baby?" he asks, as he tucks a loose strand of my hair behind my ear. Swoon.

"Yes," I breath out. "I'm sorry you had to get up so early and come over here. I'm sure you're beat."

"Maybe after coffee and donuts we can take a nap. Did you have other plans today?" he asks, running his hands up and down my back. I could go to sleep right now.

"No other plans today, but we better get going, Blue Eyes, or I'm going to fall asleep." I say, trying to push up off of him. He holds me close for a moment.

"I suppose you're right." he sighs.

I stand up and hold my hand out to him. He smiles and shakes his head but takes it anyway.

I set my alarm on the way out and lock the door. He drives me over to his grandpa's house, which isn't far from me at all. The house is a mid-century modern style and I absolutely love it.

When we come in, Brenden leads me into the living room. His Grandpa is sitting in his recliner watching sports news. He's got salt and pepper hair that's mostly salt. I can definitely see a resemblance between him and Brenden.

"Grandpa, I want to introduce you to someone," Brenden says over the TV.

Grandpa mutes the television and looks over at us. "Well, now, you didn't tell me we'd be having company today." I watch as he pushes a button on his chair and it starts to lift up to help him stand. That is pretty amazing. I wonder if he'll let me sit in it later? He walks over closer to us. He's not as tall as Brenden, but he is hunched over a little. "It's so nice to meet you, Molly. My grandson hasn't stopped yapping about you since he saw your beautiful face," he says taking my hand in both of his hands. I immediately love him.

"Thanks for playing it cool, Grandpa. Molly, this is my Grandpa, Bennett Clarke," Brenden says.

"Ben. You call me Ben," he says with a smile and a squeeze to my hand. "Are you two ready to get some donuts?"

"I sure am," I say with a big smile. "Where are we going?"

"Have you ever gone to Max's Donut Hole?" Ben says taking my arm and tucking it into the crook of his own, which makes me smile.

"My dad took me there a few times growing up. It's been years since I've been there though," I say remembering my dad sitting at the counter with me. I always got this big, whipped cream covered donut and a chocolate milk.

"Was your dad a fireman?" Ben questions.

"Cop." I answer.

"Yup. I'm sure he went there a time or two then. What's his name?"

"Dennis O'Brien. He retired almost three years ago," I say.

"Oh, sure. I know Dennis," he says.

"You do?" I ask, kind of shocked.

"Oh yeah. I was a fireman here for thirty-five years. It's hard to find a cop, EMT, or another fireman that I don't know. C'mon, slow poke. Let's get going. They'll be out of all the good ones by the time we get there," he throws over his shoulder at Brenden. I look over my shoulder and catch the smile on Brenden's face.

We pull up to the Donut Hole, and it still looks the same as when I was a kid. I kind of forgot it was here. It's got that dark wood paneling on the walls and dark brown padded booths. There's a counter top you can sit at with padded stools. That's where I remember sitting with my dad. It smells like heaven in here. I notice a lot of older gentleman inside sitting in the booths. We each order donuts, and I get one of those chocolate cream filled ones that has a mountain of whipped cream on top of it and a chocolate milk. Might as well keep up with tradition.

Ben leads us over to a group of older guys. "Hey, guys. I want to introduce you all to Brenden's girl. This is Molly O'Brien. Dennis O'Brien is her old man." I can feel my cheeks heat a little being called Brenden's girl. I get a rousing welcome. I actually know a few of the guys that had worked with my dad, and Mr. Tillton comes into the shop to get his hair cut by Caitlyn.

"How's Dennis doing? Still on the road?" one of the guys asks.

"Yeah, he and mom are near Yellowstone right now. I think they should be back to town in three weeks." I answer.

"Grandpa, you visit with your friends. Molly and I will be right over here," Brenden says. I feel his hand resting on my lower back.

"All right. I'll let you know when I'm ready," Ben tells us.

We sit by the front window of the shop in a booth. I scoot in and then realize Brenden's sitting down on the same side. "You don't want to sit over there?" I nod to the other side of the table.

"No, I like to sit next to you. Then I can touch you easier." he says.

"Oh." I try to hold back a smile. "So, do you come here with your Grandpa a lot?" I ask trying to take a ladylike bite of this monstrosity of a donut I have in front of me. I do not succeed. I end up with cream on my nose.

Brenden laughs and hands me a napkin. "Yeah, he usually

comes every Sunday to meet up with his buddies. Sometimes they play a card game I don't understand. Sometimes they just sit around and shoot the shit and talk about the old days. I've been able to come with him the last three Sundays, and when I was younger, I'd come spend time with him in the summer. We always came on Sundays. I actually think I've met your dad before too."

"That's kinda crazy, huh?" I say before I take another messy bite of my donut.

"It's pretty cool, I think. In fact, I'm almost positive that when I visited Grandpa last summer, your dad said he had a single daughter I should meet," he says while stuffing half a donut into his mouth.

"What? Are you serious?" I'm dumbfounded.

"I'm completely serious. I didn't meet you then because I didn't live here. I was only visiting. I hadn't planned on moving here. Until Grandpa fell about a month ago, I had no plans to live here. But I'm here now," he says bumping his shoulder into mine.

"Yes, you are," I lean my head onto his shoulder. We're at the donut shop for about an hour. I end up finishing my messy but delicious donut. And then I give into temptation for a second donut. Mmmmmm…. Blueberry cake donut.

CHAPTER THIRTEEN

Brenden

*A*fter the donut shop, we take Grandpa back home. On the drive home, he asks about what happened this morning, and then he badgers Molly about staying here with us. She still says she'll think about it. He settles into his recliner to watch some documentary on the History Channel as soon as we're in the door. We sit and visit with him for a bit, but then I catch Molly nodding off.

"How about that nap, baby?" I whisper to her.

"That sounds nice," she says, so I pull her up off the couch, and we head upstairs to my room. We're just laying down and getting comfy when her phone starts playing Crazy Bitch by Buckcherry. I didn't know people still put ringtones on their phones. Molly answers it and holds it up to her ear.

"Hello, Sam I Am," she says into the phone.

"OH. MY. GOD. Molls, are you ok? Jared just told me! Someone tried to break into your place last night?" Sammy shrieks into the phone.

"Yeah, they didn't come in, but they did some damage outside and left something really creepy," she says. I had almost forgotten about the pictures. Thinking about it makes me so angry and scared for her at the same time.

"Do you want us to come over there? We can bring lunch. Mom and dad have the twins until late this afternoon."

"No, I'm not home right now. I'm with Brenden," she says looking over at me.

"Ooooooh. I see. Well, I won't bother you then. I'll talk to you later, Batch!" Sammy abruptly hangs up the phone.

"Why do you two call each other batch?" I noticed they did it several times last night at McMurphy's.

She giggles. "In our early 20s we used to go out practically every weekend. One night we had had quite a lot to drink. We were walking down the sidewalk with a few other friends. I think Anna and I were lagging behind a bit when Sammy yelled, 'Let's go, batches' in stead of 'bitches.' At twenty-two and fairly intoxicated, it was the funniest thing we'd ever heard, of course. So we started saying that instead of calling each other a bitch. I'd say it's almost a term of endearment now."

"Girls are so weird sometimes," I say shaking my head. "Get some sleep, baby."

I swear she's asleep in seconds. I wait a few minutes and then creep out of the room to call Jared.

"Parker," he barks into the phone.

"Hey, man. I need a favor."

"What's up?"

"So I know Sammy called Molly a little bit ago about what

happened last night. Did you know that whoever did it painted some pretty fucked up shit on her house and garage door?" I ask.

"Yeah, it came across the scanner early when the guys at the station were out on a call. Colton is Molly's cousin, and he recognized the address. They drove the rig by when the police cruisers were still there," he says sounding pretty pissed.

"Yeah, one of the cops suggested she not stay there tonight. I'm trying to talk her into staying with me, but she might call you guys later to see if she can stay there. Anyway, I was wondering if you know if she has paint in her garage so we can fix the graffiti. She got pretty upset when she saw it," I say clenching my fists.

"Yeah, I think she's got some in her garage. I know we have spare keys to her place, but I'm not sure about the garage. Wait, her car is still here so we probably have her garage door opener," he says.

"Cool. She's sleeping right now. I'd really like to get it taken care of today. I'm gonna try to call one of the cops that were there this morning and see if I can paint over it or if it needs to stay up longer for evidence. If I can't paint over it yet, I'll see about getting some tarps to hide it for now."

"Ok, man. Call me after you talk to them. I'll come over and help you. I don't think it should take too long either way," he offers.

"Thanks, man," I say hanging up.

I call down to the police station and ask for John or Craig. Craig tells me they took pictures and picked up all evidence they found. It should be ok to paint over. He also says to pay attention to anything out of the ordinary and if we find anything to call him. He'll head straight over. I call Jared, and we plan to meet over there around one.

I sneak back into the room and crawl into bed with Molly. I set the alarm on my phone for a couple of hours from now. I lay behind her, wrap my arm around her middle, and pull her against me before I doze off.

———

I wake up hearing the alarm on my phone going off. Reaching for the phone, I realize Molly isn't in the bed with me anymore. I lay there for a minute, assuming she's in the restroom and will be back in a second. After a couple of minutes, I decide to go find her. When I open the bedroom door, I can hear her and Grandpa talking downstairs.

I walk into the living room and see she's sitting on the couch. Grandpa sits in his recliner, and they are watching some old black and white movie. "What you guys watching?"

"Your girl here knows a lot about old movies. We're watching A Streetcar Named Desire." Then they both starts yelling, "Stella!!!" and Molly giggles and Grandpa throws his head back and laughs. It's been a while since I've seen him laugh like that, and it gives me that warm feeling in my chest.

I hate to break up their bonding time, but we're gonna have to go soon. "Hey, baby, we gotta head over to your place in a bit."

"We do?" she looks at me with her head cocked to the side.

"Yeah, we're gonna meet Jared and Sammy. Jared is gonna help me paint the garage door and side of the house."

"Oh, gosh." her face falls. "I almost forgot about it." She shakes her head.

"It's ok, baby. Do you know if you have leftover paint? Or the names of the colors you used?"

"Ummmmm, I think I might have paint cans in the garage. I didn't paint the house, but I'm pretty sure the previous owners left some."

"Lets go by your house and look for the paint, and then we can run to the hardware store to get supplies and more paint if we need it," I say standing up and reaching my hand out to her.

"Ok."

"Grandpa, we're gonna take off for a little bit. We'll be back a little later."

"Ok. Molly, honey, you don't be a stranger. Come watch movies with me anytime," he says.

Molly leans down and gives him a kiss on the cheek. "I promise I will."

CHAPTER FOURTEEN

Molly

*W*hen we get back to my house, we check the garage for the paint. We find almost a full gallon of the blue house color and about a half gallon of the red paint that's on the doors and shutters. Brenden said that since we need brushes and tarps, we should take the paint to the hardware store and see if they can re-shake it, and we can have them color match them in case we need more. That's not something I would have ever even thought about doing. We made it quick since Jared and Sammy were coming over. We're standing in my driveway laying the tarps down when Sammy pulls up in my Beetle and Jared in his truck.

"I figured I'd bring your car back in case you needed it," Sammy rattles off. Then she suddenly bursts into tears and runs to me wrapping me in a hug. "I didn't know how big they wrote it. Do you think it was Hank?"

I sigh, "I really don't know. He's the most logical explanation. I feel like he would never do this. But he was weird on Friday. I've never seen him like that."

"Well, we brought some stuff for lunch. Did you guys eat yet?" Sammy asks while walking to the passenger side of my car bringing out a brown paper bag.

"We had donuts this morning. I could definitely eat though," I say, realizing that I'm hungry.

"Babe, why don't you and Sammy go and eat lunch. This shouldn't take long. I think Jared and I can handle it." Brenden offers.

I nod and lead Sammy through the back gate and in through the back door. "Are the kiddos still with your mom?"

"Yeah, they were going to take them to the zoo today. They'll be home later this afternoon, stuffed full of sugar, I'm sure," she rolls her eyes. Her mom, who was so strict about our snacks as kids, gives in to the twins' every wish.

"What did you bring me to eat? I didn't even realize I was hungry until you said food."

"Nothing huge. We just stopped at the deli and got some soup, salads, and sandwiches." Sammy no sooner says this, and my stomach lets out a big growl. We both giggle. I opt for half a corned beef sandwich and a cup of chicken noodle soup.

"So, not that the graffiti and the person trying to get into your house aren't important, but what happened after you guys left McMurphy's last night?" I smile and shake my head. She's always so damn nosy.

"Well, we got here, and I invited him in. I changed into pjs and I gave him a tour of the place. We talked about watching a movie, but then we chit chatted a little bit. He put on music, and we slow danced." I look up smiling. Sammy's got the swoony face on. "We made out for a little bit, but when things started to get a little hot and heavy, he pulled back."

"What!?" she practically shouts.

"I had told him last night at the bar that I wanted to take things slow. He was trying to respect my wishes. But then he said he should probably get going."

Sammy starts to say something, and I cut her off. "He had promised his Grandpa he'd take him for donuts this morning...early. So we said goodbye, and I locked up and went to bed."

"So when did your alarm go off?" she asks while stuffing a big bite of salad into her mouth.

"I think it was around four this morning. It scared the fuck out of me, and it took me a minute to realize that's what it was. It's never gone off before. The alarm company called my phone about thirty seconds later, and they dispatched police. Then I called Brenden and he headed over. He only lives like five minutes from here."

"That's convenient," she says around another huge bite of salad, waggling her brows at me.

"You are truly sexy when you talk with your mouth full," I say flatly.

"So then what happened?" she says ignoring me.

"So Brenden stayed on the line with me until the cops got here. John Palmer looked around outside, Craig Voss started asking me some questions, and then Brenden showed up. A few minutes later, John came in and asked if I had noticed the graffiti earlier. He told me what it said, but I still wasn't expecting it when I saw it."

"Yeah, when Jared told me about what happened this morning, I wasn't expecting it to cover nearly the whole garage door and half the side of your house. Hank is such a fucking asshole." Sammy says around another bite of food. She's not wrong about that.

"Anyway, they went out to the cruiser until it started getting light out." I'm not sure if I want to tell her about what Brenden and I did this morning. Sammy and I usually dish on all the details, but I kinda feel like I want it to be private. "So once it was light enough, they took pictures of stuff and dusted for fingerprints. Oh my GOD, Sammy! The pictures!"

"What pictures?" she says with wide eyes.

"John tells me they found an envelope under the cushion on my patio set. It had like twenty pictures of me. Like stalker-type pictures!" My eyes start to tear up just thinking about it. "They were photo shopped too. You could tell they were me, but whoever took them put this skull over my face in all the pictures." I set down my sandwich and push it away. I feel a tear fall down my cheek. "Sammy, some of them were from several months ago. One was from last night while I was on stage at McMurphy's." I swipe at the tears running out of my eyes. I chance a look at Sammy. She's got this horror stricken look on her face, and tears are starting to run down her cheeks. "There was even one with you and me with the kids, at the park." I'm sobbing now.

"Fuck, Molls. That's fucking scary. I don't think you should stay here. Why don't you come stay with us?" she asks through the tears.

"I was planning to call and ask, but Brenden is kind of insistent that I come stay with him. We were supposed to have real date tonight. What am I gonna do, Sammy? Not about the date, but about whoever did this?"

"I don't know, Molls, but you know you're always welcome at our place," she offers.

I hear the door slide open and the guys come in. "Why does it look like you've both been crying?" Jared growls.

"I was telling Sammy about the pictures we found," I say looking at Brenden. I see his jaw tick, and he looks pissed.

"What pictures?" Jared demands. Sammy rattles off what I just told her. "Holy fuck, Molls. You gotta come stay with us. I don't think it's safe for you here."

"I'll think about it." I say, looking at Brenden.

"Are you guys done painting already?" Sammy asks.

"Not yet. We got the garage door mostly done, but I think it's gonna take a few coats to cover. We might need to go get more paint," Brenden says.

"Well, you guys should eat while you're in here." Sammy says pushing a sandwich in Jared's direction. Brenden washes the paint off his hands in the sink and then comes over to see what there is. He settles for a turkey sandwich and stands next to me at the island.

"Do you have any mustard?" he asks, and Sammy bursts out in a fit of giggles. Brenden looks at her like she's nuts.

"MUSTARD MAN!" Sammy works out around her hysterical laughter.

"Would you stop?" I say shaking my head and trying to hold back laughter.

"Who is Mustard Man?" Brenden and Jared both say.

I sigh. I don't know why I'm always telling these damn stories. "Mustard Man was another failed date I had during cosmetology school. There was a little sub shop near the school where we ate most days. One of the guys that worked there would always flirt with me, and one day he asked me out on an actual date. We decided to meet at the sub shop after I got out of school one night. I thought we were just meeting there, but he bought me a sub. It was a little sweet because he made me the sandwich I always ordered, but then when we sat down, he brought out this jar of Grey Poupon and kept wanting me to try it. I told him I didn't want any, but he wouldn't stop. He kept saying 'Just try it! You'll like it.' I told him I don't really like mustard that much. You would have thought I slapped him in the face. When we were done eating, I thought maybe we'd go see a movie or play putt-putt. But he looked me in the face and said, 'I don't think this is going to work out. I don't think I could be with someone that doesn't like mustard.'" By the end, Brenden is shaking trying to hold in the laugh.

"After that, I tried to avoid going in there because, what a freaking weirdo. But on occasion, it was the quickest option if i needed to eat, so I would go in. I lucked out for a while that he wasn't working or was with another customer. Then, one day, he served me, and he wouldn't even look at me. When we got to the condiments, I asked for mayo, and he yelled, 'WHO DOESN'T LIKE MUSTARD?' He ended up squeezing the mayo bottle too hard, and the top shot off and covered the whole sandwich. He just threw the bottle and yelled at his coworker that he was going on break. That poor girl was so confused. She made me a new sandwich and I never went back in after that," I say taking a bite of my sandwich. "As it turns out, I learned later that I do kinda like mustard, but only on burgers and pastrami." Brenden is full on laughing at this point.

"It sounds like you have dated some nuts, babe." he says. "Can't wait until you tell me about Italian Job."

"You are NEVER going to hear about him!" I say shaking my head.

"Tell him about 6.5," Jared casually tosses in.

"Ugh... You guys are not helping. Ok, so we were all at McMurphy's one night, and I start chatting with this guy. He buys me a drink. We dance. Then they played Dancing Queen, which is our jam," I say pointing to Sammy. We both do a little shimmy. "Anyway, Jared and Kelli's husband, Josh, are standing over to the side, and this guy is standing near them. I'm not sure if he didn't realize I knew them or what. But he told Jared I was a '6.5' on a scale of 1 to10."

"Yeah, and I told him if he didn't get away and stay away from her, I was going to break his fucking teeth off on the curb." Jared still looks pissed about it.

"Easy, baby. Calm down. The bad man left Molls alone," Sammy says rubbing his back. Jared rolls his eyes and then smiles at her.

"So when we were done dancing, I realized he wasn't there anymore. Sammy ended up telling me the next day what he had said. So about a week goes by, and I'm standing in the coffee shop, and he taps me on the shoulder. He was trying to be all flirty. I asked what happened to him at McMurphy's, already knowing what he said and what Jared told him. He said something came up, but he'd really like to get my number. I said, 'Oh, yeah? On a scale of 1-10, how much do you want my number?' he looked pretty shocked. I said, 'You're an asshole.' Then I got my coffee and walked out."

"You're kind of a badass baby." he says, smiling.

"Correction. I am a total badass," I say, taking another bite of my sandwich.

After the guys painted the garage door and the side of the

house, Jared and Sammy took off. I'm still on the fence about staying the night with Brenden. We haven't even been on an actual date yet, but I can tell you that I really like spending time with him. I feel like this is going somewhere. Is it weird that I almost think we don't need a first date? I mean we've already hung out several times. Doesn't that count?

We decide to watch a movie at my place, and I grill some steaks, and make a salad and baked potatoes. I let him pick the movie, and I'm pleasantly surprised when he picks a romantic comedy. We're snuggled up on the couch watching the movie, and I can feel myself getting sleepy. It's only about 7:30, but I know I won't last too much longer. I think the stress of the week and what happened last night has sapped all my energy.

"I'm getting so tired. I think I should pack some stuff up and head over to Sammy's." I say, peeking up through my lashes.

"Babe, I'd really like it if you came and stayed with me tonight. I'm not ready to have you out of my sight after last night. You can stay with Sammy tomorrow night. I have to work then." He gives me a pouty face. Then he pulls me onto his lap and holds my face in his hands. "Please ,baby? I just want you safe."

"You don't think it's too soon to be spending the night together?" I say shyly.

"Baby, I know we haven't known each other long at all. But from the second I saw you, I was drawn to you. I don't know what the future holds, but I can see you in my future. I'm not trying to move too fast, and I'm not trying to freak you out. But since I walked into your salon, I haven't stopped thinking about you. And since I tasted your sweet pussy this morning, I haven't stopped thinking about tasting it again." I can feel myself getting wet thinking about him doing just that.

"We don't have to rush the sex. I can wait, Red. But please let me help keep you safe," he pleads. It's hard to say no. And if I'm being honest, I really don't want to. I want to be with him. I want to kiss him…among other things. And every time he calls me baby, I melt inside.

"Ok. I'll stay with you." He pulls me in for a kiss before I can say another word. It's a fucking fantastic kiss. I love the way he fucks my mouth with his tongue. I love the way he holds onto my face but somehow works one hand down to my ass. I love the way he kisses and nibbles on my neck. I'm lost in his kiss when he pulls back.

"Lay down, baby. I want to taste you again."

I don't have to be told twice. I slide off his lap and lay back on the couch. He comes down on top of me and puts his lips on mine. The kiss starts sweet and slow, but before I know it, we're frantically pulling at each other's clothes, and he's plundering my mouth. His hands find the bottom of my shirt, and he leans back to pull it over my head. I reach to his shirt and pull at it. "Take it off, Brenden. I want to feel your skin against mine."

"Fuck, baby." He rips his shirt over his head, and I realize he has tattoos. I mean, this is the first time I'm seeing him with no shirt, and he hadn't mentioned them before. There's one over his heart that has two axes crossed with a fire helmet and the words 'My Dad, My Hero'. Another one across his collar bones says 'Fire in my blood'. And starting on his right pec and running down his ribs and wrapping around his back, is a Phoenix with flames running through its brightly colored feathers.

"Holy fuck! Brenden, you're so hot," I say staring at him in awe. He gives me a shy smile.

"Baby, just let me eat you," he says, leaning down and pulling the cup of my bra down, sucking one of my nipples into his mouth. I arch my back and my hands find their way into his hair. His mouth releases my nipple with a pop, and then he pulls the other cup down and gives my other nipple the same treatment. I'm squirming, trying to rub against him to get some friction. Placing a little kiss on my nipple, he sits back on his knees and looks down at me. I reach for the button on his pants, and he stops me. "Baby, if you keep going, I'm not going to be able to go slow. Just let me make you feel good."

"Maybe I changed my mind. Maybe we don't need to go slow. I want you in me now," I pant.

"No, baby. We gotta wait a little longer," he says. Brenden reaches for my jeans and unbuttons them. He starts pulling my jeans and panties down my hips. Leaning down, he puts his face right at the apex of my thighs and breathes in deeply. "You smell so good, baby. I love the way your pussy smells and tastes." I think any other time I'd be a little embarrassed, but right now I'm so turned on that it only makes me more wet. He removes my pants and panties together before grabbing my legs and pushing them open. "So pink, and so pretty," he says before he lowers his mouth to me.

Brenden

"Oh! Fuck! Brenden!" she screams. I'm attacking her clit with my tongue, over and over. "It's too much." I slow down, then swipe my tongue from her core to her clit, back and forth several times, nice and slow.

"Is that better, Red?" I don't hear a response, so I slap the inside of her thigh. She moans, and I smile. "Words, Red. Tell me, or I'll stop."

"It's so good Brenden. Please don't stop," She begs.

I return to licking slowly and lazily. I bring my hand up to her breast and pinch her left nipple. She lets out a loud moan. Fuck, I love the way she sounds when I'm making her feel good. I bring a finger to her pussy and start to push it inside. She lets out a, "YES!" and I push it in fully. She's so wet. I pull the finger out and push in a second, and she starts grinding against my fingers and my mouth. I already love the way she gets a little wild when I eat her. I'm so fucking hard that it's almost painful. I want to pull out my cock and jack it while I eat her. But, I better not. I'm not sure if I'll be able to stop myself if she asks for my cock. I want to feel her so bad, but I know she wants to go slow. I'm pushing my limits right now. I'm not going to fuck her until she knows she's mine.

She's getting close, I can tell. Her pussy is squeezing my fingers, and if it were my cock, I'd be struggling not to come. That thought makes me leak a little come into my pants. I just know I'm going to embarrass myself and blow my load. Get it together, Brenden. You can jerk off after she falls asleep tonight. She's so close. I know she likes it when I say dirty things or I tell her to come. I want her to come hard. So hard that she screams my name.

"Are you getting close baby? Are you gonna come and squirt on my face?" She gasps and moans when I lick her clit again. I'm fucking her tight little pussy with my fingers, and she's starting to thrash and writhe under the pleasure. Her inner walls are squeezing my fingers so tight, it's getting harder to move them in and out. I wrap my lips around her sensitive little nub and suck hard. She's practically screaming, and her hands are in my hair and pulling. It doesn't hurt though; it's turning me on even more. I'm about to come in my pants when she starts screaming my name.

"Brenden! I'm coming! Brenden! FUCK!"

I slow my finger strokes as she starts to come down from her orgasm. I'd love to force her to have another one, but I'll come in my pants for sure if I keep going. Maybe I can eat her again before we sleep tonight.

"Oh my gosh... You are *very* good at that," she pants, and I start laughing.

"Well. Thank you, baby." I kiss the inside of her thigh while I pull my fingers out. I lick them clean. She watches while I lick her juices off my fingers, and she bites her bottom lip. I'm looking forward to the day when I get to see those pouty little lips wrapped around my cock. Soon, Brenden. Just wait.

I fall down on top of her ,and kiss her lips. She reaches for the waistband of my pants again. "Baby..." I say, dropping my forehead to hers. "We gotta stop. If you keep doing that, I'll have myself buried deep in your tight little cunt. I promised myself I wouldn't do that until you tell me you're mine."

She gasps. "Brenden..."

"We've got all the time in the world, Red. I'm not going anywhere. But you can't have my cock until you know you belong to me." She doesn't say anything else, just nods her head. "Now go get your stuff, baby. We both have to get up early tomorrow."

I was expecting her to come out with a huge bag full of clothes and shit, but she only has a small overnight bag. She follows me to Grandpa's house in her car, and then we sit and chat with Grandpa for a bit. We're both getting tired by about nine, so we head upstairs and call it a night.

"Did you want to shower tonight?" I ask.

"No, I'll do it in the morning, if that's ok." she says.

"Of course, baby. I'm gonna go jump in. I'll be back in a few." I take a quick shower and think about rubbing one out, but I'm so exhausted after the last couple days that I just get out. As much as I want to wear nothing to bed, or even just my boxers, I don't want to torture myself that much by only having one layer, or nothing, between her and my dick. So, I put on some plaid pajama pants that my mom got me for Christmas and a t-shirt. Then come back into the room. The lamp on my side of the bed is on, and the thought that I have a side of the bed, makes me smile. Molly is curled up under the covers already fast asleep. I crawl in and turn off the lamp, then I pull her back toward the middle of the bed and spoon behind her. I don't even remember anything after that, I was out like a light.

CHAPTER FIFTEEN

Molly

I walk into Common Grounds to get my caramel iced coffee, as is my usual routine and practically plow into Craig, one of the cops from yesterday morning. "Oh, gosh! Sorry!"

He smiles at me. "It's no problem. No spills. I'm good. Hey, so I think John was actually going to call you sometime this morning. We went to talk to Hank yesterday. He wasn't home, but we did get him on the phone, and it seems as though he was out of town when the incident happened."

I feel my face fall. It's not that I want Hank to have done it, but I'm a little more freaked out now thinking someone else could be following me and trying to get into my house. At least when I assumed it was Hank, I could come up with reasons why he might want to scare me. But no suspect is terrifying. "Ok, thanks." I think he can tell I'm a little upset by the news.

"We'll keep looking into things. The lab has the finger print samples and the photos. Maybe they'll be able to find something that will give us a clue. Please stay aware and call me or John if you need anything." He gives me a nod and says, "Gotta go, duty calls." And then he's out the door.

With that bit of news, I'm feeling a little down, so on top of the large iced coffee, I get a chocolate croissant and a cake pop.

I make my way to the salon and unlock the door. I'm here early this morning. We don't open for another hour, and none of the other girls will be here for at least thirty minutes. I take this time to sit in the office drinking my coffee and checking my emails.

My mind wanders to waking up this morning. Brenden's alarm was going off around 5:30 am. Who gets up that early? Well, I guess he does — at least on days that he has to be at the fire station by seven. I heard the alarm, and then he shut it off and snuggled back in with me. It has been so long since someone held me like that. I could really get used to it. The feeling of his arms around me, his breath on my neck, his hardness against my ass… Oh, goodness. I wanted to push back against it, but I'd only be teasing myself. He's made it very clear that he won't be giving me any sex until I tell him that I'm his. And I almost want to say it. I think the only thing that is holding me back is that this is moving so fast. I just met the guy on Wednesday morning. Jiminy Christmas, it hasn't even been an entire week yet, and I'm spending the night with him and contemplating saying that I belong to him. Who does that? I'm not some possession. So why am I sitting her imagining him saying it to me right before he pushes into me? Wowza, that makes my lady bits tingle. I wanted so badly to roll him over and straddle him this morning. But firstly, we're in his grandpa's house. If there is one thing Ben isn't, it's hard of hearing. Secondly, I know he's serious about not giving me sex until I say those words. It's not like it's a terrible thing to have the sexiest man you've ever seen in your life want to eat you like a starving man would eat ice cream. He's soooooo good at it. I can't even think straight afterward. I think he knew I was awake when he turned off the 5:30 alarm. After he spooned me for a few minutes, he flipped me onto my back and had my pj pants off and my legs over his shoulders before I could even say good morning. He made me come three times, and I think he would have kept going if the second alarm hadn't gone off at six. He said he needed me to come extra since he wouldn't be able to tuck me in with an orgasm tonight.

I'm a little sad he's working for the next twenty-four hours. I know it's silly, but I miss him. He promised to meet me at Maybell's for waffles tomorrow morning when he gets off. I'm also off tomorrow, and I'm really looking forward to spending some more time with him.

I'm just staring into space when I hear the bell on the front door jingle. I look at the clock, and it's still early. It could be Sammy, so I make my way to the front, and I don't see anyone. I start to get a little freaked out, and I'm contemplating running to the back to call 911 when Sammy jumps out from the other side of the desk.

I scream, "You fucking Batch! Are you trying to give me a fucking heart attack? Did you forget I'm being stalked by a lunatic?"

She's laughing until I say stalked. Then she stops laughing. "Oh my God, Tamale. I totally forgot. I really am sorry. I shouldn't have done that." I can tell she feels bad.

I take a deep breath. "It's fine. I'm fine. Just don't do that again, or I'll throat punch you."

"That does not sound fun." she pouts.

The bell rings again, and Gracie comes in followed by Anna

and Emily. "OMG, Molls, someone tried to break into your house?" Emily asks.

"Yup," I'm reminded.

"And they spray painted on your house?" Anna asks.

"Yeah," I say with a sigh. "I don't really want to talk about it at the moment, and can we all refrain from talking about it today? I really don't want or need every client in here asking about it." Everyone agrees. I give them all a quick smile and excuse myself to the back room. Of course, you know Sammy is right behind me.

"Are you going to be mad at me all day?" she asks as I plop down in my chair.

"What? No. I'm over it. I ran into one of the cops from yesterday morning while I was getting coffee, and he said Hank was out of town when it happened. He's got an alibi or whatever they say on the cop shows." I shake my head. "It's scary to think there is someone else out there could be watching me, taking pictures, that could write those horrible things on my house." Tears start filling my eyes. "When I think about what they might have tried to do to me if the alarm hadn't gone off, " I suck in a deep breath. "I don't care if you tell the other girls about what happened. I just really don't want to talk about it right now."

"Don't cry, Molls." Sammy rounds the desk and squats down in front of me. "I'll talk to the girls and tell them it's off limits for conversation today. If any clients bring it up, we'll redirect." That makes me smile and I nod.

"I'm gonna sit back here for a few and get myself together. My first client isn't until eleven. I'm going to get the supply order done."

"Ok, let me know if you need me."

"Hey, Sammy, can I stay at your house tonight?"

"Of course, Molly Dolly. We'll have a big girl sleep over. Wine and reruns of The Office!" She bounces up and down. Then she throws her fist in the air and yells, "Whoo!" as she walks down the hall.

For the most part the day was uneventful. As a good best friend does, Sammy talks to the girls, and they don't ask me a billion questions. Gracie was really concerned and asked if I wanted to come stay with her for a bit. She's like my little sister but wants to play mama bear too some days. I assured her that I'll be fine and invite her to have dinner with us tonight.

A little after six, Gracie and I close up shop. As I'm locking the door, John walks up. "Hey, Molly. I meant to call you earlier. So you have a second?"

"Sure, but I did talk to Craig this morning. He said Hank was out of town. I don't suppose you have any other leads ,do you?" he looks a little irritated.

"I told Craig I would talk to you about it," he says through a clenched jaw. I watch him try to slide on a calm face. "Sorry, we don't have any leads yet. But I'll let you know when and if we get anything." I nod. "Also, I was wondering if you might like to get dinner sometime?" I start to open my mouth. "I know you told me a while back you weren't ready to date. But, since I know you've gone out with a couple of guys now, I figured maybe you'd be ready."

I try to hide the confusion I'm sure is written on my face. I look over to Gracie for a second, and she looks confused too. I know it's not like Brenden is my official boyfriend or anything, but I would have assumed he would have gotten that idea after seeing us together yesterday morning.

"Uh.... Well, I'm actually seeing someone pretty exclusively right now." I don't feel like that's a lie. "You met him yesterday? His name is Brenden."

"Oh. Right. The fireman," he says with a bit of a smirk. "Not trying to cause any issues, but I'd make sure he's as exclusive as you think you two are." He doesn't say anything else but turns around and walks back to his cruiser which is double parked behind my car.

"What the eff did he mean by that?" Gracie questions. "Is Brenden seeing someone else?"

"I really find that hard to believe. I mean, since we met, which I realize has not been that long ago, he seems to either be at work, with his Grandpa, or with me. And he's only been here a few weeks. I mean, he's sexy as fuck, so maybe he's already met some other ladies, but I really just don't believe it." I shake my head. "I have to run by home before I head to Sammy's. I'll meet you there ok?"

"Alright. Don't be too long, or we'll send a search party," Gracie throws over her shoulder as she walks to her car.

I only brought enough stuff for last night and today to Brenden's, so I have to get stuff for tonight and tomorrow. I feel stupid admitting that I'm a little scared to go into my own home all by myself, and it really pisses me off. It makes me feel like I'm handing some power over to whoever is doing this. I take a deep breath and walk up to my front door. I'm just about to unlock the door when my phone rings.

"Holy fuck," I say under my breath while clutching my heart, which feels like its about to beat out of my chest. I pull out my phone to look at it and smile when I see it's Brenden. "Hello, Blue Eyes," I answer.

"Hey, baby. Whatcha up to?" he says in his upbeat tone.

"I just got to my house. I have to get some clothes and stuff before I head over to Sammy's," I say, trying to unlock the door with my phone sandwiched between my shoulder and my ear.

"Why didn't you bring it with you last night?" he asks, sounding a little gruffer than he did seconds before.

"Because I didn't want to haul a huge suitcase with me to your house. I just need clothes for tomorrow and pajamas for tonight," I say, going to the security panel and punching in my code. "I'm just running in to grab a few things. Do you..." I stop myself.

"Do I what, Baby?"

"Do you think you might be willing to stay with me at my house tomorrow night?" I don't want to seem needy, but I don't know if I'm ready to be home alone, and I can't stay with Sammy and Jared every night.

"Of course, baby. Now get your stuff and head over to Sammy's." I smile at him trying to use a bossy tone with me. When I get to my room, I empty the dirty stuff out of my overnight bag and chuck it in the basic direction of my hamper. Then, I go to the dresser and pull out my favorite skinny jeans and a t-shirt that says 'Sassy' across the front. I also grab a long sleeve t-shirt to layer under it, and, in case it's chilly, a cardigan, socks, undies, pjs, and my green sparkly converse. Brenden and I talk about our days as I pack my stuff into the bag, and it strikes me that I never told him what Craig said about Hank.

"So ,this morning I went to get coffee, and I ran into one of the cops from yesterday. Craig. He said they talked to Hank, and he was out of town on Saturday night. They have proof, I guess... So that means they have no leads," I say, sounding defeated even to my own ears.

"Fuck. Ok, baby. Can you do me a favor?"

"Yeah," I say, wondering what he's about to ask me.

"Can you try to make sure you're always with someone? If you leave the salon, make sure Sammy or one of the other girls is with you. I just want to make sure you're ok." He sounds so serious.

"I promise." I still have my toiletries packed from being at Brenden's last night, so I take my bag into the living room and grab my e-reader off the coffee table. I take a look around to make sure I'm not forgetting anything, and then head for the door. "I've got everything, I think."

"Ok baby. Jared said Sammy was making some cake that's 'Better than Sex' for you guys to eat tonight." I throw my head back and laugh. "Is the cake really better than sex?"

I smile, "Better than any sex I've ever had."

His voice gets low with a little growl in it, "Is it better than my tongue in your pussy?"

"No," I whisper into the phone. "It's definitely not better than that."

"Good," he growls into the phone. "I'm gonna let you go, baby. Have fun with Sammy and think of me when you eat that cake. I'll text you before lights out."

"Talk to you later, Blue Eyes."

"Soon, Red."

CHAPTER SIXTEEN

Molly

*W*hen I get to Sammy's, she's made dinner. We're having this Swiss Chicken she makes that I freaking love, and she pairs it with sautéed asparagus. After dinner, I help with getting the kids bathed, and she gets them to bed while Gracie and I straighten up the kitchen and pick up the kids' toys in the living room.

"You two don't have to clean my house every time you come over, ya know," Sammy says, as she comes back into the living room.

"I know, Sam-a-lama-ding-dong. We're just helping you out, so we can eat some cake. See, we're done now. Cake time!" I say in a sing song voice. Gracie pours the wine and Sammy cuts each of us a very large piece of "Better Than Sex Cake." Then, we head into her bedroom, where Sammy and I get our jammies on. Gracie isn't staying the night, so she just throws herself on the bed and digs into her cake. Sammy is wearing a onesie zip up that looks like a rainbow unicorn. I'm wearing a flannel two piece that has wiener dogs on them.

"Those are cute," Sammy says, pointing to my pjs.

"Thanks, mom got them for me for Christmas. They're cozy," I say jumping onto her giant bed. "Today, I was thinking that I might want to get a dog. Do you guys think that's crazy?"

"Not at all! Especially with everything going on lately. You should get a little fluffy dog that you can carry around in a purse," Sammy bounces on the bed clapping her hands.

"What would be the point in that? I want a dog that can help scare someone off or protect me from an intruder. I'm thinking like a lab or something. I might go look for one at the shelter tomorrow. I hate little yappy dogs."

"But if you had a little one, you could bring it to work, and it could be like our Mascot," Sammy says, like she's really trying to convince me.

"And will you be cleaning up after this yappy little ankle biter when it piddles on the floor? Or wants to drink the water out of the pedi bowls?" I ask.

"Fuck, no," is her only reply.

"I wish I could have a big, fluffy dog. My landlord is very adamant that I can't have pets." Gracie frowns.

"Your apartment is only about 300 square feet. Where would you keep a dog?" I question.

Gracie shrugs, "It could keep me warm at night."

"Fuck that! Find a boyfriend Graceland…then you can get finally pop that cherry," Sammy says around a huge bite of cake. I smack Sammy. I don't know why she's always telling Gracie to find some rando to sleep with.

"Pass! Men are too much of a hassle. I gotta finish school and take care of what I want and need," Gracie says.

"Good girl." I wink at Gracie.

After that, Sammy puts on The Office, and we enjoy our cake and wine. We're halfway through the Fun Run, and I'm eating the last bite of my cake when I remember. "I guess Jared told Brenden you made your 'Better Than Sex Cake.' He asked me if it was really better than sex. I told him it was better than any sex I've ever had."

"Damn!! You two haven't slept together yet, right?" she laughs.

"No. We've done some other stuff, but not sex …yet." I glance at Gracie and see her cheeks pinken. I don't usually talk too openly about sex around Gracie. She gets embarrassed easily. "He said we can't have sex until I tell him I'm his," I say shyly.

"Ooooooh, he's working on the Jared Parker rules of relationships. Aren't the women supposed to be the ones to demand a relationship and deny sex?" We all laugh. "Well, are you going to be his?"

"I feel like we're headed in that direction. I mean part of me wants to just say, 'Yes, I'm yours.' But I guess I just feel like it's moving so quickly. And what if I fall too fast, and he breaks my heart?" There it is. I finally verbalized what I've been thinking.

"Girl, I understand that. I basically moved in with Jared after our first date. We dated for all of a month before he slid a ring on my finger. I think that when it's right, you just know. Does it feel right?"

"It really does. He's gonna stay with me tomorrow night at my house. So, we'll see where it goes," I shrug. "Has Jared said anything about Brenden possibly seeing someone else?"

She looks at me like I'm nuts. "Not at all. He hasn't lived here that long, and Jared said some of the other single guys have invited him out on a night off to get a drink, but he always declines. Says he has plans with his Grandpa."

"Well, tonight, when we were locking up, John Palmer came by. You know he was one of the cops there yesterday morning. Anyway, it was really fucking weird." I see Gracie nodding in agreement with a mouthful of cake. "I told him I had already talked to Craig, and he got super pissed that Craig had already told me that Hank was out of town. Then he asked me to have dinner, like a date. He saw me with Brenden yesterday. He said he knew I'd been out on some dates so he thought maybe I was ready to date now. I told him I'm only seeing Brenden, and he said he didn't think Brenden was only seeing me."

"What? I mean, it's not like we know Brenden that well, but I just don't see it." She says shoving a large bite of cake into her mouth.

"That's what I said," Gracie chimes in.

"Me neither. But I'm meeting him for breakfast tomorrow, and we'll probably spend a good portion of the day together."

We all fall back into a comfortable silence and continue watching The Office. Before I know it, Sammy's snoozing.

Gracie tells me she's heading out, so I walk her to the door so I can set the alarm system. "Text me when you get home, okay?"

"Sure thing." She gives me a little wave as she walks back to her beat up Honda Civic.

I make my way back to Sammy's bedroom, turn off the tv and the lights, and get out my e-reader. About twenty minutes later, I get a ding on my phone, and Gracie says she's home. I give her a thumbs up emoji, and I read a little bit longer before I hear another ding. This time, it's a text from Brenden.

"Heading to bed soon. Just wanted to say good night, baby."
God, I love it when he calls me baby.

"Good night, Blue Eyes. See you tomorrow." I send a heart
emoji along with that text, and I promptly get one back. I go
to sleep with a smile on my face.

I pull up outside Maybell's, and I'm lucky enough to find a
parking spot right out front. I can see Brenden sitting in a
booth in the front window, and I take this opportunity to just
look at how gorgeous he is. He's talking to someone with an
annoyed look on his face, but that person is standing just out
of my line of sight. When I head into the diner and am kind
of taken aback when I see a skinny, bleach blonde chick
leaning over the table with her boobs right in Brenden's face.
What the fuck? I can feel my blood beginning to boil, so I
pull up my big girl panties and say to myself… 'Well, Molly.
Let's go see what the fuck is happening.' As I get closer to the
table, the annoyed look on Brenden's face is even more
apparent. I stand next to a wooden column, hoping they can't
see me. Hearing her whiney voice makes me realize the girl
is Tami-Lynn Mitchell. She was one of those semi-popular
girls in school that was really only popular for being bad.
And she is, indeed, the same person Hank cheated on me
with.

"But if she's not here yet, maybe she's not coming. Then we
can have breakfast, and you can come back to my place and
watch a movie," Tami-Lynn whines.

"Like I already said, I'm not interested. My girlfriend is
coming and wouldn't appreciate another woman
propositioning her man." Girlfriend! I know he's probably just
trying to get rid of her, but that word is doing very fluttery
things to my insides. I decide I better go save him. I walk

toward the table and around Tami-Lynn and stand next to Brenden.

"Hey, baby. Sorry I was running late." I say in a sweet voice. Then I lean down grabbing him by the face and plant a kiss on his lips that should make everyone in the diner blush. I pull away and say, "Scooch over, Lambchop. I want to sit next to you." He smiles wide and slides into the booth. I plop down next to him. I look up to a rather shocked Tami-Lynn. "Could I get a cup of coffee? Baby, do you need coffee?" He points to his cup and shakes his head with a smile on his face, like he's trying to hold in a laugh. I grab one of the menus and start looking through. When I realize she's still standing there, I say, "Oh, I don't think I'm ready to order yet. I still need a minute."

She sputters and then says, "I don't work here, Molly O'Brien"

I give her a sickeningly sweet smile and say, "Oh Tami-Lynn, I didn't recognize you. You know, you should come into the salon and let me give you a conditioning treatment and a good cut. It's been so dry this winter."

She sort of runs her fingers through her hair. Then she looks pissed. "No, thank you. I was just talking to Brandon about hanging out some time." She gives him what I assume she thinks is her sexy smirk.

Brenden starts to open his mouth, and I cut him off. "I'll handle this, Lovebug. His name is *Brenden*, and I can guarantee that he's not interested in hanging out with you. Now, if you wouldn't mind, I'm trying to have breakfast with my boyfriend. Have a nice day now." Turning toward Brenden, I give him a wink. He's got this sexy grin on his face. We just look at each other until I hear her stomp away. "Was that too much?" I barely get the words out when he grabs my face and kisses me. It's one of those kisses that seems like the earth stops spinning. He pulls back, and it takes a few seconds to open my eyes. "Wow."

"Boyfriend, huh?" I can feel my cheeks getting pink.

"Well, I mean, I might have heard you call me your girlfriend on the way in. " I look down. He tips my face back up with his finger.

"Baby, I know you might not be ready to call me your boyfriend, but I'm only interested in you. We don't have to use the titles. I just want to hear you're mine. When you're ready to say it. Now, what are you having for breakfast?"

When we finish breakfast, we walk outside. It's still a bit chilly but should be a nice day. I told him that I needed his help with some errands today, so he follows me as I drop my car off outside of the salon. Then I hop into his jeep with him.

"So, where to next, Red?"

CHAPTER SEVENTEEN

Brenden

*W*hen Molly tells me that we are headed to the animal shelter to get a dog, I'm a little shocked. It's definitely not a bad idea, and it would make me feel better about her staying at her place on nights that I'm working if she's got some protection.

When we get to the shelter, we go in and tell the lady at the desk, whose name is Lisa, that Molly is interested in adopting a dog. Molly grew up in this town, so it shouldn't surprise me that she knows the woman working there. She has Molly fill out some paperwork and then leads us back to an area with kennels. There are some smaller dogs toward the front — some Chihuahuas, a beagle mix, and some ewok looking dog, but Molly walks right past the smaller dogs and heads straight toward a big black lab.

"What a big sweetie!" she says in voice that I assume she reserves for talking to dogs. The dog immediately puts it's nose up to the door and sniffs her fingers. "What's her name?"

"Oh, we've been calling her Britney. The day she came in,

there was some Britney Spears song playing on the radio, and she started howling to it. I don't know what it is, but she howls along with any Britney Spears song we play. We've tried other artists, and she doesn't even act like she hears it. We think she's about three years old, and she's been here for about a month. We were hoping her owner would show up, but no such luck. She wasn't chipped and didn't have a collar when she was found. She has been a little skittish around men, but she warms up fast. She seems to know basic commands, and she, so far, gets along with the other dogs." She opens the kennel and puts a temporary leash on Britney while she leads all of us to a room where we can pet her and let her sniff us.

"Are you sure you want a dog this big?" I lean over to ask Molly. I'd say she's gotta weigh close to 90 lbs. She's a big dog.

"Yes! I love big snuggle pups, and I'd like a dog that makes me feel safe — not some rat I can carry around in a purse." As soon as we get in the room, Molly is down on the ground with the dog, just rubbing her tummy and telling her she's a good girl. It makes me like her even more. I'm so fucking glad she didn't want some little, yappy dog. I get down on the ground with them too. Britney seems a little leery of me, but once she sniffs me a bit, she's licking my face and trying to crawl into my lap.

"I think I might have some competition now," Molly says laughing. "Britney, do you want to come home with us? You're such a pretty girl, and you're so sweet. I think you need to come home and get some snuggles."

"She's a big girl, but she is so snuggly. You think she's the one you want?" I question.

"I honestly didn't even see any other dogs. I was just drawn to her. I think she's my girl." Molly goes back to snuggling

Britney while I poke my head out of the room and flag down Lisa. When she sees me, she walks over to the door with a big smile.

"So, Molly really loves her. What do we have to do to take her home?" I ask.

"Oh, good! She'll just have a couple of things to sign, and there's the adoption fee of $200. I'll go get the paperwork started, and then we'll get you guys on your way. " I nod and step out of the room completely.

"Can I pay a portion of the adoption fee without your telling Molly that I paid it?" She gets a big smile on her face and nods. I walk with her to the desk, and she runs my card for $125. I'd pay the entire fee, but I don't want to have Molly pissed at me. I thank Lisa and head back to the room. I catch Molly through the window in the door, and I can't help but laugh. She's got Britney up on her hind legs with her paws on Molly's shoulders. Molly's singing "Oops! I Did It Again" and the dog is howling along with her. I get out my phone and take a picture of them through the glass before stepping back into the room with my girl and her diva dog.

"You head out to the desk, baby; I'll stay here with Britney. Lisa says you need to sign some paper work." As if Britney understands exactly what I'm saying, she hops down and comes over to me. Then she sits at my feet and rubs her head against my leg.

"Ok. I'll be back to get you in a few, pretty girl!" She kisses me as she walks by. "I'll be back for you too, Blue Eyes."

I squat down on the floor and pet Britney until Molly comes back. Lisa is behind her at the door. "I'm gonna take her out back really fast to let her go potty. Then I'll bring her out the side door if you want to meet us out there."

We walk back out through the reception area. When we get

outside, we stand near the side door waiting for Lisa and Britney. Molly is practically vibrating with excitement. I stand behind he with my arms around her waist. After about ten minutes, we see the side door open, and Britney pops her head out. Lisa has her on the temporary leash still. Molly told her we would go get Britney a collar and leash and everything else she needs as soon as we leave here.

When Britney sees Molly, she gets excited and starts to run toward us, but Lisa still has a hold of the leash, and she gets pulled. She loses her balance, and even though it's only two steps down, she falls and lands hard on the concrete. We both run in their direction. Lisa somehow still has a hold of the leash, and Britney is starting to pull her to get to Molly. Molly grabs Britney and untangles the leash from Lisa's hand. I run to Lisa to see if she's ok. She's grabbing her left arm with her right, and I can see tears already streaming down her face.

"Lisa, what hurts the most? Is it your arm?" she squeaks out a yes. "Do you think you can move it?" She shakes her head. I reach out to touch her arm, and I can see that it looks like it's swelling quickly. "Is there anyone else inside the shelter?" She nods. "Ok. Molly, run inside and let the other people know that Lisa is hurt. Take Britney with you." I pull out my phone and dial 911. "Hey, this is Brenden Clarke. I'm an off-duty fireman with Station Number 4. I'm at the Happy Tails animal shelter, and I have a woman with a possible broken arm and several other abrasions." The front door to the shelter opens, and two other ladies come running out. I finish the call with 911, and the operator says they are dispatching emergency services. "Someone should be here soon to take you to the hospital." It only takes a few minutes before EMTs show up and get her on a stretcher and out of there. One of the other ladies hands Molly a folder that has copies of the paperwork she signed and updated shot records.

We get Britney loaded into the back of my jeep and both hop

in. We just sit there looking at each other for a minute. "I feel so bad about poor Lisa. I can't believe she broke her arm."

"It wasn't your fault, babe. Britney just got excited to see her Momma." She smiles at me, and I grab her hand and kiss it. "Let's go get her the stuff she needs."

Molly

I'm snuggled on the couch with my giant black lab, and I've decided that it's my new happy place. After we left Happy Tails Animal Shelter, we went to a big pet store to pick some things up for Britney. I got her a giant dog bed that I'm sure will rarely get used as she seems to be much more comfortable lying on me. We also got her food, toys, and a pretty rhinestone collar with a new, heart-shaped tag. Brenden rolled his eyes at me, but I like those things. He suggested that we get her a leash that goes on a harness, instead of the collar, since she's so big. After the pet store, we stopped by Brenden's house to see his Grandpa. Ben was just as in love with my new pup as I am. He didn't want to let her go and told me to bring her by tomorrow morning while I was at work. We brought him lunch and ate with him. Before we headed back to my house, we took Britney to a dog park where we apparently tired her out. I swear Brenden threw a tennis ball for her five hundred times. Note to self: buy one of those ball launcher things.

Brenden walks down the hall after putting his overnight bag in my room. "You two look comfy." Then he pouts. "I can already tell. Britney is going to get all my snuggles." I smile at him and then lean up so that he can slide in behind me, and I can lean against him.

"Want to watch something?" I ask handing him the remote.

"You're gonna let me pick? She really does like me." He laughs.

"What sounds good for dinner? I didn't have time to defrost anything, so we can either order pizza or Chinese, or I can make grilled cheese and tomato soup." Mmmmmm grilled cheese.

"I vote grilled cheese and tomato soup," he says running his hands through my hair. It's only about 5:30 right now, so I'll make dinner in an hour or so.

"If you keep running your fingers through my hair, you'll put me to sleep." I close my eyes and get comfy.

"You've been yawning all day, baby. Did you sleep ok last night?" he asks, pushing my hair off my forehead.

"Sammy flails in her sleep. I really need to sleep on the couch when I stay with her. I always get either hit in the face or kicked. I sleep much better next you." I didn't mean to say that last part. My eyes fly open, and Brenden is looking at me with a soft expression. I feel a little silly admitting it, but I say, "It's true. I sleep really well next to you."

"That's a good thing, baby." He continues to stroke my hair, and I eventually doze off.

CHAPTER EIGHTEEN

Brenden

*M*olly ends up sleeping with her head in my lap and the dog on her legs for a good hour. I put ESPN on for a while, but I mostly just watch her sleep. When she finally wakes up, she lets Britney out in the backyard and says she'll start dinner. I get Britney's food bowl ready and let her back in.

"I'd suggest a doggy door, but you might want to wait until we figure out who's behind the pictures and graffiti."

"Yeah, I'll wait on that. Besides, sometimes Britney will go to your house and hang out with Ben while I'm working." Her cheeks get pink, and she says, "Or you can watch her. I mean she's practically your dog too." I don't want to make a big deal out of it, but I'm glad she's thinking it.

Molly made good on her promise of grilled cheese and tomato soup. I was expecting cheese singles wrapped in plastic and tomato soup from a can, but Molly made these gourmet grilled cheeses with big, thick pieces of sour dough bread, bacon, and gouda. The soup was awesome. She had pulled out a container from the freezer and heated it up. Apparently, she and her mom make soups every fall and freeze them for the winter.

"Oh, my God. This has to be the best grilled cheese I've ever had." I say taking another huge bite.

She beams. "I watch a lot of food network. I like to make comfort food a little more fancy. I'll have to make my baked mac and cheese for you soon."

"I'm ready when you are, baby. Well, maybe not right this second," I say, rubbing my belly. She served me two grilled cheese sandwiches and a large helping of tomato and roasted red pepper soup. I don't know that I could eat another bite.

I help her clean up the kitchen, and then we settle onto the couch again to watch some television. I can't help but to think about doing this on a regular basis: having dinner together, watching tv, crawling into bed, and holding her all night. I'm lying on the couch, she's lying on me with her head on my chest, and we're watching some that show she likes that I've never seen before. I watch her wiping at her eyes and sniffling. "Red, are you crying?"

"Shut up. Just ignore me. I always tear up when I watch this show," she says still swiping at tears on her face.

"Babe, why do you watch it if it makes you cry?" I ask, trying to hold in a laugh.

She pops her head up and looks at me like I'm crazy. "If I only watch movies or shows that didn't make me cry, I'd be pretty limited on what was available. Something you gotta learn about me? I cry all the time."

"You cry all the time?" I know I'm looking at her like she's crazy.

"I am an overly sensitive person. I cry when I'm mad, sad,

happy... I cry when I laugh too hard and when I'm so angry I could scream. I cry all the time. You will see me cry a lot. Just try not to be the one that makes the sad or angry tears." She gives me a wink.

I grab her under her arms and haul her up my body. She straddles my waist, and I sit up, taking her face in my hands. "Baby, I will always try my hardest to not make you cry. I only want to see smiles on your beautiful face." I lean in to kiss her, still holding her face. The kiss is sweet and gentle. I pull back and look at her, brushing her hair off her forehead.

"I want you," Molly whispers. I can feel my cock growing under her. She's already starting to rock against. "I want you to take me to bed Brenden."

"Red. I want nothing more than to take you to bed, but I still need to hear the words before we have sex," I whisper back, trying to stop myself from thrusting up to meet her grinding against me.

"I'm yours, Brenden." The words rush out of her mouth. "I've been scared to say it because I worry I'll fall for you and then you'll break my heart. But I'm already falling. I'm already yours. I can't worry about what if, when it could only push you away. I want this, Brenden. I want you." She says looking like she might break if I refuse.

"Thank, God," I say, swinging my legs around and picking her up with my hands on her ass as I stand.

Molly

I've got my legs wrapped around his waist and I can feel his hands gripping each of my ass cheeks. I'm kissing and nipping at his jaw and neck, which must be distracting to him as he walks, because he stops in the hallway and pushes me against the wall. Holding me there with his hips while he captures my face with one of his hands and attacks my mouth with his own. I feel his hand slide down a little and his thumb rests on my throat. A flood of wetness soaks my panties, and I let out a whimper. "Brenden, please take me to bed. I need to feel you inside me," I beg while grinding myself against him as best I can. He hauls me into my room and falls on top of me on the bed.

"Are you sure you're ready, Red? Because once I feel your tight little cunt wrapped around me, I'm not letting you go. Not that I'd let you go without a fight now, but I want you to be sure you're ready, baby."

"I'm ready, Brenden. I promise. I'm ready." I whisper back.

He leans back on his knees and pulls me up to sitting. "Lift your arms, baby." I raise my arms, he must only grab the t-shirt, because only the t-shirt comes off. He looks at me, bewildered. "How many fucking shirts are you wearing, Red?"

I burst out laughing, and then he's laughing. "It was chilly today. I wore layers. You're lucky I already took off my cardigan."

"Ok, well, now I want all the layers off so I can fuck you." He reaches for my other shirt and pulls it up over my head. Then he wastes no time in undoing my bra and pulling it down over my arms. Pushing me back to lie down again, he crawls up my body and leans down to suck my nipple into his mouth while pinching the other nipple with his fingers. I find myself grinding up against him and pulling at his shirt.

"I want your shirt off, Brenden." He reaches behind himself and pulls his shirt off over his head. Then he's on me again, kissing my lips. I'm lost in the kiss when he leans back up and unbuttons my jeans. Then, he quickly grabs the waist of my jeans and panties and pulls them down my legs together. He gets off the bed and finishes removing them from my feet. Looking at me lying there naked, his eyes blaze with hunger. "Pants off, Blue Eyes. If you get to stare at me like I'm dessert, I want to see you too." He smirks at me and immediately reaches for the button on his pants, then slides them and his boxers down and stands in front of me. Fuck. He's so hot. How is it possible to be that hot?

His dick is big, thick, and pointing straight at me. I wonder how it will even fit inside me, but I won't give up until it does. I can see a little pearl of come collecting on the head, and I lick my lips. I want to taste. Getting on my hands and knees, I crawl to the end of the bed. "Fuck, Red. You're like my fantasies come to life."

"Let's see if real life is better than the fantasy." I wrap my hand around the base of his cock and my fingers don't meet. I stroke my hand up and down the length a couple times, his eyes never leaving mine. I open my mouth and take the head of his cock into my mouth. Mmmmmm. I love the way he tastes, and I want more. I take him as deep as I can, which isn't very deep because he's so thick. Swirling my tongue around the head, I take him as deep as I can again, all while pumping my hand up and down his shaft. I see his mouth part and his head drop back. He lets out a grunt, and I can tell he's trying to reel himself in. I feel one of his hands in my hair and it causes a flood of wetness to surge from my core. He holds on tight but doesn't try to force me deeper. He lets me go at my own pace. I want touch myself, but before I can, he steps back and pulls his cock out of my mouth.

"Lay down, Molly." It's not a request. It's a command, and it's one I'm all too willing to follow. I scoot back up the bed and lean back on my hands. I'm feeling sexy and brave, so I open my legs, hoping it will entice him to hurry.

He puts one knee on the bed and starts to crawl toward me, then sits back on his heels and takes one of my legs in his hands. Starting at my calf, he starts to massage my leg and leaves a little trail of kisses and love bites up to my knee. I'm ticklish, and it's taking everything I have in me not to kick my leg or laugh. "Brenden, please. It tickles. I can't take it." He smiles his gorgeous smile at me and drops that leg but then grips my other ankle and proceeds to tease me more. "Brenden. Please, baby. Please stop teasing and fuck me."

"You beg so pretty, Red. And I like it when you call me baby." He doesn't stop the torture, but he does lead his kisses and bites all the way to the apex of my thighs. He takes one big, slow swipe of his tongue from my opening to my clit but doesn't put any pressure on it. Then he continues to follow this brutally slow pace until I'm about to scream, licking everywhere but where I need it most, and I don't know if I can take it anymore. I'm about to grip the back of his head to try and guide him where I need him, but he grabs both of my wrists and holds them down at my sides while he proceeds to tongue fuck my pussy. He's got his arms over my wide-spread legs, and I'm not able move my hips to meet his rhythm. I'm locked in place with his tongue torturing me.

"Brenden! Please!" I'm so close to coming, but I just can't fall over the edge. He stops suddenly, and then he's crawling up my body.

"Your pussy is so sweet, baby. I can't wait to feel it squeezing my cock," he whispers into my mouth. I can feel the head of his cock nudging my entrance. Kissing me hard, he leaves me breathless. Then he leans up to his knees and uses his hand to guide himself into me. He's watching as he pushes inside me. I can feel the stretch of his thickness, but it doesn't hurt, I'm too wet. It takes a few seconds, but I can feel his hips hit my body. He's all the way inside me. It's so deep but so perfect.

He fills me up completely. "Lean up, baby. I want you to see how pretty it is when you take my cock."

I lean up and try to hold myself up as I watch him pull out of me slowly and push back in even slower. "Oh, God," It feels so good, and watching him push into me is almost too much to take. He wraps one hand around the back of my neck and kisses me deeply. He never stops his slow pumping in and out of me, and after a minute, he starts to lean me back onto the bed.

"Baby, your pussy was made for me." His slow thrusts start to pick up speed. With every stroke, he hits my clit just perfectly that I'm getting close already. He throws one of my legs over his forearm so he can get that much deeper. It's so deep, and I'm lost to the feeling. Then I hear the sound of a high pitched squealing...Wait, I think that's me.

"I'm gonna come, Brenden," I scream as he keeps thrusting over and over hitting the perfect spots. I finally fall over the edge of the orgasm that's been building. It hits me like a tidal wave, and I'm convinced that I black out. When I come back from my orgasm, Brenden is still thrusting in and out of me, deep and slow. I'm surprised to feel the low pull of another orgasm building.

"You're gonna come again, Molly." He starts to pick up more speed. "You're gonna come with me this time, and I'm going to fill your Tight. Little. Cunt. With. My. Come," he says with a deep hard thrust on each word.

"YES!!! Yes I'm almost there, baby!" I shout.

"Rub your clit, Red. Let me see you touch yourself," he says as he leans up again. I reach down and touch myself. I can feel the zing run through me, and I'm so close to falling over. "I changed my mind. Pinch your nipples while I rub your clit." He reaches down and pushes my fingers away and rubs his thumb right over my little bundle of nerves. I run my hands up my stomach and over my ribs until I reach my breasts. I palm both breasts and then squeeze my already sensitive nipples. I cry out, and I'm about to crest when he slaps my clit and says, "Come, baby. Come NOW!"

I know it sounds ridiculous that I'm coming on command, but it happens. And it's the most powerful orgasm I've ever had. I feel like it goes on and on. I look at Brenden, and he's got his head tossed back, the tendons in his neck are stretched, and he's making the most delicious grunts and growls. Still thrusting over and over, I can feel his hot come shooting into me, and I just keep coming. He finally falls down on top of me, but he's still moving, just slower now. It's ridiculous that this orgasm is still going, but I can't stop it. And why would I ever want to? "Keep moving, Brenden. I'm still coming, and I can't stop. I need you deeper." He picks up speed and thrusts hard and deep. Somehow, he's still hard, and he doesn't stop fucking me.

"Give it to me, baby. I want to feel you squeeze my cock and come all over it." He's hitting the perfect spot, and as soon as his fingers find my clit again, I'm screaming with pleasure. Right about the time I finally start to come down, I feel him coming again, rolling his hips into me slow as he keeps filling me full. When he lets out his last grunt, he falls on top of me completely. He's a big guy, and you would think it would be crushing me, but I love his weight on me. After a minute, he rolls us to the side, my leg draped over his hip. He's still inside of me, and I don't think I ever want him to pull out. "Fuck, I've never come like that, baby. You have some kind of magic pussy."

I start to laugh. "I'll take that as a compliment."

"Question, which in hindsight, we probably should have talked about before. Are you on birth control?" I feel my eyes go wide. Wow. Neither of us even thought about it. Luckily, I am.

"I am. I take the pill. We should be all good."

"Good, because I'm not sure I want to come anywhere but inside your tight little pussy." Why does it turn me on so much to think about him coming in me? I feel him start to pull out of me, and I let out a little gasp at the feeling. "I'll be right back, baby." He kisses me quickly, and then I watch his naked body with all those muscles as he heads out of the room. I hear him start the shower, and before I know it, he's back. "C'mon baby, lets go take a shower."

CHAPTER NINETEEN

April
Molly

*I*t's been about a month since I told Brenden that I'm his, and it's been awesome!! I've been able to rework some of my schedule at the salon so that I have a day off with him during the week. On most of his nights off, we have dinner with his Grandpa, and then he spends the night with me. Ben has been dog sitting for me during the day, and he loves Britney just as much as Brenden and I do. Nothing weird or dangerous has happened since St. Patrick's Day, and my mom and dad should be home this weekend. YAY!

I'm very excited for my mom to meet Brenden. They did a brief FaceTime last week. Or, rather, she called me, and he was there. So he popped on screen and charmed her, of course. When I told my dad I was seeing him, he said he remembered meeting him before and thought he was a really nice guy.

My parents will be around for a few months before they take

off for a trip to Alaska in their RV. I'm glad they are getting to do all the things they want to do and see what they want to see, but I miss having them close. My mom and I used to cook dinner together almost every Sunday evening, and sometimes Sammy, Jared, and the kiddos would come too. My dad was the one that did all the work in my attic space, and that's part of the reason it's still unfinished. I've thought about hiring a contractor to finish it, but as my dad reminded me, it's just me here, so we can take our time getting it done. He really enjoys working with his hands, and I'd hate to take it away from him if he's still interested in doing it. Besides that, Brenden offered to help too. Do I smell bonding time between my boyfriend and my dad? Eeeeeeek! Yes, he is my boyfriend, and I am his girlfriend! And I am about five seconds away from blurting out that I love him every time we are together.

I work ten to six today, but I have some paperwork to do, so I gotta be there by nine at the latest. Brenden is cooking dinner at his grandpa's tonight. I've learned that he has some hidden culinary talents. He makes a delicious meatloaf and mashed potatoes. I don't know what he puts in the potatoes, but I could eat an ungodly amount. Mmmmmmm. Mashed potatoes.

My third alarm goes off, and I know I need to get up. Brenden already ravaged me this morning. Then he rolled out of bed and went for a run. I don't know how he has that much energy. I went back to sleep for another forty-five minutes. I have to get up now, and my only option for hair styling today is a big, messy bun. At least I can do it in a, "I'm a hairstylist. It's supposed to look like this." kind of way. It's either that or forego my stop at Common Grounds for my iced coffee, and that is *not* something I'm willing to do.

I throw my comforter off and my robe on. I walk out to the living room and expect to see Britney on her big puppy bed, but Brenden must've taken her out to run. I thought she'd be trying to sleep with us every night, but on the nights Brenden is here, she stays on her bed. I start the shower and brush my teeth while the water heats up. I reach for my brush to run through my hair, but it's not here. I'm hoping Britney didn't decide that it's her new chew toy, but I won't be surprised if I find it in pieces in the backyard. Searching through the vanity drawers, I don't find that particular brush, but I do find another one that works. Piling my hair on my head and hopping in the shower, I make a mental note to look under the couch for my brush. That's where Britney stashes things that she claims as hers.

I'm in the middle of applying my mascara when I hear the front door slam and the unmistakable sound of Britney's tags jingle. Brenden pops into the door way and says, "Hey, how much time do you have before you have to go?"

I look at the time on my phone. It's 7:35, and I have to leave by eight. "I've got about twenty-five minutes before I have to go.Any later, and I can't get coffee," I say, pouting.

"Well, it looks like the tire on your rear driver's side is low. So how about if I jump in the shower and drive you to work. I'll get you coffee then come back and deal with your tire. I talked to grandpa a few minutes ago. He said he wanted to get a burger tonight. We can pick you up after work and go to Maybell's."

"That sounds perfect! Mmmmmm. Cheese fries." He wraps his arms around my waist and kisses me on my neck. "Mmmmmm. Get in the shower, or I'll be late." He smirks at me in the mirror and then slaps me on the ass before he strips off his clothes.

"Hey, Red, eyes up here," he says with a smile. "I'm not just some piece of meat for you to ogle."

"I'm not ogling. I'm taking mental pictures of you to think about until I see your naked ass later tonight." He gets that dark, sexy look in his eye. "Get in the shower!" I yell throwing a washrag at him.

He was actually showered and dressed, and we were out the door by 8:05 am, giving me time to get coffee and a muffin and unlock the salon. Brenden follows me in and back into the office while I put my purse away. He walks around and sits in the office chair before patting his lap for me to come sit. I smile and shake my head at him.

"You are a dirty boy. I know what you're thinking, and I don't have time for your naughtiness this morning. Everyone will be here by 8:45. I've got paperwork to do, and Mrs. Milton will be here at 9:15 on the dot. If I come over there and sit on your lap, I won't have time to eat my muffin or finish the salon order before I need to set up." I'm speaking from experience. This is not the first time he's tempted me with messing around in the office. "Besides, last time, Sammy was banging on the door before we finished."

"Red. I just want to have you on my lap for a few minutes," he says. I know he's a lying liar that lies, but he's so damn sexy that I'd rather sit on his lap than anywhere else anyway. I walk to the office door, close it and lock it. When I turn around, he's got his big, sexy smile on, dimple on display, and everything.

I sit on his lap, and he immediately starts unbuttoning my pants. He spreads my legs over both of his with my back leaning against his chest. "I just want to feel how wet you are, baby. Your pussy determines whether I eat you or fuck you. I know you need to come again, and I need to have your taste in my mouth before I leave."

I moan as he slides his fingers over my already slick pussy, then plunges a finger into me. "Your pussy is soaked, baby." He rubs his fingers up to my clit and back down several times making me moan again. I feel his other hand cup my breast through my blouse, and he pinches my nipple. I let out yet another moan. "Stand up, baby, and try to be quiet this time. I don't like anyone else hearing you come." I don't waste any time standing up, and he doesn't waste any time pulling down my pants. "Bend over baby."

I put my forearms on the desk in front of me, and I can feel his hot breath on my backside. He pulls my panties to the side, and his tongue is suddenly attacking my pussy. Sliding it from my clit to my core over and over again. I'm already on the brink when he stops, and I feel him stand close behind me. His hands rub over the curve of my ass, and then I feel him guiding himself into me. I've gotten used to the size of him, and he fills me with one quick stroke. I gasp and moan at the feeling. "Ok, Red. It's time to be quiet. If anyone hears you come, I'll spank your ass later." I moan even louder as he pulls out slowly and pushes back in hard and fast. "You're a naughty girl, baby. I think you *want* me to spank you later."

I definitely don't mind when he gives me a swat, but he's never just spanked me. "I'll try to be quiet. I promise," I whisper.

"I'm gonna go hard and fast. Hold on tight, baby." He grips my hips in his hands and starts to pick up his pace, slamming into me. It feels so good. I'm trying to hold in any noise, but I know some little moans and squeaks are slipping out, and I can feel my orgasm starting to build. His right hand travels from my hip around to my clit, and he starts to rub. I'm trying to hold in the sounds that want to escape, but I'm not doing a very good job, and I think I may have heard the front door bell jingle. "You gotta be quiet, baby, or I'll have to stop."

I turn my head to look at him over my shoulder. "Don't you dare stop fucking me."

He smirks at me, pulls out, and spins me around with my ass up on the desk before I can even protest. "I'm so fucking glad you wore these little slide-on shoes instead of the boots today," he says, pulling my shoe off and one leg out of my pants. He pushes me back until I'm leaning up on my hands and slams back into my pussy. I let out a small cry that he captures in his mouth. He eats all my sounds while he fucks me. His left arm is wrapped around my lower back, keeping my ass right at the edge of the desk while his right hand starts picking up the pace on my clit. I'm close, so close I'm gonna fall over any second. "Come for me, baby. I want to fill you up with my come. Then put your panties back in place so you walk around with me leaking out of you all day."

His filthy words always push me over the edge, and I come so hard. I'm sure I'm practically shrieking, but he's muffling the sound with his mouth on mine. I feel him start to come, and he didn't lie when he said he was going to fill me up. I sit there with his cock still hard inside of me, leaning his forehead against mine we both try to catch our breath.

"You're definitely getting spanked later," he whispers, and I start to giggle.

"Looking forward to it, Blue Eyes."

"I bet you are. How did I fall in love with such a sexual deviant?" he says with a smile.

"What?" I'm certain I just heard him say he's in love with me.

"You're a dirty girl and a sexual deviant, baby." He says with an ornery smile on his face.

"You know very well that's not what I said 'what' about," I say looking at him, hoping he didn't say it on accident or want to take it back.

"I love you, Molly," he whispers to me.

"I love you too, Brenden." I whisper back. Then he grabs my face and kisses me. I start to lay back, pulling him down on top of me when I hear a loud bang on the door.

"Are you two almost done in there?" Sammy yells through the door. "Some of us would like to put our bags away so we can work. Molly, you know you've only got about fifteen minutes before Mrs. Milton is here."

"We'll be right out," Brenden says smiling at me. He pulls out of me and puts my panties back in place. I can feel his come leaking out of me. My panties will be soaked with it all day. God, I really am a dirty girl, because it turns me on so much to know that. We both get dressed quickly, and I take a look in the mirror to make sure my hair and makeup aren't messed up.

I walk to the door and unlock and open it. Sammy is still standing there along with Anna. Both smirking, they walk in to hang up their coats. "It smells like sex in here," Sammy says. I just shake my head and look over at Brenden who is back to sitting in the chair trying to hold in a laugh.

I just walk back around the desk and sit in his lap. Then, I, ever so gracefully, shove half my muffin into my mouth.

When Brenden leaves, he gives me a quick kiss, and we exchanged I love yous. These nosy batches I work with all gave a collective "AWWWWWWWWE." After that, the day flies by pretty uneventfully.

I wake up suddenly, and I don't know why. It takes me a

second to realize that Britney is standing on the bed, facing the door and growling a low growl. I listen to see if I can hear anything. Brenden's not here tonight. He's working. I've never seen Britney do this before, so I'm kind of freaked out. I switch on the lamp on my nightstand and reach for the phone to call Brenden. He answers on the second ring.

"Baby? Everything ok?" he sounds sleepy but concerned.

"I woke up, and Britney is standing on the bed, looking out into the hallway, and growling," I whisper. "I've never seen her do this before. She's kinda freaking me out."

"I'm on my way, baby. Call the cops."

"Do you really think I should call the cops? What if she's just being weird?" I no sooner say that than I hear the 'beep beep beep' that my security system makes when you open the back door. Britney jumps off the bed and runs toward the noise. "Britney!" I scream. "Oh MY GOD, Brenden! Someone was in the house. I just heard the door beeps. Britney ran out to the living room."

"PARKER! We gotta go! It's an emergency. There's someone in Molly's house. I'll have Jared call and dispatch police on the way there. Baby, lock your bedroom door and stay there until I get there. I'll stay on the line."

I get out of bed and creep over to the door. I whisper shout, "Britney!" into the dark hallway. I can hear her still growling out in the living room. I hate to do it, but I close the door and lock it, hoping like hell that Britney will be ok out there. The fire station Brenden works at is about a fifteen minute drive from here.

"Jared called 911 and told them the situation. They are dispatching police. We should be there in ten, baby. Just breath for me, ok?" I nod. "Baby?"

"Sorry. I'm nodding. I'm ok. I'm just worried about Britney."

"She'll be ok, baby. We'll be there soon. Did you forget to set the alarm tonight?"

"No!!! I absolutely set it. I remember distinctly punching in the numbers. I don't understand how someone got in without setting off the alarm." I'm starting to freak out even more.

"Ok, baby. What did you and Britney do before bed?" I know he's just trying to keep me calm.

"We watched television for a bit, then I read for a little while before I started getting sleepy."

"Are you still reading that naughty book about the millionaire?" He says with a hint of jealousy in his voice

I giggle. "You should let me read you some of it. Especially this part where they're in his playroom."

I hear Jared in the background, "The playroom parts are good, man. Trust me."

I giggle again. Then I hear a scratch at the door. "I think Britney is scratching at the bedroom door. Should I risk opening it and letting her in?"

"I think you'll be ok. Hopefully, whoever it was has run far away before I get there," Brenden growls.

I unlock the door and crack it open. Britney sticks her nose in through the crack, then with all her size she just shoves the door open and comes in. I quickly lock the door behind her. When I turn around and look at her, she's already up on the bed lying on her back looking at me as though she's waiting for her tummy rubs. I hop on the bed with her and give her the reward she deserves.

Brenden keeps asking me silly questions to keep me calm.

Then I notice red and blue lights outside the house. "Babe, I think the cops are here. I can see the lights out my bedroom window. I'll let you go. I know you'll be here soon."

"We're just about four minutes away, baby. See you soon."

I walk out to the living room, turning on every light as I go. Britney follows close behind me. I walk to the back door and let her out. Sometimes she gets a little excited when new people get here, plus, if the person is still out there, maybe she'll scare them away. I hear a knock on the door. When I get there, I look out the peephole and see John. I haven't seen him much since he stopped by the salon that night. He'll wave if he sees me as he drives by, but he hasn't called to talk about the attempted break in from before.

I swing the door open right as he's about to knock again. "Hey! Sorry to have you come out ...again." I give him kind of half a smile.

"It's no problem," he says as he steps into my house. "I was patrolling nearby and heard it come over the radio." He runs his eyes over me, and I realize I'm in a tank top and sleep shorts that are pretty damn short. I cross my arms over my chest trying to hide myself a little. I see the cardigan I had on earlier today tossed over the arm of the couch, so I pick it up and put it on, pulling it closed over me as much as I can.

He straightens himself up and tries to be professional. "So what happened?"

"I was asleep, and something woke me. I'm not sure what. I don't know if it was Britney or hearing the door open."

"Is that the dog's name?" he asks, flipping open a little notepad.

"Yeah. Wait, how did you know I have a dog?"

"Well, for one, I can see her sitting at your back door through the glass. And two, I heard she broke Lisa Pinski's arm at the shelter."

"Right," I say nodding. "Do you mind if I let her back in?"

He looks a little iffy, then he says, "That's fine. Now, when you say heard the dog, what do you mean?" he asks as I walk to the back door and let her back in.

Britney comes in and immediately starts growling at him. "Hey, girl. This is John. He's a friend. It's ok," I look at him. "Sorry, she's very skittish around men, especially new men." Britney lets out this sonic boom of a bark and keeps growling at him. John puts his hand on the butt of his gun. "Britney!" I yell. "Calm down, baby girl." I look at him. "She won't hurt you. She's just protective of me."

The front door opens up, and John spins around and pulls his gun out, aiming it straight at Brenden and Jared.

"What the fuck?" Brenden shouts. Britney is getting wild. I've got a hold of her collar, but she's trying to get loose, and she's pulling me with her.

"John, put the fucking gun down, man," Jared says. John slowly puts it back in his holster.

"You don't knock? You just barge into her house like that?" John looks at the guys like they are criminals or something. He turns around and looks at me wrestling Britney, trying to keep her from jumping on him. "You better calm that fucking dog down, before I shoot it."

"You touch my fucking dog, and I'll beat the shit out of you, man. Cop or not," Brenden yells. "Britney. Sit." He walks past John and squats down in front of her. "Calm down, girl. It's ok." Britney sits, but she lets out a barely audible growl in John's direction.

Brenden stands back up and turns around to face John. "And

another thing, I'm her fucking boyfriend. I don't have to knock. I have a fucking key." He turns around to look at me. "You ok, baby?"

I nod at him, unable to speak. I realize I have tears running down my face. I really thought John might shoot Britney for a second. Brenden pulls me into a hug. He turns to face John again with me tucked under his arm. Britney's sitting at my feet, still letting out that low growl. "Ask your fucking questions and write the goddamn report. I'm calling your captain in the morning to report you. I don't want you near my girl or my dog anymore. Pass it off to some one else."

John looks pissed. His face is red, and he's breathing hard. "You don't get to tell me how to do my job, and you don't get to decide who is on what case."

"John," Jared says, gaining John's attention. "Just do the report and go man."

John asks me a couple of questions before he flips his little notebook closed. "My guess is, you probably forgot to set the alarm. Try to be a little more careful." Then, he turns around a walks toward the door, sneering at Brenden and Britney as he walks by.

I know I didn't forget. If there is one thing I am completely anal about, it's setting that fucking alarm and locking my doors. Jared offers for me to go stay with Sammy until morning, but its so late. It's nearly 3:30. I don't want to risk waking her and the kids up, especially when I'd have to be up in three hours anyway. I'm positive I will not go back to sleep tonight. We finally decide that Jared will take Brenden's jeep back to the station, and I'll drop him off there on my way to work, since Brenden only had a few hours left on his shift.

After Jared leaves, Brenden and I shut the lights off and head back to the bedroom. I feel like there is no way I'll sleep, but he insists I try. He promises he'll be right there, and with his reassurance, I do eventually doze off, but it's not a restful sleep. I dream that a snarling Britney is trying to lunge for John who has his gun pointed at Brenden. In my dream, I hear a pop, then my eyes fly open. Brenden is there, with his arms around me.

CHAPTER TWENTY

Brenden

*Y*ou know the thing about living in a smaller city? A city your grandpa and father grew up in? Everyone knows who you are, even if you only had short visits over the years. And if you're the grandson of Bennett Clarke, you've met most of the higher ups in law enforcement at the Donut Hole. Another possibility is that they knew your father. I mean, not everyone gets to call the Police Chief 'Uncle Bill'. Bill Garrity was my dad's best friend growing up. When we came to town to visit my grandparents, he and his family always came for BBQs and holiday parties.

After Molly dropped me off to get my jeep this morning, Jared followed me to the precinct. Sure, I could have called and talked to Uncle Bill, but I didn't want to deal with the possibility of getting his voicemail. He's an early riser, and I knew he'd be in already, so I wasn't surprised to see him standing in the doorway of his office with a screw driver messing with the hinges. "Uncle Bill!" I say, getting his attention. "What are you doing?"

"Brenden, get over here and help me with this damn door," he says.

"Don't you have maintenance to fix these things for you?" I ask.

"They are over-worked and underpaid and by the time they get around to doing it, this damn thing will be falling completely off the hinges."

"Maybe you should stop slamming it all the time," I hear my Aunt Doreen say. She works part time here as his administrative assistant. "Brenden, get over here and give me a hug." She opens her arms to me. Doreen is the best and practically a second mother to me. She and my mom are still good friends, and she has been campaigning for mom and me to move here for years. Jared goes to help Uncle Bill with the door while I'm properly hugged.

"Hey, Aunt Doreen," I smile and wrap my arms around her.

"How's your grandpa? I stopped by last Thursday, and he had a big black dog with him. He said it was your girlfriends dog? When do I get to meet this girl?" It's just like her to be nosy and need the inside scoop. I'm sure she's already had several conversations with my mom since then. Mom knows about Molly, but they haven't met yet. She's planning to come here next month over Mother's Day weekend.

"It's highly possible you already know her. Molly O'Brien? Her dad was a cop, Dennis O'Brien. And her mom was a schoolteacher, Suzanna O'Brien. Molly owns a salon downtown.

"Oh, my goodness. Yes! I know her parents, and actually, Kelli at Bombshells cuts my hair. Molly is such a lovely girl." She gives me another hug and then notices Jared standing behind me. "Now, who is this young man behind you?"

"Aunt Doreen, this is Jared Parker. We work together at the station. You might know his wife too. He's married to Sammy Parker from the salon."

Jared reaches out his hand to shake Doreen's, and she pulls him in for a hug.

"Oh, yes! Sammy does my nails! She's such a sweet girl, and your kiddos are just precious. And Sammy was right! You sure are handsome." I see Jared's cheeks get pink.

"Thank you, ma'am," he stutters out.

"Alright, alright. I assume you boys came by this morning for a reason?" Uncle Bill says.

"Yeah, I've got a problem I need your help with." He must see the seriousness on my face.

"Step into my office," he gestures with his head.

Once we're in, he rounds his desk and takes a seat. Jared and I sit opposite him in the club chairs he keeps for guests.

"What's up?"

I launch into the story about Molly and the previous attempted break in, the pictures, and the graffiti. He nods as I talk, and then I start telling him about last night.

"So, Jared and I walk in the door, and John pulls his gun out and points it at us. Jared had to talk him down to get him to holster it. Then our dog was barking and growling at him, and he threatened to shoot it. I can go to his precinct and talk to his direct supervisor, but that doesn't mean anything will get done. I want him off her case, and if anything else escalates with whoever is terrorizing her, someone else can handle it."

"I can understand your concern, and he definitely handled it badly. I'm just not sure that's cause to remove him from her case. And in an emergency situation, if he's the closest officer, wouldn't you rather have him there than have her wait for someone that might be patrolling further away?"

He makes sense, but something about John just rubs me the wrong way.

"I can definitely understand how you feel though Brenden, if some guy kept asking my girlfriend out, I might want him to stay the fuck away too," Jared says.

"WHAT?! He's been asking her out?" I want to go find him right now and kick his ass.

"Fuck." Jared mutters. "I thought Molly would've told you. Seeing as my wife is her best friend, I hear a lot of shit. I think he asked her out not long after her and Hank split up. She told him she wasn't ready to date yet. Then, I think he asked her out again about a month ago."

"Since we've been dating?" I say through gritted teeth.

"Yeah, Sammy said he stopped by when Molly was closing up shop and asked her out. Molly told him you guys were seeing each other exclusively."

"Alright boys, if you're done gossiping," Uncle Bill interjects. "Look, Brenden, I don't know if I can get him off the case, but I'll talk to his captain and suggest it. As far as your girl being stalked and terrorized, I'll also ask the captain to go over the report to see if he can find anything. I'll even have him send it over to me, and I'll take a look myself."

"Thanks, Uncle Bill." I stand up. "By the way, mom's coming next month. We'll have to plan dinner." He agrees and rounds the desk to give me a hug.

When we get outside, Jared looks at me. "Sorry to rat Molly

out, man. I just figured she'd have told you about John asking her out."

I just nod and clench my jaw.

"I'm gonna head home. I've got a headache," Jared says. "See you Thursday night, man."

"Alright, man."

As I climb into my jeep, I have to reel in my anger. I'm pissed for a few reasons. Number one, I'm pissed that there might not be anything that can be done about that John asshole being on her case. I don't fucking trust him, and I don't want him near her. Number two, I'm really fucking pissed that Molly failed to mention that some fucker asked her out. If I didn't know Molly had a full day today, I'd march into the salon and spank her ass for leaving that out.

To tamp my temper down, I head home to check in with Grandpa. He's in his recliner, as usual, watching highlights on ESPN.

"Hey, Grandpa," I say, coming in and plopping down on the couch.

"Was there a fire last night? You look exhausted."

"We had a small fire in the Chinese restaurant, but that was still early. Molly called me at 2:30 this morning. Someone was in her house."

Grandpa sits up suddenly. "What happened? Is she ok?"

"Yeah. I don't know how, but someone got in. It woke Britney up, which woke Molly up. She called me because she didn't know why Britney was standing on the bed, growling into the hallway. Then she heard the backdoor beeps from her alarm. She swears she set her alarm, so I don't know why it didn't go off like last time. Do you know John Palmer? He's a cop."

"Yeah I think I recall meeting him a time or two at Max's Donut Hole. He's kind of a smug little bastard." Leave it to Grandpa to call it like he sees it.

"Well, he's been on duty both times Molly had break ins. Last night, he drew on Jared and me and threatened to shoot Britney. I talked to Uncle Bill about it this morning."

"He pointed his weapon at you and threatened to shoot the dog? There's something wrong with that boy. I'd talk to his captain as well."

Nodding, I say, "He apparently has a little crush on my girl." That last part is said through clenched teeth. "I'm hoping he'll get pulled off her case. I'll definitely stop into the station and talk to his captain. I'm going to go buy a few extra security camerass for Molly's house. She's only got the doorbell camera, but you can't even see the side of the house." I'm kicking myself for not having thought to put up extra security cameras before.

"Well, who wouldn't have a crush on Molly? She's pretty and smart. She's got her own business and can take care of herself. I'll tell you right now, bud, you better start looking for a ring sooner than later. You need to stake your claim and make sure everyone knows she's yours. If I were forty years younger, I might throw my hat in the ring," he says with a wink.

I don't know what's crazier, that it seems perfectly logical to ask a girl I've known for just a month to marry me or that I'm adding stop by the jewelry store to my list of things to do. "It's crossed my mind. How long did you know Grandma before you asked her to marry you?"

"Your Grandma and I knew each other since we were kids. She was two years younger than me. We started dating officially in high school, but she was always mine. She was fourteen and I was sixteen. I asked her to marry me when she turned sixteen, but her daddy said we had to wait until she turned eighteen and had graduated high school. And he made me promise that she'd go to college if that's what she wanted. We got married two weeks after she graduated high school, and then she started school that fall to become a paralegal. We waited a few years before we started working on kids. Your grandma wanted a whole house full. We lost quite a few before she got pregnant with your daddy, and she never was able to get pregnant again after him." He looks into space with a sad smile. Then he looks at me. "I loved your grandma from the day I first saw her until the day she took her last breath. If I have any regrets, it's that I didn't marry her sooner. I'd suggest you get on it before someone else beats you to it."

I don't wait around long after that. I head to the electronics store to get some cameras for Molly's house. I plan to put several up. Something tells me that whoever is doing this is not going to stop. Molly promised she would change the code to the security system and that she'd pick a code that is random. Her first code was her mom's birthday, and the second code was her dad's birthday.

After I get the cameras, I head to the precinct that John works at to talk to his captain. I don't know him, but I'm hoping he's willing to hear me out. I walk in and ask the officer at the front desk if the captain is in. I don't have to wait long before he comes out to meet me. His name is Captain Sharp. If I'm being honest, he looks like he's not going to give a good goddamn what I have to say. He's just placating me to get me out of his hair.

"Captain Sharp," I say reaching to shake his hand. He shakes mine back. "I'm Brenden Clarke, and I'd really like to talk to you about one of your officers in this precinct." Recognition fills his eyes.

"Why don't you step into my office." He motions with his head and then leads me in, closing the door behind us. "Brenden, I'm gonna let you know I was expecting you to pop in. I talked to Bill this morning and had a phone call from both Dennis O'Brien and your Grandpa in the last hour."

"Well, I was expecting Bill to call. I did not know that Dennis or my Grandpa would call you, but neither surprise me, if I'm being honest. So, I guess the question is, can you remove John Palmer from Molly's case and possibly from patrolling in that area?"

He takes a deep breath, then leans forward with his elbows on the desk, and scrubs his hands up and down his face and through his hair. He lifts his head up and looks me in the eye. "I'm gonna be perfectly honest with you about his whole thing. Ordinarily, if you had just strolled in here and talked to me, I'd say there is nothing I can do. Officer Palmer was within his rights to draw the gun on you because you surprised him."

"He was within his rights to threaten to shoot my dog?" I question.

His eyebrows knit together. "He threatened to shoot the dog?" He picks up a document, that must be copy of the report he filled out. "He states here that the dog was barking and growling at him, and he instructed the owner to calm the dog down."

"When Jared Parker and I walked in, he turned and aimed at us. Jared told John to put the gun down. He holstered it, then the turned to Molly, who was doing her best to calm the dog and keep her from jumping on him. He told her to calm the dog down before he shot it. Britney, the dog, is very protective of Molly and extremely skittish around new men. Being that she had just chased someone out of Molly's house, she was looking at John as a threat in that moment."

"Aw hell, do you want to file a formal complaint? You have two other witnesses to that."

"If that's what it takes, I'd definitely like it on the record."

"Alright, let me just finish what I was going to tell you. Then you can decide." He reaches into his desk drawer, pulls out a cigarette, and puts it in his mouth. He doesn't light it but pretends to puff on it before he pulls it out of his mouth. "I'm trying to quit. Stress creates the cravings. This helps somehow." He shakes his head. "I've known your grandpa my entire life. He was friends with my dad, and I was pretty good friends with your dad growing up. I worked with Dennis and was even partners with him at one point, and your "Uncle" Bill is not only my boss but a damn good friend. I'm getting pressed on this from every angle. I'm going to speak candidly with you, Brenden. You have the right people on your side, and that makes me trust you. John Palmer is a bit of a pain in the ass. He's a by the book type of cop, but he's smug and thinks he's smarter than everyone. We've had complaints about him before, but because he's by the book, there's never been anything I could do. He watches what he does and says. Since I have the request of the Chief and a former partner, I'm willing to work with you guys. John will be pulled off the case. I will switch his patrol with another officer. So if, by chance, something else happens at your girl's house — and I'm hoping it won't — he will not be the one that answers."

I feel like I can breathe a little easier hearing this. "I really appreciate that, sir." In the end, Captain Sharp has me file a formal complaint, and he puts it in the paperwork he has to do to take John off the case. At least that's one less thing I have to worry about at the moment. Now I gotta get the cameras up.

CHAPTER TWENTY-ONE

Molly

I was hoping to get out of work a little early today, but I had a client that took longer than I expected, and it threw my whole day off by twenty minutes. My mom called me earlier. My parents got into town around ten this morning, and she wants Brenden and me to come by for dinner. What kind of crazy person is on the road for three months straight and then wants to host people for dinner the day they get back into town? Something tells me that my mom inviting us over has more to do with her wanting to meet Brenden than anything else. I'm really excited to see them though, so if she's willing, we'll be there.

I called Brenden earlier to let him know we were going to my parent's tonight, but I just got his voicemail. He texted later and said he'd been busy, but he is fine with meeting them tonight. It's about 5:45 by the time I get home, and mom wants us over at her place by seven, so I've got time to jump in the shower to get all the hair off of me from the haircuts I did today. I know Brenden is here because his car is parked out front. I make my way inside and am met at the door by Britney's sweet face. I set my bag down and give her all of my attention because I missed my sweet girl today. I look up and notice Brenden is standing there watching us with a serious look on his face.

"Hey, baby! What's up?" I ask laughing and trying to get off the floor. Britney doesn't agree with that idea though and keeps knocking me back down and licking my face.

"Britney, go lay down," Brenden says sternly. Britney is a good girl and listens to him. Then he walks over to me and reaches his hand down to help me up. When he pulls me up, he jerks me against his chest and holds me there hard. "You and I need to have a little chat."

"What's wrong?" He sounds mad, and I can't think of anything I could have done or said that would have made him angry. He grabs my chin and kisses my lips hard, walking me back against the wall as he plunders my mouth.

He releases my mouth and stares at me. "Has John Palmer asked you out?"

"Yeeeeesss," I say slowly, feeling a bit confused.

"Since we've been together?" he growls.

"Yes. But I told him we were together."

"Why didn't you tell me he asked you out?" still growling

"I don't know. I guess it slipped my mind. I'm not interested in him, and I told him no. I didn't know I needed to give you a list of guys that have asked me out." I say, probably sassier than necessary, but what the fuck?

He smirks at me. "Well, let me make one thing perfectly clear. Especially where he is concerned, I want to know if he or any other fuckers ask you out from now on."

"So, do I get a list of every girl that comes on to you?" I toss back at him.

"What girls?" He has the audacity to look at me with a puzzled expression.

I roll my eyes. "You can not tell me you don't get flirted with on a daily basis. I've witnessed it myself. Hell, 99% of the time when we go out to eat, the waitress flirts with you. Half the girls at the salon treat you like a piece of meat when you stop in."

"I don't see any of them. I'm only looking at you when I'm with you. And when I'm not with you, I'm thinking of you. Only you."

"And growling at any guy that looks in my direction too." I roll my eyes again and smile at him. "Look, I didn't tell you about John asking me out because it didn't matter. I hadn't even thought about him asking until you just brought it up. I'm not the least bit interested in him. And if it's possible, I'm even less interested since he pointed a gun at you and threatened to shoot Britney." I can tell that this calms him a little, but he's still got me pinned against the wall with his hands on my face. I lean forward and give him a peck on the lips.

"We've got about an hour before we need to leave to go to my parents' house for dinner. I need to shower and change because I'm covered in tiny hairs. Would you like to shower with me?"

"I just got out of the shower about thirty minutes ago, but I'd like to help you get clean." He picks me up and hauls me into the bathroom where he proceeds to get me clean and very, very dirty.

We pull up outside my parents' house about ten minutes past when I told my mom we'd be here. Damned sexy shower. They don't live too far from me. They're not as close as Brenden's grandpa, but it's still the same area of town. My parents live in a Victorian style house. I loved this house growing up. It's yellow with a big wrap around front porch, and there's a porch swing I used to sit on and read for hours.

"Are you nervous?" I ask Brenden.

"No, I've kind of met both of them. I mean, your dad wanted to set us up. I think we'll be fine." He kisses my hand and then exits the car. He didn't want to ride in my Beetle over here. He says the car fits me, but it doesn't fit him. He's afraid one of the guys from the station will see him riding in my car and make fun of him, so naturally, I insisted we take it.

We meet in front of the car, and he gives me a sweet kiss before taking my hand and walking with me onto the porch. Before we even get to the door, my mom throws it open and is pulling us both into a hug. "Oh, Molly Wally, I missed you so much!" she says pulling back from the hug. "Wow. Nice job on getting a cute one, Molly," she cups her mouth and stage whispers. I laugh and shake my head. "Brenden, you're even more handsome in person than over the phone." She pats him on the cheek. "Well, come in, come in. Dinner's ready, and your dad is about to die from starvation."

"Mom, you didn't need to cook! We could've picked up pizza or something." I hate that she went out of her way to make us dinner tonight.

"Your Dad has been going on and on about having spaghetti for the last month. I already had a jar of my sauce made, and I used frozen meatballs. I sent your dad to the store earlier for garlic bread and a bag of salad." She gestures with her hands at the table. Dad walks out of the kitchen and places the breadbasket on the table.

"Cupcake!" He bellows. My dad is a big guy, and he's very loud. I love that about him though. He's called me cupcake since I was born, and it always makes me smile. I run over and wrap my arms around him. "How's my girl?"

"I'm doing pretty good, Dad." I look over at Brenden. He's got his big, handsome smile on.

Brenden steps forward with his hand out. "It's nice to see you again, Mr. O'Brien."

"Call me Dennis," Dad says, shaking Brenden's hand. "It's nice to see you again, Brenden. I'm glad you two finally met. Now, can we please eat? I'm wasting away over here." My dad says while patting his tummy.

My dad is pretty fit for a guy in his early 60s. He and Brenden are probably about the same height, but he's gotta have at least thirty pounds of "extra love" as he calls it. My mom is pretty much my twin. Her red hair isn't as bright as it was when she was younger, but it's still long and still red. We're the same height, but I'm pretty sure I weigh more than she does. What can I say? I love sugar…and bacon.

Once we sit down and start eating, my dad starts the conversation that I knew was coming. "Now, tell me every goddamn detail about these break-ins." We go over the timeline of what happened on St. Patrick's Day. I tell him about the pictures and the graffiti on my house and garage. Brenden has pictures of it on his phone that he shows my dad. "And what about the incident with Hank a few days before?"

"He showed up at the salon on Friday and asked me to talk. We went out front and got into an argument. When I turned to leave, he grabbed my arm. I told him to let go, but he just smirked at me. I broke the hold, punched him in the throat, and then stomped on his hand when he went down."

"That's my girl," my mom says while slurping up some noodles. Brenden throws his head back and laughs.

"And nothing happened with him?" Dad just carries on with his questions.

"Well, I said I wanted to press charges, but the judge only made him pay a citation for public disturbance and let him go." Dad makes a huffing sound as he scoops more food into his mouth.

"And you're sure he's not the one that's tried to get in?" Dad asks while biting into some garlic bread.

"I mean, I have't talked to him since then. The cops said he had an alibi and was out of town," I shrug.

"Maybe I should pay him a visit," Dad mumbles.

"Dad," I sigh. "I think you better let the cops that are still on the job handle it."

He lets out a low, growly noise. "Tell me what happened last night?"

"I think I woke up because Britney was growling. She was standing on the bed facing the door and growling toward the hallway. I'd never seen her do that before, so I called Brenden. While we were on the phone, I heard the beeps the door makes when it gets opened. My alarm never went off, and I know for a fact that I set it. Brenden and Jared rushed over and called 911 on the way. John Palmer was the cop that showed up, and he started to ask me what happened. I had let Britney out before I let him in, and she was scratching at the door, so I let her back in. She did not like John, and while I was trying to calm her, Brenden and Jared came in. John pointed the gun at them. Jared told him to put the gun down. Britney was freaking out, and John said to calm her down or he would shoot her. Brenden got her calmed down. Then he and John had words. Ultimately, John said I probably forgot to set the alarm, even though I am 100% positive that I set it."

"Did you reset the code on your alarm today?" Dad asks.

"I did, and I chose random numbers instead of a birthday or something," I say nodding.

"I also put up some other security cameras today," Brenden says.

"You did?" We didn't talk about him doing that, so I'm a little surprised.

"Yeah. I put them on each corner of the house. They can rotate to scan the area. I'll put the app on your phone later. It will alert you if there's movement, and it records 24/7."

"You didn't tell me you were going to do that." He's thoughtful and such a good boyfriend.

"I want you safe when I can't be there, and if it keeps going on, we need to figure out who is doing it," he says grabbing my hand and kissing it.

"Anything else strange?" Dad says interrupting our moment.

"When can I meet my grand-puppy?" Mom chimes in.

"I thought about bringing her tonight, but she's a little shy around new people. You guys will have to come over soon."

"I was planning to come over tomorrow to check out your security, but it sounds like Brenden's on top of that. I do want to go over the plans for your attic space soon though." Dad seems a little calmer knowing Brenden's got my back.

We sit around the table chatting about their trip. Mom shows me a slideshow of photos she took on her phone. It has a lot of selfies that she didn't mean to take and pictures of my dad frowning in front of various signs and historical sites. Dad excuses himself to go to the other room for a minute.

"Does anyone have room for dessert? I used Sammy's BTS cake recipe," I start to giggle.

"Molly, really?" My mom tries to scold me, which only makes me laugh harder.

"What's BTS cake?" Brenden asks looking at me like I'm crazy.

"Better than sex cake. Mom just can't say sex in front of me," I laugh.

"I can too. Sex sex sex. There. Are you happy?" she shouts.

"What the hell did I walk back into?" Dad stands in the doorway looking completely confused. This causes me to laugh even harder, until tears are running out of my eyes.

After we all eat cake, Brenden and I head back to my place. We make plans for my parents to stop by on Sunday to meet Britney and have lunch. Dad wants to look at the attic and talk to Brenden about some of his plans for it. I knew they would bond over power tools. My mom is so excited to see Britney and is already offering to come walk her when we are both working. Since our family dog passed a few years ago, my mom just couldn't bring herself to get another pup, but she never passes up a chance to pet and snuggle other people's dogs.

I brush my teeth before bed and decide to sleep in my panties and a tank top. I'm so tired, I'm not sure I could stay awake even for an orgasm tonight. I've got a full day of clients tomorrow, and then we're having girls' night for Gracie's twenty-first birthday. I crawl into bed, and I think I'm out before my head hits the pillow. When I wake up in the morning, it's to Brenden's mouth between my legs, and all is right with the world.

CHAPTER TWENTY-TWO

Molly

oday was exhausting at work. I don't know why I always think it's a good idea to work a full, busy day and then go out on the town. I'm sure it mostly has to do with remembering how I used to survive on minimal sleep and go out five to six nights a week. Sure, I'm off tomorrow, and I took Monday off too, but I'm not twenty-one anymore, and it's getting harder and harder to stay up and party.

Brenden spent the day with his grandpa, and he'll meet us at McMurphy's later tonight since it's a Ladies' Night dinner. Gracie has been a bit down this week and doesn't seem to want to talk about it, I'm hoping this will perk her up a little bit. I'm putting the finishing touches on my makeup when I hear the front door open and the security code being punched in. I know it has to be either Brenden or Sammy. They are the only ones with the new code. Also, anyone else would be screaming for their life right now since Britney's out in the living room.

"Well, you sure do clean up nice, Molly Dolly." Sammy puts on a southern drawl.

"Thank you kindly, Sammy Sue." I drawl right back. "You're lookin' pretty sexy yourself. I'm surprised Jared let you leave the house like that." She's wearing a short black dress. It doesn't show any cleavage, but it's *very* short and dips pretty low in the back. She's wearing some hot pink heels with it too. Sammy loves to antagonize Jared with her clothing. They're always having arguments about what she wears. She does it on purpose because she loves how possessive he is and the reaction he gives her. She will buy clothes and say, "I wonder how long it will take for Jared to rip this off of me?"

"He was actually sleeping when I left. I don't think he's gonna come tonight. He's got another migraine. You almost ready to go? I'd like to be on time for the reservation, and we still have to stop and get Gracie. Plus, I'm starving."

"Just gotta slide my dress and shoes on." I laid my dress out on the bed already. It's a dark green flowy chiffon maxi dress with spaghetti straps. It's loose and comfy, and I can wear my jellies without anyone knowing. My feet hurt. I didn't sit today until I got into my car to go home, so comfort is a must. Then I grab a black cardigan off the end of my bed, in case I get chilly. I give Britney an extra cookie for being a good girl and set the alarm on the way out.

We pull up outside of Gracie's apartment about ten minutes later. It's a big, old house that was reconfigured years ago into a bunch of apartments. On the outside, it's a bit rundown, but Gracie has her little apartment fixed up adorably. When she answers the door, she's still in her work clothes.

"I thought you'd be ready! C'mon, lady! Chop, chop," I say walking into her apartment.

"I don't really feel like going tonight, you guys." She turns and walks back to her little living room, which is also her bedroom, and plops down on her bed, which is also her couch.

"Too bad, chickadee! We gots to *go*. Everyone will be waiting on us, and we gotta get you *crunk*," Sammy says, raising her arms likes she's raising the roof before plopping down next to her.

"I definitely do *not* want to get crunk." She throws herself back onto the bed.

"What's up, Gracie? You haven't been your bright and shiny self this week. Is everything ok? You can talk to us about anything, you know?" I assure her, sitting down on her other side.

"I don't want to talk right now," Gracie says. She's got her arm thrown over her eyes. Was I this dramatic at twenty-one? Please. I was probably ten times worse.

"Well, the options are talk or get ready so that we can go," I say.

She lets out a big sigh. "Fine. I'll get ready." She pulls herself up and heads to the closet. She pulls out a cute little dress she bought a couple of months ago when we went shopping. Then she stomps into the bathroom.

"Whatever's going on is definitely going to end up with us forcing it out of her," I turn and say to Sammy.

"How are your waterboarding skills?" Sammy smirks at me.

About ten minutes pass before she emerges from the bathroom. Gracie is a gorgeous girl as it is, but she looks smokin' hot right now. She must be wearing contacts because her glasses are gone. Her inky hair is down in its natural curls. She never wears it down. She put some fake lashes on and bright red lipstick. The dress is skin-tight and hits mid-thigh. It's dark grey with a little ruffle at the bottom of the skirt and little sleeves that are off her shoulders.

"Wowza, Gracie! You look hot, girlfriend!" I say.

"Can I gets some fries with that shake?" Sammy asks.

"I love you guys, even if you are both crazy." She tries to hide her smile as she walks back over to the closet and digs out some black strappy sandals with at least a four-inch heel. She grabs a purse a little bigger than a clutch and puts in her lipstick, a small wallet, and her keys before throwing in a pair of those little flats that fold up tiny. "I'm ready."

All the girls from the salon are waiting for us when we get to the restaurant. We somehow made it before our reservation time, and they seat us almost immediately. Dinner is so good, and we all eat until we're stuffed. After a couple of cocktails, Gracie seems to loosen up a little bit. Toward the end of dinner, Sammy slips from the table to tell our server that we want to sing Happy Birthday and to bring out the cake. We got a turtle cake from the bakery, and its mouthwatering in all its chocolate and caramel glory. It also happens to be her favorite treat from there. They sell it by the slice. Mmmmmmm. Turtle cake.

The server brings it out with candles in the shape of twenty-one, and we all sing happy birthday to her. Gracie seems to have done a complete 180 from the mopey girl we picked up an hour and half ago, which is awesome. And before I know it, we're all marching down Main Street and heading toward McMurphy's.

It's about 9:15 by the time we get there, and karaoke is in full swing. Brenden texts me about fifteen minutes ago and said he and a few of the other guys from Station 4 were here. One song is ending as we head to find the guys' table, and Emily runs up to the Karaoke DJ to tell him that it's Gracie's twenty-first birthday. So he plays Happy Birthday as everyone sings along, and we all shout "GRACIE" when it gets to that part. She's bright red but smiling and seems to be holding onto the happy feeling.

I notice as we're sitting down that a couple of the guys from the station are admiring Gracie's dress and heels. Most days, she's wearing slacks and flats, and her curvy figure is usually hidden under boxy tops and cardigans. Her hair is almost always slicked back in a ponytail or bun, and her oversized glasses cover her tiny face. But tonight, it's like she went from the girl next door to a sexpot in the ten minutes she was in the bathroom. They are all good guys, but I ask Brenden to keep an eye on them with Gracie. She doesn't need the ten shots they are already offering to buy her.

I've been coming here long enough to know the staff pretty well. On karaoke nights, as long as I give the Karaoke DJ a wave, he puts me on. He likes to play what he refers to as Karaoke Roulette with the "regulars." He keeps a box of note cards on which we've all written down songs we can and will sing. Then he calls us up and picks from the list. I give him a wave, and he signals to me that there are four people in front of me.

Brenden gets drinks for Sammy and me. Sammy's is nonalcoholic because she's the DD tonight for Gracie. Sammy says she doesn't want to be hungover tomorrow because she and Jared are taking the kids to the children's museum. But I have a suspicion that there might be a bun in that oven that she hasn't told me about yet. I don't plan on getting drunk either. We're supposed to have my parents over tomorrow, and I'd prefer not to be hungover for that. Like I said, I can't bounce back like I used to do.

When Ken, the karaoke DJ, calls my name to sing, I hear the familiar guitar riff of I Love Rock n Roll by Joan Jett and the

Black Hearts. I try to be upbeat when I sing and get everyone to do the "Owwwwws" with me. When I'm finished, I ask him to put Sammy and me on the list for a duet, and I'm surprised when I see Gracie's name on the list to sing. "Did Gracie put her name in?"

"The birthday girl? Yeah, she ran up her right after you guys got here." Hmmmm. I've never even heard her sing along in the car. This should be interesting.

I make my way back to the table and sit. Leaning over the table, I ask Sammy, "Have you ever heard Gracie sing?"

She looks at me like I'm crazy. "No. I can't picture her singing in front of anyone. You didn't put her name in did you?"

"I'm not an asshole. No! Her name was already on the list. Ken said she ran over right after she got here. She's probably up soon." An older guy, named Barry, who I see here often, is singing Margaritaville right now. I glance at Gracie who is swaying in her seat with her eyes closed and mouthing the words. I point her out to Sammy, and we both laugh. Who is this girl, and where did our timid receptionist go?

Barry finishes, and sure enough, Ken calls Gracie up on stage. I am shocked when she steps up and starts belting out 'I Touch Myself' by The Divinyls. She's got an awesome voice, and I cannot even believe this is the same girl who didn't want to come out with us hours ago. I look around our long table, and everyone has the same shock that I feel written on their faces. Sammy's mouth is hanging open. All the girls have their eyes bugged out. I look back at Brenden, and even he is bewildered. I think a couple of these guys will be ready to ask her for a date as soon as she steps off the stage.

When she whispers her last lyric into the microphone, I notice a big, muscular guy with tattoos up and down his arms and a well-kept beard reach out his hand to help her down. Then he leans down and whispers in her ear. Gracie looks up at him and throws her head back and laughs. To be a fly on the wall of that conversation. She whispers something back to him and pats him on the chest, then walks back over to our table and takes her seat between Sammy and Emily. We all ask what that was all about. Does she know him? She says, "Nope," and pops the P. Then she merely smiles and sips on the water we insist that she drinks before she can have more alcohol. The rest of the night, I notice her shift her eyes over toward the brooding stranger in the corner. He looks familiar, but I can't think of anyone I've ever met with tattoos on their face. Gracie doesn't get back on stage again, but she sings along to every single song at the table. By the time we're ready to leave, Gracie has sobered up quite a bit, but Brenden and I walk her and Sammy back to Sammy's car before we head home.

It's about 1:30 when we finally head home. My head is leaning against the window, watching the streetlights go by, when I feel my phone vibrating in the pocket of my cardigan. I assume it's Sammy or Gracie, but when I look at the screen, I see that my doorbell cam is alerting me that someone is on my front porch. I click on the app, and I see a person, dressed in black from head to toe, with a hood around their face, just standing on my porch. I can't make out who it is. I can't even tell if it's a man or woman. Then they lay a package on the porch and turn and run away into the darkness.

"What the fuck?" I whisper.

"What's up, baby?" Brenden looks over at me. "Is everything ok?"

"There was someone on my porch. They were dressed in all black, and they put down a package and walked away."

"What?!" He pulls over to the side of the road abruptly and reaches for my phone. Rewinding the video feed, he watches it until the person runs off. Then he goes to my contacts and calls my dad. It's late, so the call wakes him up.

"Dennis, we are heading home from a night out with friends. Molly got an alert that there was someone at her door. She watched on the video and saw someone on the porch dressed in black. They left a package. I think we need your help," he says in a clear and calm manner.

I can't make out what my dad is saying to him, but he must say he's on his way. Brenden hands me back my phone and pulls his out to call his Uncle Bill, who is apparently the chief of police in our little city. The conversation pretty much sounds the same, and I think he'll be on his way as well.

When we pull up to my house, we can see that there is something sitting there on the porch. Brenden suggests that we wait in the car for my dad or his Uncle Bill. While we wait, he brings up the app that connects to the cameras he put up the other day. You can see the person walking from down the block. After they drop the package on the porch, they take off running, trip at the edge of the yard and then run off with a limp. Maybe that can help us figure out who is doing this?

It's not long before my dad pulls up. As we get out of the car to meet him, a police cruiser pulls up with Craig Voss, the cop from the first incident. As he makes his way over to us, a black sedan pulls up, and an older man I assume is Uncle Bill, gets out.

"Bill," my dad says nodding.

"Dennis, good to see you, man. Not under these circumstances, of course," he says as he claps my dad on the back. "Craig, do you have any gloves in your cruiser?"

"Yes, sir." Craig gets gloves from his trunk for all of us, and we make our way to the porch to get the package. Being that the last envelope we found had pictures of me in it, I'm nervous to see if this is more of the same.

Uncle Bill squats down to get it. "Let's get inside, and then you can introduce me to your girl," he says to Brenden.

I unlock the door and then punch in my alarm code. Britney is waiting, and she starts to growl at the strange men following us in. Brenden gets down and pets her before he takes her collar and pulls her over to her dog bed, telling her to lay down. She always listens to him.

My dad wraps his arm around my shoulders and kisses the top of my head. "C'mon. Let's go see what's in the package, Cupcake," he whispers guiding me into my living room.

"First things first, Molly. I'm Bill Garrity. You can call me Uncle Bill." That makes me smile. I feel at ease with him already. "The last time I think I saw you, you were probably only five or six. I remember that red hair, and my wife says you're the sweetest." I look at him for a second wondering who his wife is. Then it clicks.

"Oh! You're Doreen's husband. She's such a sweet lady." He nods.

"Now, tell Officer Voss and me what happened tonight."

"We were on our way home after being at McMurphy's tonight for my friend Gracie's birthday. While we were on the way, my doorbell cam alerted me that someone was on the porch." I pull up the video and let him see it. Then he passes it to my dad.

"We've got video from additional security cameras also." Brenden hands over his phone with the video of whoever it is limping as they run.

"Looks like he fell right at the edge of the yard," Bill murmurs. "Craig, can you go out and look for any evidence that might have been left and cordon off that part of the yard?" Craig nods and heads outside, and then Bill continues, "Alright. Do you two have any ideas what might be in this box?"

"The first time someone tried to get in, they left an envelope with pictures in it. They were all of me, but they photo shopped them ,and there was a skull filter over my face. You could tell it was me though."

"Ok, then. We'll see if it's more of the same," Bill says, opening the box and removing some of the contents. I feel like we're all holding our breath waiting to see what it is. Bill stares for a few seconds at a slip of paper. He hands it to me, and I see it's a note with one sentence written on it.

When you dress like a slut and act like a whore, you get treated that way.

I suck in a deep breath. I don't know if that is a threat or just a really fucked up observation in this crazy person's eyes. I pass the note to Brenden.

"Easy. Brenden. Don't crumple it up. It's evidence," Bill says. "Molly I think you might want to look through these without your dad present."

"Why? What the fuck is there that I can't see?" my dad grits out.

"Just calm down a minute, Dennis. Let Molly see if she's comfortable with you seeing them," Bill says trying to calm my dad's nerves. It makes me more nervous. What could it be?

He walks me over to the kitchen island and lays a stack of pictures down in front of me. The top one is of me wrapped in a towel in my bedroom. Only the angle isn't through the window like last time. I gasp and cover my mouth.

"Molly? Baby? Are you ok?" Brenden says from a few feet behind me.

"Brenden, you should probably look at these as well. I believe you're in them also." Bill doesn't stand over us while we look. He walks back over to my dad and has a quiet conversation with him. I assume he's giving him the gist of what is in the pictures.

I flip the top picture over to see the next one. It's Brenden and me on the bed. I'm on my knees facing toward the camera. He's behind me. In another time and place, I might look at this and think it's sexy. But it just causes me to let out a sob. We flip through each picture. Every one of them is of Brenden and me in various sexual positions. None of them are too close. They are all from the same angle. When we get to the last one, I'm a wreck. Brenden is standing behind me, his arm wrapped around me. I can hear him breathing heavy. He spins me around and holds me close to his chest while I just cry. I let out everything until I feel like I might collapse into a heap on the floor.

"I'm going to call the CSI team to come over and sweep your place for any other devices." I look over at Bill. He's standing there with what looks to me like a tiny flashlight in a clear bag. "From the angle of the first picture, I could tell it was across from your bed. It was in the vent on the wall above your dresser."

Bill tells Craig to make the call to the station to get CSI down here. "Molly, there was one more thing in the box."

"I don't know if I can handle seeing anything else," I say through the tears that are still falling down my cheeks. Brenden leads me over to the couch and makes me sit. My dad sits down next to me and wraps his arm around my shoulder. Bill pulls out a hairbrush from the box. It's my hairbrush. I recognize it. "Oh my God!" I say continuing to sob. "It's my hairbrush. I've been looking for it. I though Britney had taken it to chew on it. I figured she had it hidden somewhere."

My dad rubs my back, and Brenden brings me over a glass of water. I finally calm down enough to ask, "So what do we do now?"

"It might take a little bit, but they'll come to sweep your place to look for any other devices. They'll take the package and all of its contents back to the lab to look for DNA and finger prints as well as dust in here to see if we can get an idea of who could have done this. Is there anyone you might suspect?"

"Well, after the first incident, I assumed it was my ex-boyfriend, Hank."

"And what would lead you to think it was him?" Bill asks.

"Well, the day before, he and I had an argument that ultimately sent him to the emergency room and got him arrested. I thought he was retaliating."

Bill's eyebrows shot up when I said sent him to the emergency room. "What exactly happened that sent him to the emergency room?"

"He showed up, and we got into an argument. I tried to walk away, but he grabbed my arm and wouldn't let go. I broke his hold, punched him in the throat, and stomped on his fingers when he hit the ground." He looks even more surprised when I say this.

"She takes self-defense classes." Brenden says with pride in his voice.

"But Craig," I say nodding in his direction, "told me that Hank had an alibi and was out of town. And the video from tonight definitely wasn't him." Craig nods in confirmation.

"How can you be sure?" Bill asks.

I sigh. "Because Hank is 6 foot 5 and weighs over 300 pounds. The person on the video was not that big."

"Ahhh, yes. I guess we can at least rule him out for dropping off the package. Tomorrow morning, we'll go to the neighbors and find out if any of them have security cameras that might have picked something up. For tonight, you might want to collect some things and go stay somewhere else. I'm not sure how long the team will be here."

"You can come stay with us tonight," Dad says.

"Thanks, dad, but I'll probably go stay with Brenden." Brenden wraps his arms around me. My dad seems to understand, thankfully.

I head into the bedroom to grab some clothes for tomorrow and Monday, just in case. Then I grab some of my toiletries and stuff them all in my overnight bag. I really hate that all of this is happening, but at least I've got the next two days off to deal with it.

Brenden

While Molly is getting her things together, I pull Uncle Bill aside. I can't help but wonder if the person doing this could possibly be John Palmer. I don't want to accuse him in front of Craig. I don't know if they're buddies, and I don't want to stir up shit if it's not warranted.

"I'm not saying I have any kind of proof, but is there any way to check to see where John Palmer was tonight? I don't know what it is about him, but I just don't trust him." I say quietly.

"Brenden, I know you have issues with the guy, and he hit on your girl." I start to interrupt him to plead my case, but he stops me. "I will look into it, quietly. But do not say anything to anyone about it. If he didn't have anything to do with this, you could start a lot of trouble for yourself with him. I don't want your imagination running crazy. Just make sure you and Molly keep an eye out and call me if anything else happens."

I decide not to press him too far on this. He said he'd look into it. I nod and walk down the hallway to find Molly.

CHAPTER TWENTY-THREE

Brenden

On Sunday morning, I wake up and check the clock. It's early still. I think I've only slept for a few hours. It was after four by the time we got to my grandpa's house. It feels strange to sleep here now. If I'm not at the station, I'm usually sleeping at Molly's house. I look at Molly, sleeping on her side facing me. She's fucking beautiful. How did I get lucky enough to find her? I lay there for a while just holding her, trying so hard to get back to sleep, but the sun streaming in through the blinds is making it impossible. I've always been a morning person, so I roll out of bed and make my way to the bathroom. Since I'm up, I decide to go for a run with Britney. I think I need to burn off some of this nervous energy. It's hard to relax with all this bullshit happening. I just wish there was more I could do to put a stop to it.

When I sneak back into the bedroom to grab my running shorts, Britney perks up. "You wanna go run, Brit?" Her tail is wagging, and she stretches, then stands up, and walks to the door. It never fails to amaze me how smart this dog is.

We make our way down the stairs and find Grandpa already in his recliner watching television. "I thought I heard you come in early this morning. I figured you'd be sleeping at Molly's house." Britney goes to grandpa and forces her head under his hand for a pet.

"That was the plan, but someone left a package on Molly's doorstep last night. Uncle Bill suggested we stay here instead. Molly's upstairs sleeping still."

"What was in the package?" he asks, scratching behind Britney's ears.

"Pictures of Molly and me, taken from inside her bedroom. Uncle Bill found a spy camera in the vent above her dresser. Also, there was a hairbrush Molly had been missing. She thought Britney had taken and hidden it. Someone has been inside her house without us knowing."

Grandpa looks at me with worry in his eyes. "That poor girl. Why would someone want to do this to her?"

"I don't know, and besides her ex-boyfriend, Molly has no ideas of who it could be. I have my suspicions, and Bill is checking into them, but there might be nothing to back it up besides my own possessiveness over Molly."

He looks at me for a second, "You think John Palmer could have something to do with it?"

"I do."

"What makes you guys think it's not the ex-boyfriend?" Grandpa asks, still petting Britney.

"On the first incident, he was out of town. Then, last night, the person who left the package came right onto the front porch. They were dressed in black with a hood up, and you couldn't see a face. But her ex was a huge guy, and this person was much smaller. They are going to sweep her house to look for any other devices and check with neighbors to see if any other security cameras caught anything."

Grandpa just nods.

"Alright, I'm gonna take Britney for a run. I shouldn't be gone too long. I don't think Molly will be awake before I get back." I put Britney's leash on, and we head out the door and down the street.

I take this time to think about everything going on. I'm sure this is wearing Molly down. I'd love to be able to get her out of town for a few days, but between me being new at the station and her being booked ahead of time at work, it would be nearly impossible. Britney and I run to a nearby park that has some walking paths. The sign says the complete loop is two miles, so we run that before heading home.

When we get back to the house, I see a black sedan in front of the house. I think it might be Uncle Bill. Sure enough, when I walk in, he's on the couch chatting with Grandpa.

"Hey. Do you have any news?" I ask as soon as I see him.

Uncle Bill gives me a tight smile. "Not anything huge, but a few pieces of information. I should talk to both you and Molly. Why don't you go get her?" I nod and head up the stairs.

Opening the door, I see Molly sleeping soundly. I hate to wake her up for this because I know she's exhausted. I'll promise her an early bedtime tonight. Sitting on the edge of the bed, I rub her back and whisper her name. Her eyes flutter open, and it takes her a few seconds to wake up. "Baby, Uncle Bill is here with some news. He wants to talk to both of us. Can you come down for a few? You can go back to sleep when he leaves."

She nods her head, then pushes herself up to sitting. "Can

you tell him I'll be down in a few?" I smile and nod, then head out of the room and back downstairs. It doesn't take long before Molly is descending the stairs. She's gotten dressed and even braided her hair.

She sits next to me on the couch, and we both stare at Uncle Bill. "Sorry to wake you, honey. I just had a few pieces of information for you and a couple of questions." Molly nods, and he continues. "Well, first, we haven't found any other devices. The team will probably be there for most of the day, so that could always change, but so far, it seems that the camera in the bedroom might be it."

I think Molly and I both let out a collective breath. "Second, we have detectives checking with neighbors to see if anyone caught anything, I haven't gotten an initial report on that yet because it's still early. Now, as far as suspects, this stays between us for now. Brenden, I followed up with the whereabouts of John Palmer last night. He was supposed to be on patrol in another area. As far as we know, he was. We are checking to see if there was any way he had been near Molly's house.

Molly looks at me. "You think John had something to do with this?"

"I don't trust him. I think he's up to something." I look to Uncle Bill. "What else?"

"Something else interesting — we tried to contact Hank. He did not answer at the number we had for him, so we sent someone to his apartment. He was not home, but his car was there. We contacted his parents; his mother was not very forthcoming, and just between us, that woman is quite a pill."

Molly laughs, "You have no idea."

"Anyway, it took some time, but she finally admitted that Hank has been in rehab since the Sunday after your incident."

"Rehab?" Molly seems confused. "He was on drugs?"

"Apparently, he had been using anabolic steroids for quite some time. The outburst he had with you that day may have been due to side effects of the steroids. He is in New Mexico, so I definitely do not believe Hank has been involved with this."

"Well, I'm glad to know he's getting help. And I guess that explains the weirdness." Molly mutters.

"Now, Molly, I'd like to ask if there is anyone else you can think of that could want to scare or harass you," Bill says looking hopeful.

"I've been wracking my brain since the first time someone tried to get in. I went on a whole slew of terrible dates before I met Brenden, but I can't think of one that would do this. Besides that, rarely did I go past a single date, and I always met them in a public place. I don't think I even gave any of them my last name."

"Ok, darlin'. Well, if you do think of anything or come across anything that would be helpful, Brenden has my number." Uncle Bill stands up and gives both of us hugs. Then he pats Britney on the head, and waves to Grandpa on the way out the door. "See you at Max's next Sunday, Ben."

I turn toward Molly. She looks like she's deep in thought. "You ok, baby?"

She looks over at me, "I just wonder how long he's been on the steroids. Did he start when we were still together?" she shrugs. "I think I'm going to go lay down for a while."

"I'll be up to lay with you in a few, baby. I'm just gonna get Britney some breakfast." She nods. Then goes over and kisses my grandpa on the top of his head, before she heads back upstairs.

"Hopefully, they'll find some security video of whoever is doing this." Grandpa says.

"I hope so." I get Britney some breakfast, then head up to hold my girl while we both get some more much needed sleep.

Molly

When we finally get up for the day, we make our way into town to grab a bite to eat. We decide to keep it simple and head to Maybell's for cheeseburgers. Last night feels like a bad dream, but I keep remembering that it was real and shuddering when I replay seeing those pictures. I suppose I should be thankful that they only sent us the creepy pictures and that they weren't plastered all over a billboard.

Brenden's been quiet, and I worry a little bit that he's feeling like he picked the wrong girl and that he could have found someone that wasn't constantly calling him in the middle of the night because someone is breaking in or leaving creepy pictures. This whole situation has me on edge, and I'm sure I'm freaking out for no reason.

Sitting down at a booth in the front of the diner, we both look at the menu. I already know what I want, but I still look. Francine, one of the servers, takes our drink order, and then I sit there, looking out the window. "Babe," Brenden says grabbing my hand.

"Hmmm?" I say, looking back at him.

"You ok?"

"Not really. It's just that I don't know what to do about all this. I can't keep living every day, waiting to see what else they do. Waiting to see if it escalates."

"I know, baby. I'm sorry that you have to deal with any of this. We'll figure this out. I promise." I nod and wipe away the tear that I feel running down my cheek. "Hey."

I look up at him again. "What?"

"What concert costs forty-five cents?" He asks with a silly smile playing on his lips.

I can't help but smile when I ask, "What?"

"50 Cent featuring Nickelback." He's got that blazing smile, and I can't help but laugh.

I shake my head. "What's wrong with you?" I say still laughing.

"There's that beautiful smile." He reaches across the table and brushes his fingers down my cheek. "I love you Molly."

"I love you too, Brenden."

Francine makes her way back over to take our orders. We both put in our regular orders and settle into a casual conversation about the upcoming week. We're waiting for Francine to bring the check when I spot Betsey.

"Fuck." I say under my breath. Brenden looks at me, then looks over his shoulder to see what caught my attention. Before I can warn him, Betsey is practically at our table. She's walking with a cane, which is new. She's got a pissy look on her face, and I just know she's coming over here to give me a piece of her mind.

"Molly, I do not appreciate having the police at my door this morning asking questions about my Henry. I can't believe you would accuse him of anything." She snips out.

"Betsey, I didn't accuse him of anything. His arrest for grabbing me is public record. The cops asked me if he could be involved with other things that have been happening lately." I try to whisper. I don't want to make a scene, but Betsey is the type that wants all the attention on her, even if it's negative. She finds a way to make herself the victim. Always.

"What things? What could you possibly be thinking Henry did? He's been out of town. He's not involved in your drama any longer." It drives me crazy that she calls him Henry. He prefers Hank.

"It's really none of your business, Betsey. We know Hank wasn't involved. Let's just leave it at that." I notice Brenden just laid the money on the table so we can get out of here.

"You always have to say something snarky, don't you? You are an awful girl, and I'm so glad Henry finally came to his senses and left you." She says with a smug smile.

"You and I both know that's not what happened. I can send you the video again if you'd like. You know, just in case you forgot why we actually split." I slip my arms into my jacket. "You have a lovely day, Betsey. I hope Hank is getting the help he needs."

I try to step around her, but she grabs my upper arm. "You better watch yourself, Molly O'Brien."

"Kindly remove your hand from my arm before I do to you what I did to Hank. Just because you have a cane now doesn't mean I won't defend myself against a bully," I'm still trying to remain somewhat quiet so as to not draw attention from the other diners.

She lets go but then start talking very loudly, "Did you all hear that? Molly O'Brien threatened me. She slanders my son then threatens me with violence! I wouldn't even be able to defend myself. I'm still healing from surgery. You are an awful young lady, Molly O'Brien."

"Excuse me, ma'am, but I think you should walk away. We were just leaving. You don't need to cause a scene," Brenden chimes in. I can tell he's trying to remain calm.

"I don't believe this has anything to do with you," she says to Brenden with a sneer. "Just another one of the many men Molly has coming and going from her house. You might as well install a revolving door, you little trollup."

"That's ENOUGH!" Brenden shouts. Betsey grabs her chest like she can't believe someone would raise their voice to her.

"C'mon, Brenden, let's go. I'm not going to waste any more of our time on her." I put my hand into his and tug. It takes him a second, but eventually, he comes with me. When we get outside the door, I take a deep breath. I'm half expecting to have her hobbling after us, waving her cane around , and yelling that I'm a hussy. I hear the door open behind us, but thankfully, it's not Betsey. It's Francine.

"Molly, are you ok, honey?" Francine has worked at Maybell's for as long as I can remember. She's known me since I was tiny.

I nod. "Yeah, you know Betsey loves to cause a scene and get attention. She's awful."

"Well, Larry is telling her that she's not welcomed here anymore." I start to protest, but she puts her hand on my forearm. "Darlin', we all saw what happened and heard it too. She thinks she's making you look bad, but really, she's just letting everyone see what kind of crazy she usually keeps hidden under her roller set and turtlenecks." That makes me smile because she's not wrong.

"I just don't want to cause Larry any trouble. You know

Betsey will be spreading the news that you all kicked her out and were rude. I'd feel so bad if he lost business because I got into an argument with Betsey."

"You just let Larry worry about that, honey. You and your handsome fella are always welcome here. And I'll see you in a couple weeks for a cut." She wraps her arm around me and squeezes, then heads back into Maybell's.

Sometimes I forget how much support I have in this town, and that thought helps me feel like I can get through this.

Brenden

It's Tuesday morning, and I'm back at work. I hate that I'll be away from Molly tonight, but she's agreed to stay at Grandpa's.

We found out from Uncle Bill, that a few of the neighbors have doorbell cameras, but only one caught the person from the other night, and it was just briefly. It wasn't a very close neighbor either. It was someone who lives down the block and around the corner. Other neighbors said they would keep a closer eye out.

I'm in the workout room in the station punching the bag. A couple other guys are lifting weights. Jared is doing some curls with a dumbbell when I ask him, "Do you think Sammy could help me with a couple of things?"

"Probably, but you'd have to ask her. What kind of things do you need help with?"

I smile and look over at him. "Ring shopping."

"It's about damn time." He smirks at me. "That's awesome, man. Congratulations."

"Thanks. I'm smart enough to know Molly has a style she likes; I just don't know what that is."

"It's fitting. Molly came with me to find Sammy's ring. It took some convincing, too, because Sammy and I had only been together for a couple of weeks when I asked her."

"I thought *I* was moving fast," I say with a laugh.

"I just think that when you know, you know. Just call Sammy later and ask. I'm sure she'll help you out. No problem."

Later that afternoon, I call Sammy. She almost blows my cover because she is eating lunch with Molly. We plan to meet on Friday afternoon because she'll be off work around two that day, but Molly works until six. So that should give us a few hours to find something. She said she'd do some reconnaissance and find out exactly what Molly would like. I have an idea of how I'd like to ask her. If I'm being honest, I'm a little worried about talking to her dad. I know he likes me, but he might not love the idea of me asking her so soon. We've been working together on Molly's attic space, and we're supposed to work on some of the drywall tomorrow.

On Friday, I meet Sammy at Meadow Hills Mall. We have a plan go into several chain jewelry places.

"In the past, when we've talked about rings and weddings and stuff, Molly always says she wants a gemstone. She likes color. She doesn't want a diamond ring. After you called the other day, we were having lunch in the back. Taylor has bridal magazines all over the place. So I started flipping through one and making comments about ads. She seemed to like the vintage style rings the most. Then I checked her Pinterest. Like most women I know, she has a dream wedding board.

All the rings saved were vintage style with emeralds, sapphires, and opals," Sammy rattles off.

"Um....ok. I really have no idea what most of that means, so I'm glad you're here."

We wander in and out of a couple stores, and nothing is grabbing either of our attention. I feel a little discouraged. I know I don't have to find one today, but the sooner the better.

"Absolutely none of these looks like Molly," Sammy says, leaning over the jewelry case in the third store. "Ya know, there is a custom place about two blocks from downtown. We should go check it out," she says, getting an evil eye thrown her way from the sales lady standing on the other side of the display case.

"Ok, let's go." The sales lady whips her head in my direction and gives me the same stink eye.

The custom place is tiny. I've driven past here pretty regularly, and I didn't even realize it was here. It's not much bigger than a two-car garage. In fact, I'm pretty sure it was a service station or something similar at one point. The parking lot out front looks like it might have had gas pumps at one time. It's not cluttered or dusty, but there are display cases lining every inch of available space, and they are filled with jewelry the owner has already made. Photo albums filled with pictures of jewelry he's created and sold and drawings of designs sit on the display cases.

"So what style are we looking for here?" Gordon, the owner of A1 Custom and Estate Jewelry, asks. He's a short, skinny, bald man with a thick white mustache. Sammy knows him, of course. He used to own the house behind her parent's house but moved years ago. He, like most people here in Rockplaines, knows Molly as well.

"Uh....vintage? With gemstones?" I say, trying to remember exactly what Sammy said.

Sammy touches my arm and then rattles off the specifics for me.

"You know, I've got one I think you might be interested in." He glances around like he's trying to figure out what case he has it stashed in. "I designed it and made it years ago, assuming someone would buy it up quick. Everyone always says it beautiful, but no one has ever even tried it on."

He leads us over to a case and pulls out a ring that is displayed in an iridescent, octagon-shaped ring box. Maybe it's the lighting in the store, but I am mesmerized by it.

Just as I say, "I'll take it."

Sammy says, "That's the one."

I don't think we could have found a more perfect ring for my Molly.

CHAPTER TWENTY-FOUR

Molly

*I*t's been a couple of weeks since the package of personal pornography ended up on my porch. For three days after it happened, we stayed with Ben. But that came to an end when Ben mentioned us making too much noise the night before. I just about died of embarrassment and told Brenden that I'd be staying at my own house after that.

Nothing out of the ordinary has happened since the last incident. On nights when Brenden has to work, I don't sleep well, but Gracie and Anna have both stayed with me a couple of times. Tonight will be the first time that I'm staying here all alone. Brenden and my dad are not on board with it, to say the least, but I can't spend my life being terrified of what could happen. I have to hope the person doing this has gotten bored and moved on or is afraid of finally being caught. Brenden bought me a taser to be on the safe side. He wanted me to get a gun. While I'm not against that idea for the future, I need to take some gun safety classes first. I've never shot a gun in my life, and I don't want the first time to be when I'm scared for my life.

I'm just sitting down with a bowl of ice cream to watch The Masked Singer, when my doorbell rings. I look on my phone to see who it is before I answer the door. To my surprise, Hank is standing there. What do I do? Do I answer it? Do I pretend I'm not home? Britney is barking her head off. My car is in the driveway, and there are lights on in the house. I'm sure he knows someone is home. I might as well hear him out. It's not like I don't know that I can defend myself. I just hope I don't regret giving him a chance. I get closer to the door and shout, "Just a minute!" Then I run to my bedroom to grab the taser out of my nightstand. I'm wearing a long cardigan that has pockets, so I put it in my pocket for safe keeping. Then I fire off a quick group text to Brenden, Sammy, Jared ,and my dad knowing that someone will show up sooner rather than later.

When I get to the door, I take a deep breath before I open it. Hank is standing at the bottom of my stoop, looking guarded. "Hank? What are you doing here?"

"I don't mean to bother you. I just wanted to talk for a minute, if you have the time." He looks skinnier, but not skinny by any means. He's still a big guy — but smaller than the last time that I saw him. I expect that happens when you stop taking steroids.

"I don't know if that's such a good idea, Hank. I mean, last time didn't turn out so great." I'm peeking my head out the door, trying to keep Britney from squeezing through the crack.

He gives me a little smile. "Yeah, you could say that. I'll make it quick, and I'll stay right here." He cocks his head to the side and looks down at the opening in the door. "Did you get a dog?"

I smile. Hank has always been a dog lover. "Yeah. This is Britney." I open the door a little and keep a good grip on her collar. She's not growling at him, so we step onto the porch, and I let Britney go to the edge to sniff his hand. He gives her a good pat on the head and scratches her ears. I immediately feel at ease because I trust Britney's judgement.

Hank stands back up and Britney comes back over and sits next to me like she's satisfied, and we may proceed with our conversation. "Soooo…...?"

Hank takes a breath before he starts talking. "Molly, I just wanted to apologize to you about what happened that day outside your salon. I wasn't in my right mind, and I deeply regret anything I did to upset you, scare you, or hurt you." He sounds sincere.

"Thank you, and I'm sorry I hurt you physically. Was it the steroids? Did you have 'roid rage?" he doesn't look surprised that I know about this. He nods. "Were you on them before we broke up?"

He nods. "Yeah, I had started taking them a few months before."

"Why didn't you tell me you were taking them?" I ask.

"Because I knew you would try to talk me out of taking them. I wasn't going to get any bigger without them, so I thought it was worth taking them." He's right. I would have tried to talk him out of it, and I probably wouldn't have stuck around if I'd known he was on them.

"Why did you come to the salon that day?" I ask, wondering if his answer will be different than before.

"I really did come there to see if you'd take me back. I wasn't lying when I said I missed you and that I wanted another shot. I definitely wasn't expecting you to be so mad."

"But…you do understand why I was mad, right?" I say kind of slowly. I realize I'm speaking to him like he's an idiot, but

I'm afraid he doesn't get it. "You cheated on me, Hank. I thought we were going to get married and have kids. I wasn't expecting to find you in bed with another woman."

"Molly, it was your idea!"

"Hank, I don't know why you keep saying that. I would never be ok with the man I'm with sleeping with other women. I don't know why you think it was my idea." I stop myself before I say something that I shouldn't. "I'm not going to fight with you again. Let's just leave all of it in the past and move on with our lives."

"I don't want to fight with you either, but I have proof that you told me to do it."

I know I'm looking at him like he's out of his mind, but before I can say anything else, Brenden's Jeep comes flying up in front of the house. He's barely got it into park before he's jumping out. He runs up to the porch looking cautiously between Hank and me.

"You ok, baby?" he asks, looking me over like he thinks I might be hurt or something.

"Yeah," I nod. "Brenden, this is Hank. Hank, this is my boyfriend ,Brenden." They do that head nod thing that guys do. Brenden comes up on the porch to stand next to me. I turn my attention back to Hank. "What proof?"

He pulls out his phone and messes with it for a minute. Then he holds it out to me. I see an email that is from me to Hank. "This is the specific one, but there were a few back and forth where you mentioned it."

Hank,

I know we're getting to the point in our relationship where we are both ready to settle down and move on to the next

*steps, but I worry you'll always wonder what if. I think the
best thing to do is get those urges out of your system
now — before we get engaged. I'm giving you a hall pass.
If you still want to marry me after you get it out of your
system, then we can do that. I wouldn't feel right tying
you down if you're not ready.*

Love,
Molly

I look at the email again. What the actual fuck? I feel like I'm
living in the mother effing twilight zone. I read through the
email again, then something catches my eye. It isn't my email
address in the sender line. I missed it at first, but there is a
period in the address, that isn't in my address. "I didn't write
this. This isn't from my email address. There's a period
between my names, and that's not in my email address."

"What?! You're kidding, right? Are you just saying that
because he's here?" he questions. Like I would joke about
this?

"No, I'm not kidding, and why would Brenden being here
make a difference? And why would you not talk to me about
it first? You didn't think we needed to have a serious face to
face conversation about something like this? When did I ever
email you instead of calling or texting? And anytime I left you
a note, did I ever sign it Love, Molly?"

He looks stunned. "No. You always signed with a heart and
Angel." I feel Brenden stiffen next to me. Hank stands there
for a minute. "There were other emails, before and after this
one. The first ones were just short 'how's your day' kind of
stuff. After this one, we talked about it over email more. I
don't know. I thought it was what you wanted. I think part of
the confusion must've come from the steroids."

I hand his phone back. "I don't know who wrote this to you, but it wasn't me." I don't have it in me to start telling him what an idiot he was for believing I would have written this email. He looks sad and confused.

"Hank, have you heard about the stuff that's been happening to Molly?" Brenden asks.

Hank just shakes his head with a defeated look on his face.

"The day after you two had your fight outside the salon, someone spray painted horrible words on her house and garage, and they tried to get into her house. We thought maybe it was you at first," Brenden says. Hank's head flies up.

"Why would you think it was me?" his eyebrows are knitted together. He looks hurt that I would think he could do something like that.

"Because, I hurt you. I broke your fingers. You weren't yourself that day. Never in all the time we dated, did you put a hurtful hand on me. I honestly didn't know what you might be capable after that."

"Yes, you hurt me." He shakes his head. "They took me to the hospital to get my fingers splinted and ran a tox screen. I knew they'd find the steroids in my system. Someone came in and offered me information about a rehab program specifically for steroid use. I was still raging, and it pissed me off that anyone would suggest something like that. I was convinced I had it under control. When they took me before the judge, the lawyer they assigned me showed me the video that some bystander took. I saw myself grab you, and you told me to let go. I deserved what I got. I didn't remember grabbing you, and I didn't even remember you defending yourself. I was convinced someone jumped me until I saw the video." He shakes his head. "I never wanted to do anything to threaten you or scare you."

"There have been other things too — creepy stalker pictures, and it turns out someone had put a camera in my bedroom," I say.

"Do the police have any leads?" Hank asks, looking between us.

"No," Brenden says. "There were partial fingerprints on the box left a few weeks ago, but so far nothing that leads to a suspect."

"Let me know if I can help in anyway. Again, I'm really sorry Molly." He looks at Brenden. "Take care of her." Brenden nods, and Hank gets in his truck. He waves as he drives away.

"That went surprisingly well," I say looking toward Brenden. He's looking at me with his jaw clenched.

"I cannot believe you came outside with him and didn't wait until I got here. That could have been a dangerous situation." He sounds seriously mad.

"But it wasn't dangerous. Britney was with me, and I have the taser in my pocket. I also texted you, Dad, Sammy, and Jared."

"Yeah, well I'm the only one here. What if I hadn't seen the text?" he grits out.

"I don't think he was here to hurt me, Blue Eyes," I say trying to lighten the mood. "Besides the closest he even got to me was when you were here. Britney didn't even growl at him. I really think he just came to apologize." I shrug.

"Maybe because I showed up. What if I hadn't come? What if he hurt you?" he practically growls.

"What if frogs had wings? They wouldn't bump their butts so much," I sass back at him.

"Don't fucking joke right now, Red. I'll take you inside and spank your ass!"

Turning around, I walk to the door. Then I peek over my shoulder at him. "Promise?"

He tries not to smile, but fails. Shaking his head, he mutters, "You're such a fucking pain in the ass." He grabs me around the waist as I walk through the door, and I squeal.

Kicking the door closed behind him, he flips the lock before pushing me against the wall. He puts his face in the crook of my neck and breathes. "You drive me crazy, baby," he whispers into my skin. He's got my front pressed to the wall, and I can feel him getting hard. I push my ass back against him. Kissing down the side of my neck, he then nibbles on my shoulder. He snakes his hand down the front of my leggings and cups my sex. "Maybe I should keep my hand right here while I spank your ass. See how wet you get? Your little pussy is already wet for me. I bet it would be dripping off my fingers by the time I finish spanking your ass. What do you think, baby? Is that what your pussy wants?" He reaches for the top of my leggings and begins to peel them down. He gets them right below the curve of my cheeks and rubs his right hand over my ass slowly. I can feel myself getting wetter already. He pulls his hand back, and I'm waiting anxiously to feel the sharp slap of his hand, holding my breath in anticipation. Suddenly, there's a pounding at the door.

"Molly! It's dad."

"And Sammy!!"

"Are you ok?" Dad yells.

Brenden rests his forehead against the back of my head, and I feel him shaking, trying to hold in laughter. "Hold on! Be right there!" I yell. "Let me get the door before they break it down."

"We will continue this tomorrow night. I'm going to go to the bathroom for a minute." He pulls my leggings back up and then turns to walk down the hall, adjusting himself.

I'm about to unlock it when the door is thrown open, and Sammy is pulling her keys out of the lock. "I said I was coming."

"Are you OK?" Dad asks. He grabs me and pulls me into his big Papa Bear hug. I hug him back for a second.

"I'm fine. He really just came to apologize for that day outside the salon. Brenden showed up. Hank didn't even come onto the porch. Britney didn't even growl at him."

Brenden comes back down the hallway. "I'm going to have to get back to the station. Maybe you should go stay with Sammy tonight."

"I don't need to go stay somewhere else. Nothing happened. Hank wasn't here to do anything more than apologize."

"You can come stay with your mom and me," my dad suggests. "Go pack a bag."

"Am I speaking another language over here? I just said I'm not going anywhere. I'll be fine right here. Britney is with me. I have a taser."

"A taser isn't going to stop someone with a gun from shooting you, Cupcake." My dad says putting his hands on his waist.

"I feel like nobody is listening to me. I'm not going anywhere. I'm not going to live my life being terrified of some invisible boogey man. Nothing has happened for a while. I don't want them thinking they can scare me out of my own house. Then they win. I'm going to go back in there, eat my now melted ice cream, and watch the Masked Singer." I point at Brenden, "You should go back to work." Pointing at Sammy, "You should go home to your kids." Looking at my dad, I put my hands on my hips to mirror his stance, "And you should go home to mom." Britney chooses this moment to jump up on the end of the couch and lie down with a harumph, like she's as exhausted with this conversation as I am.

"Molls, we just want you to be safe. C'mon. Come have some peach cobbler and watch reruns of New Girl." Sammy gives me a cheesy grin.

I ignore all of them, walk back to the couch, and curl up. Grabbing my ice cream, I un-pause the TV. "You all have a nice evening." I can see them all out of the corner of my eye, just looking at me. Brenden sighs, then walks over and leans down to kiss me.

"Call me if you need me. If, before you go to bed, you feel uneasy, please go stay with one of these guys. I'll see you in the morning." He kisses me on top the head.

"Molly, please understand..." my Dad starts to say, but I cut him off.

"Have a lovely evening. Tell mom I love her." I don't even look away from the TV. I know I'm maybe being childish. But I'm not going to let other people decide what I can and cannot do. I will not let this psycho run me out of my house.

My dad shakes his head. "Call me if you need anything."

After dad walks out the front door, Sammy prances across my living room and plops down on the couch next to me. She's so fucking annoying, and yet I love her so much.

"Batch... you don't have to come stay with me. But I'm gonna watch this with you. Mom is with the kids. And since I'm missing out on my warm peach cobbler, I'm gonna need some dessert. AND WINE!"

"There is ice cream in the freezer, cookies in the cabinet, and I think I have a bottle of that three dollar wine from our White Trash Bash on New Year's Eve." We sit in moderate silence, eating ice cream and cookies. I dunk the cookies into my melted ice cream and wonder why haven't I ever thought of this before? The wine isn't the worst thing in the world. It's blueberry though — which is kinda weird.

"So, what did Hank have to say?" Sammy asks, finishing her wine.

"He said he was sorry. He confirmed he was on steroids and that he actually didn't remember me kicking his ass. He thought someone jumped him until the lawyer showed him a video of it. He went on about me saying it was ok to sleep with someone else. Then he showed me emails that were his 'proof.' The emails were from an email address that looked like mine, but it wasn't mine. Which tells me that someone has been trying to fuck me over for a while now."

"What did the email say?" she looks at me with her eyebrows drawn together.

"Something like, 'I don't want to tie you down until you're ready. Have a hall pass and get other women out of your system.' He said he had started the steroids when we were still together, so I think maybe his judgement was clouded. He seemed really lost once he put it together. I think he spent all this time thinking I had punished him for something I told him to do."

I feel Sammy's hand on my arm. "Do you regret breaking up with him? Do you feel like you made a mistake?"

"No. I can say without a doubt that I do not regret breaking up with him. I'm not saying I didn't love Hank. But the way I feel about Brenden? There's no contest. I love Brenden. I am in love with him. I want to marry him and have all the babies."

Sammy laughs, and we both shout, "ALL THE BABIES!"

CHAPTER TWENTY-FIVE

Molly

After everyone, namely my dad and Brenden, giving me a hard time about being home alone, I feel the need to get back to my self-defense classes. I haven't gone in a couple weeks because Brenden's been off on the last couple of Fridays, and that was my night to go. Sammy finally agreed to go with me tonight. Brenden and Jared are both off, and Brenden is going over to have pizza with Jared and the kids tonight. Sammy and I haven't had a friend date, just the two of us, for quite a while. So after class, we're gonna grab dinner and a drink at McMurphy's.

"It smells like the wrestling mats in the high school gym." Sammy says scrunching her nose.

"Well, I mean, they spar on the mats. Jack teaches karate classes too. People do get down on the mats and roll around sometimes." I roll my eyes at her. Any time I try to get her do some kind of exercise or activity that isn't dancing, she complains.

"Are you sure it's sanitary?" she whispers to me.

"Suck it up, Princess Crybaby. I promise you'll enjoy this," I whisper back.

Jack is the owner of the "Luck of the Dragon Karate Studio." He teaches different classes. I haven't ventured into any of those, but I've thought about it. Maybe I can get Sammy or Gracie to start karate classes with me.

He's finishing up with an adorable group of kiddos. They are probably four or five. So cute.

"You should put the twins in karate when they are older. I've heard it can help them learn to be better listeners and more respectful," I whisper to her.

"Well, hell! Where do I sign?" she whispers back.

"I think the starting age is four years old. You can ask Jack about it though."

We notice a couple of ladies that we know from the salon that are waiting for their littles to finish their class, and we chit chat with them until Jack is done.

"Alright ladies, everyone line up," Jack yells. There're only five of us tonight. I've seen the other ladies here at various times. Sammy's the only one that's brand new.

"Jack, this is my friend, Sammy. She's new tonight," I say.

"Welcome Sammy. The other ladies have been here before, so we'll mostly be going over things that are a little more advanced than the beginner session. But if you're interested in coming back, we can catch you up on that quickly." He nods in her direction. We start the class by stretching, and then he teaches us a few things about breaking the hold of an attacker. He goes over the best places to hit your attacker to get away. I have a smile on my face because I know what's coming next. Jack heads to the back for a minute while we practice how to break a hold if someone's got you in a headlock.

"What are you smiling about, Tamale?" Sammy asks while wiping the sweat off her forehead with the back of her hand.

"Just wait," I say.

Soon, Jack comes marching out of the back room in his foam padded suit. The rest of us in the class have seen it on several occasions. I think he put it on tonight for Sammy's benefit. I look over at her and she's laughing.

"I'm the assailant," Jack says, though slightly muffled since he's got the foam helmet on too.

"Boo! What's the assailant's name?" Renee, one of the other ladies, cups her hands and yells.

"You know my name," Jack says, again muffled.

"Sammy doesn't know what your name is," I yell.

Jack shakes his head under the foam helmet, then yells, "I'm Captain Foambeard." He places his hands on his sides in a superhero pose. "I'm here to teach you how to protect yourself."

We're all smiling, trying to hold in our laughter.

"And release stress," Renee shouts back at him again.

"Alright smartasses, who's first?" One of the other girls, Lindsay, raises her hands. She steps forward and close enough for Jack to grab her. He grabs her arm and she breaks the hold by jerking her arm down. Then she grabs his padded shoulders and knees the crap out of his balls.

"So, we just get to beat the hell out of him now?" Sammy leans over and asks.

"Pretty much. He will grab you or try to restrain you in some way, and you use the techniques you've learned to break the hold and get away. Sometimes, in order to get away, you have to do things like throw knees to the crotch, poke eyes, or punch throats."

She rubs her hands together, "Ohhhh! I'm so glad you brought me. This is awesome."

We each get a turn at beating up Captain Foambeard. Sammy watches all of us and goes last. When it is her turn, he grabs her the way we learned tonight. It takes her a few seconds, but she figures it out. When she tries to knee him in the crotch, she somehow gets her knee wedged right in between the pieces of foam where the leg and the crotch pieces meet. Poor Jack... She doesn't get the twig and berries, but she knees him hard right in the top of the inner thigh. Sammy apologizes profusely while Jack stands bent over. I assume he's trying not to throw up. He eventually walks it off and heads to the back to get out of the pads.

We wait for him to come back so she can get signed up for regular classes. Jack reassures her; it wasn't the worst accidental injury he's sustained in his years teaching.

"How old do kids have to be to take karate?" Sammy asks.

"Typically, they start around four years old. Sometimes we'll start them at three and a half if they have older siblings who they've watched take classes. Do you have kids?" he questions Sammy.

"Two- and half-year-old twins — a boy and a girl. They are rowdy. I'm always looking for activities to burn off their energy." Sammy smiles.

"I bet they can be a handful," he says smiling at her just a second too long. Then he must realize he's staring, and he gets a bit flustered. "Well, you probably have a year at least before we can sign them up, but you can bring them in to watch anytime. "I'll see you ladies next week?

"Yup." I say, shaking my head. I find it hilarious, yet not surprising, that Jack seems a little interested in Sammy. I'm even less surprised that Sammy didn't seem to notice at all. She only notices when other people flirt. Somehow, she's blind to any other guy's advances or flirtiness unless they flat out ask her out. She only has eyes for Jared. Part of me wants to rib her for it, but I don't want her to be uncomfortable coming back to class. I'll just try to make sure Jack knows she's married and off the market. He's cute though. He keeps his head shaved and has a goatee. He's probably around thirty-five years old. I wonder if Anna would be interested in him? Maybe I can talk her into going to classes too. Brilliant idea!

"Maybe we should have another team builder and have Jack teach this time. It would be fun if more of the girls from the shop joined the class. Maybe we could hook Jack up with Anna or Jess," I say, looping my arm through Sammy's.

"Yes! I love playing match maker." Then we both start singing "Matchmaker" from Fiddler on the Roof as we skip the four blocks to McMurphy's for corned beef nachos and a Woodchuck.

After we eat, we decide to head back to my car and over to her house. It's so funny how, as you get older, you can't hang like you used to do. In our early twenties, Sammy and I would go out and not tumble into bed until the sun was rising, sleep an hour or two, and then get up and go to work. Now, we're both tired from class, creeping back to my car, bitching about the fact that we didn't drive down to McMurphy's instead of walking.

The karate studio is on a corner, and I parked on the side street. When we turn the corner, I can see John Palmer putting something under my windshield wiper. I almost stop to hide so I don't have to deal with the confrontation, but I've had just about enough. I'm immediately seeing red; I grab Sammy's arm and stomp toward my car.

"Can I help you, Officer Palmer?" I say sweetly, though I'm feeling nothing but red-hot anger at the moment.

"The sign says no parking after 8pm on Friday-Monday." He nods to the sign in flat tone.

"It's 8:05," Sammy says putting her hands on her hips.

"The law is the law," he says. He takes a few steps toward me and then leans down and says, "Unless you want to work out some kind of deal to make this go away," as he runs the end of his pen down my arm.

Sammy can hear him as well as I can, and she shouts, "What the fuck is wrong with you, John?"

I knock the pen away and look at him in disgust. "You are a sleaze ball, John Palmer. I would sooner pay a hundred parking tickets than make any kind deal with you."

"Lower your voice," he says through gritted teeth, looking around to see if there are any onlookers.

"What? Would you like me to pretend that you didn't just proposition me to get out of a bullshit parking ticket? Do you think Sammy didn't hear what you just said to me? For a cop, you are not a smart man." I walk around to the driver's side of my car and snatch the ticket off the window. "C'mon Sammy."

Sammy walks past John giving him the same disgusted look that I'm sure is on my face. John and I stare each other down while she gets into the car. "Stay away from me, John."

I get into the car and shut my door. He stares straight at me as I back up. I only break eye contact when I put the car into reverse. I glance over as I drive away, and he's still staring.

"I can't fucking believe he just said that to me." I say, seething.

"Brenden is going to kill him," she says.

"Shit. He will kill him." I take a deep breath.

"Maybe you should just call Bill, and report it to him," Sammy says seriously.

"He would tell Brenden, and then Brenden would be pissed that I didn't tell him. No, we gotta go tell him now. I'm gonna need Jared to help restrain him so he doesn't go after John, and I am not kidding." I think about the best way for me to tell him as we drive back to their house.

When we got to Sammy and Jared's house, the guys are out in the garage messing with Jared's motorcycle. I'm assuming that they got the kiddos to bed since they are nowhere to be seen at the moment.

"Hey, baby! How was your class?" Jared asks wrapping his arms around Sammy.

"It was fun. I got to beat up Captain Foambeard. Well, I kind of hurt him in real life," Sammy says looking over at me with an oops look on her face.

"She was trying to knee him in the balls and hit him right between the padding instead. He walked it off." I shrug.

"Wait. Who the fuck is Captain Foambeard?" Jared queries, looking between us.

"Jack, the instructor, puts on this big foam suit at the end of class and lets us hit and kick him. I think it's what he calls it when he wears it for the kiddie classes. But we always make him say it," I say laughing.

"Did you have your nachos for dinner, baby?" Brenden asks, wrapping his arms around me.

"Yeah. They were delicious as always. But, uh… I have to tell you something that happened, and I don't want you to freak out," I say looking over my shoulder at him. His hold tightens around me.

"What happened?" he's already starting to clinch his jaw.

I look at Sammy for help. She starts, "We left Molly's car parked next to the karate studio and walked down to McMurphy's. When we came back, John Palmer was by her car, giving her a parking ticket."

Brenden's hold on me gets tighter. "When we walked up and asked what he was doing. He pointed at the sign that said no parking after 8pm. It was 8:05, so although he was within his rights to give me a ticket, he was being an asshole on purpose."

"Why do I feel like there's more to this story?" Brenden asks, still clenching his jaw.

"When we pointed out to him that it was only 8:05, he said 'the laws the law, unless you want to work out a deal,'" I say in a deeper voice, trying to imitate him. Brenden obviously doesn't find any humor in my impression of John.

"He said *what*? I'll fucking kill him." He starts to let go of me, like he's going to go find him and kick his ass. I grab his shirt and get in front of him.

"Baby, calm down. You can't go kill him. They don't give conjugal visits to murderers in this state," I say, trying to calm him.

"Don't fucking joke right now, Molly. It's not fucking funny."
He huffs out.

"I think the best thing to do would be to call Bill and tell him.
Let him handle it. If you go knock his block off, you'll get
charged for assaulting an officer. Take a deep breath, and call
Bill... Please," I plead with him. "Also, I told him he was a
sleaze ball and not to come near me again.

"I'll call Bill. But you better believe that if I ever see that son
of a bitch again, I'm beating his ass," he grits out.

We decide to head back to my place after that. Brenden calls
Bill and makes me tell him what happened. Bill says he will
see if John was equipped with a body cam or dash cam. I can
only hope that he was, and they can see what kind of dirt bag
he's turned out to be.

CHAPTER TWENTY-SIX

May

Molly

he Saturday before Mother's Day is always crazy busy in the salon. We run a couple of package specials for Mother's Day gifts. The mani/pedi and blowout is a big seller. We also have a spa package for a facial and a thirty minute massage. A lot of our clients, especially the men, buy packages for their wives or mothers. They don't have to use them today, but quite a few are. Luckily, Sammy was able to hire another nail tech recently. She's twenty, which makes her the new baby of the salon. Her name is Alexa, and so far, we've had only positive feedback on her nail work. She's super sweet, and she and Gracie have really hit it off which is really nice to see.

I'm glad today has been busy. It means that I haven't had much time to worry about tonight. Brenden is picking his mom up from the train station today, and we're going to dinner. I've talked to her on the phone, and she's been nothing but sweet, but meeting in person is stressing me out. I know it might sound crazy because Brenden and I haven't been together that long, but this could be my mother-in-law someday. I have to make a good impression.

I finish with my last client about thirty minutes before we close. Luckily, one of the esthetician treatment rooms is open. They are equipped with showers for the clients that get treatments like body scrubs. So, I jump in quickly to wash off all the little, itchy hairs. I brought a cute floral dress to wear with a purple cardigan and my silver jelly shoes. Our reservation is at 6:30, so I have to hurry. Ben said he didn't want to be up all night eating dinner like some sort of Jersey Shore kid. He apparently discovered the show and is now addicted. He shouted "GTL" at Brenden the other day.

I'm just finishing fixing my makeup when Sammy comes sauntering into the office and plops down in the desk chair.

"How was your day Sammy Lammy? You guys were slammed all day," I say adding another coat of mascara to my lashes.

"Yeah, I'm glad I get to sit down to work, but I'm still exhausted. Alexa is really picking up the extra slack though. Thank God we found her." She yawns as she kicks her feet up on the desk.

"Ok, do I look like I'm ready to meet the mom of the man I'm in love with and want to marry and have all the babies with?" I say twirling around.

"Yes, you most definitely look mom worthy." She yawns again. "Alright, Batch. I'm going home. Jared got another migraine today, so my mom came over a couple of hours ago so he could get a nap. Still on for a lunch picnic with the kids and me on Monday?"

"You know it. I'll bring the treats. I'm thinking cupcakes." Mmmmm cupcakes. "And hey, Happy Mother's Day!"

"Thanks! Give your mom extra kisses for me tomorrow... And your dad." She waggles her eyebrows at me.

I pick up a blush brush and chuck it at her, but she runs out the door and it hits the wall anyway, because I can't throw for shit.

Brenden

Driving down main street with Grandpa and Mom, we're just about to drive by Bombshells when I see Molly through the window. I swing into a spot and park.

"This is the salon Molly owns with her friends. I'm going to run in and see if she's ready to go. Then she can just ride with us instead of meeting us there," I say opening the door.

"Oh, I'd love to come in and see her shop. I'll go with you," Mom says opening her door as well.

I suppose we might as well get the first meeting out of the way. "You want to come in too, Grandpa?"

"No, I've seen the shop. Molly cut my hair last week. I'll wait here. But shake a leg, I'm starving." Grandpa says pulling at his collar.

When we get to the door, it's locked, so I knock. Molly's behind the reception desk, probably going over the books for today. She looks up, and I get hit with that smile that always makes my chest tight. She walks around the desk to unlock the door, smoothing her dress as she goes. I can tell she's nervous to meet my mom.

She unlocks the door, and as soon as I get the door open, I grab her and pull her to me. "You look gorgeous, Red," I whisper into her neck.

She hugs me back just as tight as I'm holding her. Then she pulls her head back and taps me on my back, whispering, "Introduce me to your mom."

"Mom, this is my girl, Molly." My mom's eyes soften looking at us. "Molly, this is my mom, Celia."

Molly reaches her hand out to shake my mom's. My mom, being my mom, grabs her hand and then pulls her into a big hug. "It's so nice to meet you, Molly." Mom pulls back and looks at Molly. "You are so pretty! The two of you will make some beautiful babies."

"Mom! Jeez. Take it down a notch," I say smiling. It's not like I'm not thinking about it, but I don't need mom announcing it.

"I'm just saying. I'm not talking about tomorrow. But down the road, they *will* be beautiful babies."

Molly just smiles, then looks at me. "She's right. We will make beautiful babies." I can't help but smile. "Do we have a few minutes? I can show you around really quickly and introduce you to a couple of the ladies that are still here."

Molly leads us around on a quick tour of the salon. She introduces my mom to Anna, Emily, Caitlyn, and the new girl, Alexa.

"Anna, I'm gonna head out. Can you lock up?" Molly asks Anna, who looks like she's just finishing up some paperwork.

"Sure thing! Have fun at dinner. Somebody get the cheesecake. It's so good!" She yells as we head to the door.

Both mom and Molly yell back, "Will do." Then they laugh and both say, "Jinx!" This is going to be interesting. On the way to the restaurant Mom and Molly talk up a storm. I knew there was nothing for her to worry about. Everyone loves Molly, she's perfect.

Molly

After dinner last night, we dropped Ben and Celia off at Ben's. I told Brenden that he could stay with them, but he said he wanted to be home with me. Which leads me to realize that Brenden totally lives with me. I glance around the house and notice little bits of his things that have made their way in. I shouldn't be surprised. If he's not at work, he's here. Ben doesn't need him as much now, and he has a nurse that stops by a couple times a week to help organize his meds.

Britney meets us at the door when we get home. I brought a literal doggie bag home for her, with a bone from Ben's steak. I give her the bone and let her into the backyard so she can do her business. I'm standing by the kitchen island, looking at the mail that Brenden checked for me today, when I notice mail with his name on it. I'm about to acknowledge the fact that he lives here now, but I feel the back of my dress being lifted and Brenden's hands and mouth start exploring.

I'm lying across Brenden on the couch, having just made love when I finally blurt out, "So you like... live here now." Smooth, Molly.

"What?" he asks.

"You live with me. In this house. You live here," I say slowly.

He's quiet for a few moments. "Yeah, I guess I do. Is that a problem?"

"No," I say smiling. "We should get your stuff from Springfield and bring you out here for good," I say looking over at him. "You want to be here for good, right?"

He flips me over to my back, climbs on top of me, and settles himself between my legs. "I would love nothing more than to stay here with you for good. I have no plans to be further than the fire house away from you, ever. You are my home."

After I'm done swooning, he takes me again. That night, I fall asleep smiling with a feeling of overwhelming happiness.

This morning, I've got Brenden out back hosing off the patio set and picking up Britney's "presents" in the backyard. I'm inside making potato salad, cucumber salad, and brisket baked beans to go with the burgers and brats we'll be grilling later.

Mom insisted on bringing dessert, even though I told her that it's Mother's Day and not necessary. She said she had a recipe for some strawberry cheesecake bars that she wanted to try. Far be it for me to deny her the pleasure of making dessert.

Celia and Ben are planning to go to Max's Donut Hole this morning before they head over here. I tell Brenden that he should go, but he says that they'll be going early, and he'd rather have me for breakfast. And he did. Twice, before taking me in the shower. Then he made me a bacon and egg breakfast burrito, so I officially have the best live in boyfriend ever.

Around noon, my mom and dad show up. Mom brings in dessert and somehow finds room in the fridge for it, and Dad wanders out back and chats with Brenden while we wait for Celia and Ben to get here. Ben doesn't drive much anymore. Typically, Brenden takes him anywhere he needs to go, but he still has an old Cadillac which I'm sure Celia is driving today.

"Celia and Ben should be here soon. We'll eat at the table outside, but we'll do buffet style serving in here on the island. I don't think all the food will fit on the table," I tell mom. "I made iced tea, and there's diet coke, unless you want some sangria."

"Molly Sue, you know your momma wants some wine. It's five o'clock somewhere," she says while pulling the pitcher of sangria out of the refrigerator.

Brenden comes in the house with the grill scrubbers. "Do you want me to put the burgers on, Red?"

"Yeah, I'm sure Grandpa will be ready to eat when they get here." He leans down and kisses me quickly.

"You're not wrong about that." He picks up the tray of meat and heads back outside.

Hearing the doorbell ring, I wipe my hands on a dishtowel and head to answer the door. Ben and Celia are standing there, each holding a bouquet of flowers. I can't help but smile. "Please come in! Happy Mother's Day," I say as Celia walks into the house.

"Molly, your house is so adorable. I love it. I need a little place like this, and you could help me decorate it." She says, handing me the bouquet she's holding — daisies and green mums. I love it so much.

"Find a house? Are you thinking about moving here?" I ask.

"We'll talk about that in a bit," she says, wrapping her arm around my shoulders. "Now where is my baby boy?"

"He's grilling out back. Let me introduce you to my parents. Then I'll show you the rest of the house." My mom is standing in the kitchen as we come in. She rounds the island and is pulling Celia into a hug before I know what's happening.

"It is so nice to meet you. I'm so glad you're here visiting," my mom tells her.

"Celia, this is my mom, Suzanna," I say laughing at the fact that they are hugging one another like long lost friends.

"Ben, it's nice to see you again too," Mom wraps him in a hug, which Ben returns. She has met Ben before, but she doesn't know him that well. If there's one thing that Suzanna O'Brien is, it's a hugger. Dad wanders in, and I do the introductions.

Brenden comes in the sliding door with a plate carrying cooked burgers. "Hey, Mom! Happy Mother's Day." He wraps his free arm around his mom. "I just have some brats to grill, and we'll be ready to eat." I give her a little tour while we wait for Brenden to finish grilling.

Once the brats are done, we all load up our plates and eat out on the concrete slab in my back yard. I have a patio table with a big red umbrella and a big round swing in the yard that is large enough to hold Brenden and me. Britney's on it now, basking in the sun and enjoying the rocking motion.

"How long are you in town for, Celia?" my mom asks between bites of potato salad.

"Well, I don't really have a specific return date at the moment." She looks at Brenden and then me with a warm smile. "I've been thinking about it since Brenden left, and I've decided to sell my condo and move out here."

"Are you serious?" Brenden asks. "Mom, I'd love for you to be closer, but please don't uproot your life for me."

"Brenden, I'm not uprooting anything. I work from home. Most of my friends are too busy to even get together for a brunch or happy hour anymore. My family is here. Hopefully, one day I'll have grandkids to spoil, and I'll need to be much closer to do that properly."

"Definitely." My mom says nodding in Celia's direction.

"Well. Alright, then. Looks like you're moving out here." Brenden is just beaming. I know he has been missing his mom. "Molly and I were just talking about going back to Springfield to get my stuff out of storage and move it out here. So maybe we can just make it one big trip instead."

"We'll work out the details. Ben said I can stay with him, if need be, until I find a place. My friend Rhonda is a realtor, and she is actually showing the condo all this week while I'm out of town. Hopefully, it sells soon. I'm hoping to find a realtor while I'm here and maybe even see a few places. I'd love to find a place like this, Molly. It's just so cute."

"Thank you! My best friend Sammy's mom is a realtor. She helped me buy this place. She is semi-retired now, but I'm sure she could help you out. I'm having a park date with Sammy and her kids tomorrow. If you want, I can ask if Vicky can come with Sammy, and you can come along and meet her. Then you two can chat," I offer. "Mom do you want to come too?"

"Vicky's the best. She helped us buy our house nearly thirty years ago. She's been in the business a long time and can definitely help you out. And, of course, I want to see the twins!" my mom throws in.

"Perfect!" Celia says. I can see it already. Celia, Vicky, and my mom — the three amigos. My mom and Vicky are already besties like Sammy and me. I know Celia will fit right in.

Before Celia and Ben leave to head back to his place later that afternoon, we gave our moms a little gift. I had found these beautiful charms at a shop in town a few weeks ago, so I made each of them a charm bracelet. I figure that, over time, I can give them charms to add to it as well. Moms has a little RV, an apple because she used to be a teacher, a wine glass, and a charm with a citron in it, which is her birthstone. Celia's was trickier because I don't know her well, but Brenden helped me out. Celia's has a wine glass, a fireman's helmet, a tennis racket because Brenden said she loves to play, and an amethyst birthstone charm. They both love their bracelets, and that makes me so happy.

CHAPTER TWENTY-SEVEN

June

Molly

*I*t's mid-June, and things have been great. Celia sold her condo the week she was here for Mother's Day. I was right when I said Vicky could help her find a new house. Her little cottage is about five minutes from mine. It's very similar and so cute. It's a little smaller, but she's the only one living there. Brenden went back to Springfield last weekend and drove a truck with his stuff from storage, and he helped his mom pack up her bigger furniture. We video chatted while he went through his furniture and a few other boxes to see what he wanted to bring or sell. I was completely in love with his bedroom furniture, and it will look beautiful in the master suite once it's done. That should only be a few more weeks away. YAY! He also had this gorgeous brown leather club chair that I think would be perfect to curl up in and read.

Celia should be on her way out here now. She needed to stay behind to finish up with the closing of her condo, and one of her girlfriends hosted a going away party for her. I know she's going to miss her friends there, but she really did hit it off with my mom and Vicky. The week she was here, they had lunch and went to happy hour one afternoon, and they invited Doreen Garrity too. My mom even went with Celia and Vicky to look at houses. They were talking about doing a book club and taking pottery classes once she settles in. You can bet that my mom, Vicky, and Doreen will be over there helping her unpack too. It's just who they are.

I'm about to leave work when I see I've got a text from Brenden. "Babe, I have a surprise for you. When you get home, find a box on the bed. Put what is in the box on, and then I need you to text me. I'll send you the address of where to meet me after that."

I'm giddy thinking about what he might have up his sleeve. I text back, "I thought you were working tonight? What are you up to?" I already knew he wouldn't tell me, but I had to ask. I tell Sammy I'm heading out, since I'm done with clients and anxious to get home to see what he has in store.

When I get to the house, I unlock the door and head in. I'm halfway down the hall to the bedroom before I realize I didn't turn off the alarm, and it's not alerting me to punch in my code. I'm positive I set it this morning. Brenden must've forgotten to reset it when he put the package on the bed, I tell myself, trying not to let the uneasy feeling that's settling within me ruin the excitement I felt moments before. Taking a deep breath, I start to head to the bedroom again when I realize Britney didn't meet me at the door like she usually does. A cold chill slides down my spine. I pull out my phone to call Brenden. I'm about to hit the call button when I feel a painful blow to the back of my head.

I feel my body being jerked up and the sound of a thunk. Jerk and thunk. Jerk and thunk. The fingertips digging into my upper arms are painful, and I can't help but think I'll probably have a bruise. Heavy breathing. Jerk and thunk. Jerk and thunk. One more jerk, and then I feel like my whole body being dragged across the ground. No. It's a hardwood floor. Whoever has me must make it to their destination. They drop my arms, and my head bounces off the floor. I want to open my eyes. I want to know what's happening, but I can't. I can't do anything but lie here.

A shooting pain pulls me from sleep. Remind me to never drink again, I think. Wait, no. I wasn't drinking. I think someone hit me. I can hear someone talking, but I can't focus on what they're saying. All I hear is a murmuring and this high-pitched ringing that's drowning it out just enough. I'm not sure how long I try to listen before the sleep pulls me under again.

I'm leaning against something. Furniture maybe? I can't open my eyes. "Ouch." I try to lift my arm to feel where my head is throbbing, I can't move my hand. Why can't I lift my hands? I think my hands are tied behind my back. "Fuck."

"Molly? Are you ok?" I realize I'm leaning against someone, not something.

I squint my eyes open. We're in my upstairs room. I try to turn my head. Fuck, that hurts. "What's happening? Who's there?"

"Molly, it's John. Are you ok?" he asks.

"John? Why are you here? What the fuck is happening?" I'm starting to feel panicked.

"I was driving by when I saw someone sneaking in your back gate. I stopped to see who it was, and she got the drop on me and hit me in the face with something when I came through the gate. I'm not on duty. I don't have my gun or anything.

She has a gun. She made me come up the stairs then tied me up."

"Who? Who is doing this?" I cry.

"She has a hood on. I couldn't see her face," he says.

"How did I get up here?"

"She dragged you up the stairs, then tied us together. Can you pull your hands loose?" he asks.

I move my hands around to see if I can get a hand loose. "It's too tight. I'll keep trying though. Where did she go?"

"I think she's just downstairs. What about now?" He does something, and surprisingly, it loosens mine up a little.

"Yeah, that made it looser. I can almost get a hand free." I get my hand almost all the way out, when I hear footsteps coming up the stairs. "Listen to me, John. I'm going to pretend I'm still asleep. Try to keep her talking. We'll figure this out. Ok?" I whisper to him.

"Ok," he whispers back.

Footsteps hit the hardwood, and I try to make my body slack.

"Well, now. I only have a little more time to figure out what to do with you and the little tart." Her voice sends chills down my spine. Holy fuck! It's Betsey. What the fuck is happening?

"I hadn't planned on having to deal with you. I shouldn't be surprised that this little slut has another man sneaking around," Betsey says with her holier than though attitude.

"Ma'am, I think you need to really think about what you're doing here. If you untie us and let us go, you'll have time to get away," John pleads.

"You *would* want me to let you go, so you can run away with this little slut," Betsey says with venom in her voice.

"I'm not with her, ma'am. She has a boyfriend. We're just friends. We grew up together. I was driving by when I saw you sneaking into her gate. I was just checking in on her," he says.

"You expect me to believe that? You expect me to believe you weren't stopping by for a quickie before her other boyfriend got home? She's a little hussy. You should have seen the line of men she had trailing behind her. She ruined my son's reputation and his life. My Henry never would have taken to drugs if it wasn't for her!"

"I urge you to think about what you're doing. I'm a cop. If you kill me, you'll surely go down for it," John threatens.

"Oh, a cop? So she's got law enforcement wrapped around her slutty little finger. I should've known. That's why she didn't get arrested for assaulting my Henry. This whole town is corrupt trash!" she shouts, and I hear a grunt come from John. It takes everything in me not to scream at her.

"I think the only thing to do here is shoot you both." I hear her footsteps echoing off the hardwood floor. I've almost got one hand loose. It's hard to work at it when I don't know if she can see me.

I hear my phone ringing, and it's close. Betsey must have it. It stops ringing and immediately starts again.

"Ugh!!! I better get busy taking out the trash before Molly's little fireman shows up here and I have to kill three of you." I hear her footsteps coming toward me. What should I do? We've practiced taking someone down if you're on the floor in my defense class, but we've never had a scenario where they have a gun. My left hand is out, but my right hand is still in the ropes. I have to try to free it. And if I can get it free, maybe John can get it free too.

She's at my side now. I can feel her. She grabs a hand full of my hair and yanks my head back. "Wake up, you little tramp!" she yells in my face. I let my head lull to the side a little and try to look like I'm barely awake. "I said wake up! I don't have much time, and I want you to see my face when I pull this trigger." I can see she has a small gun with a pink handle. Why am I not surprised?

"Look at me!" She screams in my face again. I pretend to pass out again. "Well if the little hussy won't wake up, maybe I should start with you," Betsey says letting go of my hair. I can hear her walking around to John. I'm able to get my right hand out, and I reach back and squeeze his hand.

"Please ma'am! Please think about what you're doing." John pleads with her. I'm about to call her when I hear the pop of the gun, and John cries out.

"You fucking shot me! You shot me in the fucking leg!" John yells.

"I've got plenty of bullets. So, I'd stop with the swearing and be a little more gentlemanly if I were you," she says with a little laugh. I can feel John moving his hands, trying to loosen the rope.

"Betsey," I say quietly, with my head still hanging forward.

"Well, it's about time you woke up." She starts to walk around me.

I'm lucky because she walks past me and isn't looking down. I reach out, grab her ankle, and pull as hard as I can. She's loses her balance and falls, the gun skittering across the floor. I jump up and lunge for Betsey. Maybe a smarter person would get the gun, but I'm confident I can restrain her while John gets the weapon. She rolls over to her back as I attempt to tackle her. She surprises me by putting her foot up and kicking me in the stomach as I come down on top of her. It pushes me back, and *fuck* it hurts. She starts to stand as I lunge again, and I'm able to knock her back into the wall and straddle her waist. She reaches up, grabbing a handful of my hair right at the roots, and starts pulling. I try to pry her hand out of my hair but she just keeps pulling, so I finally pull back my fist and clock her in the jaw. The momentary shock from the punch makes her loosen her grip on my hair, and I'm able to pull her hands over her head and hold her down at the wrists.

"What the hell is *wrong* with you, Betsey? Why are you doing this?" I scream in her face while she's bucking her body against me, trying to throw me off.

"You are a terrible person, Molly O'Brien, and the world doesn't need the likes of you and your trampy ways," she says with a sneer.

John struggles with the rope and finally frees his hands. Then he takes the belt off from around his waist and tightens it on his leg like a tourniquet.

"John, give me the rope and help me tie her up so we can call 911." It takes him a second, but he hobbles over and loops the rope around one of her wrists. Then he helps me roll her over and I tie her hands the best that I can at her lower back. "Betsey, where's my phone?"

"Wouldn't you like to know?" she says, then laughs.

"I think she's lost her fucking mind," I say out loud.

"I think you're right," he mumbles, limping his way over to the gun.

Glancing around the room, I look to see if she set my phone

somewhere. I don't see it, so I feel around in the jacket she's wearing and find it in the pocket. She tries to roll to keep me from getting it, but it's hard to roll when your hands are tied and you've got someone sitting on you.

"Betsey, don't make this harder on yourself. Just let me have the phone." I'm getting really fucking irritated with her.

I feel around until I find the pocket of her hoodie, and I pull my phone out. I see that I have three missed calls from Brenden. I'll call back him after I call the cops. I'm about to dal 911 when I hear the front door crash open and Brenden yelling, "MOLLY!"

"Brenden! We're up here!" I shout back.

Pushing the send button on the call to 911, the operator answers, right as Britney comes flying up the stairs with Brenden just a few steps behind her. He takes in the scene. After he sees me sitting on top of someone with the phone in my hand, he looks at John who is holding the gun now. Britney has John backed against the wall growling at him.

"What the fuck is happening?" he looks around at all of us in complete confusion. "John, put the gun down."

"This isn't my gun, man. I didn't do anything. Please call the dog off!" John yells, sounding terrified.

"Britney, come here!" I yell, surprised when she comes over and lays down. I'm trying to hear the 911 operator asking me if I'm ok while Betsey laughs like a fucking maniac and Brenden and John are yelling at one another. "Would all of you shut the fuck up? Please?!" I ask the operator to please send an ambulance for a gunshot wound, and I reiterate several times that it's for a cop. I also tell the operator that we have the shooter restrained but to hurry up because I can only sit on the woman for so long.

"John? Should we stay here until the cops get here, or should we try to get her downstairs?" I ask, assuming he would be the best person to assess the situation.

"I... I don't know," he says. "I think I need to sit down." I notice the whole leg of his khakis is soaked through with blood, and he's a white as a ghost.

"Brenden, Betsey shot John. You have to help him." Brenden looks at me and then looks at John. His face changes like he's just noticing his blood-soaked pants. Brenden springs into action and runs over to John.

Betsey starts screaming and kicking, "I caught these two having a an elicit affair. She's a little slut and always will be!"

I mean, what do I even say to that? I'm not sure Brenden is paying any attention to her. He's dealing with John's leg. I can only trust that Brenden knows me better than that. It seems like forever, but I can just barely hear sirens over Betsey's cackling, and I am hoping it's the sound of the emergency vehicles heading here. Britney is lying on the floor near me and looking back and forth between John and Betsey, rumbling out her low growl. Betsey gets quiet for a minute, and I think, maybe she's come to her senses a bit. Suddenly, she starts bucking and screaming again, which makes Britney jump to her feet, letting out her sonic boom bark over and over. It doesn't deter Betsey though; she just keeps screaming, and I'm about to fucking lose it.

Finally, we hear someone yelling about being there to help. Brenden runs down and leads two EMTs and Officer Craig back upstairs. I can only imagine the scene these first responders are walking in on. Me sitting on a tied up woman who is kicking and screaming and calling me a "cheating hussy." John sitting in the corner, his bloody pant leg ripped up to the crotch. Is he crying? I mean, if I got shot in the leg, I'd cry too. So he gets no judgement from me.

"John got shot in the leg," Brenden says leading the EMTs over to see to his wound.

"Craig, can you help me over here?" a stunned Craig finally looks in my direction. He runs over to us and squats down.

"So…what exactly is happening here?" Craig questions.

"This is Betsey Walker. She's Hank's mom. She, apparently, is the one that has been stalking and harassing me!" I say, still trying to hold her down.

"What would give you that idea?" he asks looking at me in confusion. I'm starting to feel like some of the cops in Rockplaines aren't playing with a full deck.

"Well, for starters, she hit me over the head and tied me to John. She threatened to kill us both and shot John in the leg," I say looking at him.

"How did you get loose if she tied you up?" he questions.

"She didn't tie it tight enough. I have little hands. I was able to get them loose. Once I was loose, John was able to get his hands out too. Are you going to help me restrain her, or should I call 911 to send another cop?" His eyes go wide, like he just realized that's why he's here. I realize he walked in on a shit show, but isn't this the kind of thing he's supposed to handle?

Craig gets down and puts cuffs on Betsey and lets me crawl off of her. He then removes the rope I have around her wrists and helps her sit against the wall. When I stand up completely, I feel a little light headed, and I must stumble a little. Craig notices and yells to the EMT's to come check me over too. For the first time, I reach up to feel the back of my head where she hit me, probably with the butt of the gun. I can feel wetness, and when I pull my hand back to look at it, I see blood. That makes me feel queasy, and I think I better sit down.

Brenden comes over and squats down in front of me. "You ok, baby?" he asks, running his hand down my cheek.

"I'm bleeding from the back of my head. She hit me with something." He runs his hand behind my head and feels the bloody goose egg I have back there.

"We'll have to take you to the hospital to see if you need stitches." He kisses me on the forehead and wraps me in a hug. "I called Uncle Bill. He's on his way." I realize that Brenden is dressed in a suit. It's light grey, and he's got a button-down shirt on that is open at the collar.

"Wow!" I say, pulling back from him to get a better look. "You look so hot."

Brenden smiles at that. "Thanks, baby. I see you didn't get to put your dress on yet." He runs his fingers down my face again. "As soon as Bill gets here and says we can go, we'll get you looked at. You might have a concussion from the hit you took."

Craig gets Betsey up on her feet and starts leading her toward the stairs. She's finally stopped screaming, but she's giving me the evil eye as they walk past. Just as he's about to lead her down the stairs, she looks back over her shoulder at me and smirks. Before anyone can stop her, she throws herself against Craig at full force, and they both tumble down the stairs.

Brenden and I jump up from the floor and run to the stairs, to see that they are both at the bottom, a tangle of arms and legs. Betsey moans in pain, while Craig lies there, unmoving, with his arm bent at an odd angle.

Brenden starts down the stairs, and we see Bill poke his head through the doorway. "What the fuck is going on here?" he asks looking at both of us.

Bill ends up calling for back up. They send out more ambulances, another squad car, and a fire truck from Station 4 shows up too. After they were able to untangle Betsey and Craig, they loaded them and John up in ambulances. Bill said it was ok for Brenden to drive me to the hospital and that the cops could take our statements there.

They had to shave a small patch of hair off the back of my head and gave me six stitches to close the gash. At least it was underneath so no one will notice. I've got a few bumps and bruises from being dragged up the stairs and my scuffle with Betsey, but considering the rest of them, I'm no worse for wear.

Once they get me stitched up, Bill comes in to talk to me. "We've got a lot to figure out here, Molly. What can you tell me?" I tell him everything I can remember.

"What made you go to the house, Brenden?" Bill asks.

"I had sent Molly a text telling her to go home and put on a dress I got her and to text me for the address of where to meet me. I figured even if she went home and showered, she'd meet me within an hour." He looks over at me. "I was just in the park two blocks away. When she didn't text me back after an hour, I sent her a text. She said she'd be ready to leave soon. So, I waited another twenty minutes, and when she didn't ask for the address, I called. It rang a couple times then went to voicemail. I got worried, so I got Britney in my Jeep, and we headed for home."

"When I talked to John before they took him in to surgery, he said he was stopping by the house to talk to you when he saw

Betsey go in through your back gate. Any idea what he wanted to talk about?" he asks.

"No." I can feel the confusion on my face. I shake my head. "I told him a few weeks ago to stay away from me. He told me he was just driving by when he saw her." I say looking over at Brenden.

Bill pats my hand again. "We have the report about the interaction you two had outside the karate studio. Don't worry. John admitted what he said there. I'll let you rest a little. Hopefully, the doc will let you go home soon."

When Bill leaves the room, I look at Brenden. "Baby, I promise you nothing is or has ever gone on with me and John Palmer."

"I know, Red. I know." He just kisses the top of my head. "I just wish it was me that were there to save you instead of him."

"He didn't save me," I scoff. "He was tied up; I got loose and took her down. Not every woman needs to be saved or taken care of. Some women are just badass," I smirk at him. Brenden just smiles and shakes his head at me.

CHAPTER TWENTY-EIGHT

Brenden

They only keep Molly at the hospital for another hour after we talk to Bill. Uncle Bill told me that they got the bullet out of John's leg, and he would be out for recovery for a while. Craig wasn't quite as lucky. He broke his left arm, fractured his cheekbone, bruised several vertebrae, and got a pretty bad concussion. Betsey was lucky that she landed mostly on top of Craig. He took the brunt of the fall. She broke her wrist and had to get stitches in her elbow.

The doctor told me to wake Molly every two to three hours through the night because of the concussion, so my plan is to get her home and feed her so she can go to bed early. Unfortunately, when we pull up to her house, we are greeted by Dennis, Suzanna, Sammy, Jared, the twins, Grandpa, and Uncle Bill.

I take a deep breath and look over at Molly. "I was hoping to get you inside and let you relax before bed."

"It's ok, baby. They just want to see that I'm ok," Molly, says grabbing my hand. "Let's go show them that I'm fine, so we can go to bed."

The next thing I know, Molly's door is being pulled open, and her mom is practically crawling into her lap to give her a hug.

"Molly Wally, you scared the bejeezus out of me! Are you ok?" Suzanna doesn't even let Molly answer before she's talking again. "Please don't ever scare me like that again!" she yells in Molly's face and then pulls her in for another hug.

"Ok, Suzanna, let Cupcake out of the car, and you can snuggle her in the house." Dennis says, trying to pull his wife out of the car.

Molly just smiles and lets her dad help her out. Everyone heads into the house like they were invited for a get together. Molly comes in and heads straight for the couch. Jared tells the twins to be gentle with Aunt Molly, and surprisingly, they each curl up next to her and snuggle in. Damn. Seeing her snuggling those kiddos makes my chest tight.

I catch movement in the kitchen out of the corner of my eye, and I see Suzanna unpacking a bag. She sees me looking, "You said on the phone that she had a mild concussion. I didn't know if she would be hungry, but I figured something light would be best. I brought her chicken noodle soup, and I got you both a salad and a corned beef sandwich for you." She smiles.

Dennis claps me on the back. "Is there much damage done upstairs?" he asks.

"I honestly can't remember. We can go up and check it out." Dennis, Grandpa, Jared, and Uncle Bill all follow me upstairs to survey the damage. Surprisingly, there doesn't look to be too much to do. There is a trail of blood from John that needs to be mopped up and an area of drywall that is dented in.

"I'll get the mop and get this cleaned up so you two don't have to worry about it," Dennis says, making his way back down the stairs.

"So, I take it you didn't get a chance to pop the question?" Grandpa asks.

"No, didn't get around to it." I smirk at him.

"You will," Uncle Bill says putting his arm around me.

Dennis comes back up with a bucket and mop. "Why don't you go back downstairs and eat, Brenden. We'll clean this mess up. Next week some time, we'll get this wall fixed too. You let me know if you find anything else that needs to be repaired."

"Thanks, Dennis." I say, then head downstairs.

Sammy catches me in the hallway. "Hey, Jared and I went to the park after you called and picked up all the picnic stuff. Sorry your night got ruined, but I'm glad they got Betsey. Maybe you guys can get on to a normal life now."

"Thanks, Sammy. I really appreciate it," I say squeezing her upper arm.

Walking into the living room, I take in the sight of Molly still snuggled up with the twins. All three are sleeping. "They love their Aunt Moll-wee and their Uncle Bundun," Sammy whispers.

"Bundun? It could be worse, I suppose." I smile at the name.

No one stays too long after that. Sammy and Jared are the first to go, trying to get the twins without waking them up. Uncle Bill takes Grandpa home, and not long after that, Dennis and Suzanna head home too.

I wake Molly to take her to bed. I'm sure she's exhausted, and

I'm hoping she can finally sleep soundly — except for the fact that I have to wake her up every three hours. I help her into a loose t-shirt to sleep in and crawl into bed. For the longest time, I just lay awake listening to her breath, feeling her head lay on my chest. I don't fall asleep until I wake her up the first time.

I wake her around three and again around six. I can't go back to sleep after that one but instead lie in bed with her for about an hour. I can't stop thinking about what happened last night, what she went through and how much worse it could have been. I did have a sweet picnic planned for us last night at the park. It was nothing crazy or too showy. I just wanted to ask her to marry me. It's driving me crazy that that psycho ruined my plans. And this ring is burning a hole in my pocket, so I have to get it on her finger.

I head into the kitchen and see what we have for breakfast. I'm going to make this happen as soon as possible. Luckily, Molly loves to cook and she keeps the fridge pretty well stocked. I decide to go with bacon, eggs, and toast. It's something I cook often, so I'm confidant I won't screw it up. Before I cook, I hop in the shower and get dressed. I'm not in the suit I had on last night, as that fucking asshole, John, got his blood all over it. I realize that wasn't exactly his fault, but I can't stand that guy. I do realize he wasn't the one stalking Molly, but he was still hitting on her, knowing we are together. So, fuck that guy.

I keep clothes that need to be hung up in the spare bedroom closet — at least until we move upstairs. I find a button-down shirt and a pair of black slacks to put on. I've never had the need to wear suits, so it's the best I can do at the moment.

After I get dressed, I go back in to see Molly. It's around 7:30 now, and I know she probably won't sleep much longer. I put the box that had the dress that Sammy helped me pick out for Molly on the bed with a note telling her to get dressed and meet me out back. I set the alarm on the clock radio for ten more minutes, and then I head back into the kitchen. I hate to wake her up, but she's not going to work today. Sammy said she would reschedule Molly's appointments for today or get one of the other girls to cover them.

Molly taught me to make bacon in the oven, which is awesome, because I usually splatter bacon grease all over myself. While that's cooking, I scramble some eggs and make a few slices of toast. I had flowers and champagne set up last night, but since I left everything there, and I stupidly pre-opened the champagne, Sammy threw it out. She said some animals must've made off with the steaks I had made for us also, because they were gone. Sammy was able to save the flowers and brought them in last night, so I put them on the patio table out back and set the table.

I'm just finishing, putting everything together when Molly appears in the doorway. And, just like I knew she would be, she looks breathtaking.

Molly

I really didn't want to get up when I heard the alarm go off. The clock is on Brenden's night stand, and after it buzzed a few times I realized he wasn't there to turn it off. When I reach across the bed to hit the button, I notice a box in the place where I would have expected Brenden to be. He did leave a note on top of the box that said:

Red,

Put this dress on and meet me in the backyard. I promise you can take a long nap later.

Blue Eyes

How can I say no to that, right? I sit there for a second, and the throbbing in the back of my head reminds me of what happened yesterday. Dragging myself from the bed, I head to the bathroom in the hall. The smell of bacon hits me when I open the bedroom door, and my stomach rumbles. I didn't eat much of the soup my mom brought me last night. After I do my business, I turn on the shower. I can't wash my hair yet, which is killing me, because it still has dried blood in it. I carefully whip my hair up into a messy bun and jump into the shower. After I wash myself, I wrap a towel around my body. I brush my teeth and then take my hair down and use a wide tooth comb to get some of the tangles out, gently. I wipe off the steamed up mirror and notice black finger tip bruises on my upper arms. I have a few little bruises on my knee and my hip — probably from my scuffle with Betsey. It's too early, and I'm too tired and banged up to do too much, but I put on some mascara and a little concealer. There's not much I can do with my hair, so I pull my sides back with a little claw clip and head back into the bedroom to get dressed.

Seeing the box on the bed again, I can't believe I didn't throw it open before I got in the shower. I open the box and move the tissue paper. The dress inside is so me. It's a light green swing dress with a full circle skirt and tulle overlay. I love the little cap sleeves and the sweetheart neckline. This is something I would have picked out for myself. Smiling as I slip it on, I zip the side zipper, then I dig through my shoes in the closet until I find some gold jellies. I don't think I have it in me to walk in heels at the moment.

Sneaking down the hallway, I stand where I can see Brenden

taking plates full of food out to the patio. He's singing along to music he has playing, and I'm not surprised it's another Celine Dion song. His musical tastes always crack me up. He'll blast Metallica and rap along with Biggie, then he'll belt out a Celine Dion song. He's completely unashamed, and that makes me love him even more.

Britney's already outside laying in the grass, watching Brenden sing and set the table. I walk to the door and stand there watching him until he notices me.

"You look beautiful, baby." He walks over and takes my hand to help me down the stairs. "I made breakfast."

"Thanks, Blue Eyes. I'm starving. I didn't eat much of the soup mom brought last night." Brenden pushes my seat in and then takes his seat. I don't waste any time before I dive into breakfast.

"I figured, since we didn't get to have our date last night, we could make it work for breakfast."

"Thank you for the dress. It's so pretty. It's something I would buy for myself," I say smoothing my hands down the skirt.

"Sammy may have helped me with that," he says smiling.

"Well, I love it," I smile back.

After we eat, Brenden clears the table. I finish my coffee while watching Britney pounce on one of her toys in the yard. I'm a bit lost in thought when Brenden makes his way back outside. He pulls his chair directly in front of me and sits down. I look at his handsome face. He seems concerned — or nervous maybe?

"Molly," he takes both of my hands in his. "Yesterday, when you didn't show up at the park and I realized something was wrong, I immediately thought the worst thoughts my mind could imagine. And walking into the situation last night, I was obviously worried but also incredibly surprised that you were, for the most part, just fine. I feel a certain amount of guilt that I wasn't here to save you, to prevent what happened from happening at all. But I also feel this enormous amount of pride, knowing that you really did take care of yourself. There's a certain level of relief I feel knowing, that if I'm not here, you can pretty much handle it. But, if I'm being honest, it's a bit emasculating to think you might not really need me."

I'm taken aback by his admission. "Brenden, you are right. I don't need you to be here to protect me or take care of me," I smile at him. "More than needing you, I want you. I'm not in this to be taken care of. I'm in this because I *want* to be with you. I *do* need you, but not to protect me. I need your arms around me and your sweet kisses. I need your silly jokes and your dirty words."

"I want to be with you too, Red. I've wanted to be with you from the first second I saw you. I wanted to claim you as mine from the first time your fingers touched mine. I can't go another day without the promise that we'll be together forever." Brenden stands up, pushing his chair back, and then gets down on one knee. He pulls out this pretty pearlescent glass box. "Open it."

I lift the top and see what I can only describe as the most beautiful piece of jewelry I've ever laid eyes on. "Oh, my God. That is gorgeous." I look up at him in shock.

"Molly Elizabeth O'Brien, will you please marry me?" he asks, like he's nervous that I might say no.

"YES!!! Yes! Oh my God, Yes!!!" I shout and jump on him. Like the twins often do to me, I knock him back on his ass. He laughs and then situates me so that he can sit up. He takes the ring out of the box and slides it on my ring finger.

"What kind of stone is this?" I look at it in complete awe.

"The guy said it was a black opal, and these little stones are sapphires. The band, which you can't wear until we are married, has emeralds on it."

"It's so perfect! It's like a mermaid ring," I say, watching the opal change color in the light.

"That's exactly what Sammy said."

"Great minds, Blue Eyes, great minds." I smile then wrap my arms around his neck.

CHAPTER TWENTY-NINE

Molly

*B*renden insisted I take the weekend off at the salon. I felt fine besides that big, sore goose egg on the back of my head, but I gave in and spent the weekend basking in the happiness of being a newly engaged woman. Taking four days in a row off work wasn't something I had ever done since we opened, but Brenden convinced me to take the time to relax with his mouth between my legs, so who was I to argue. I spent a good portion of the weekend with him buried inside of me, ignoring calls from our family who wanted to come celebrate our engagement. Brenden would answer after a few calls in a row and say, "No company today," before hanging up and going back to what he was doing. Which was usually me.

Mom and Sammy both already knew it was going to happen, so I'm looking forward to showing my ring off to the other girls at work this morning. Brenden had to get back to work too, so he left early this morning to get to the station. I drop Britney off with Ben and head to work a little early, stopping for an iced coffee and muffin, of course.

While waiting for my order, I see Uncle Bill's black sedan pull up outside. He's just getting out when I walk out of the coffee shop.

"Picking up your morning coffee, Bill?" I ask.

"No, I'm actually here to talk to you a little bit, if you've got the time. I called Brenden this morning, and he said he was at work and you would be heading here soon."

"Oh, sure. Here, come on into the salon. No one is here yet." I unlock the door, and he opens the door for me. Once inside, I put my stuff down on the reception desk and ask, "So, what's up?"

"Well, I just had a little bit of information for you about the case." I nod at him, and he continues. "I learned late on Thursday night, that we had had some information brought to light from your ex-boyfriend, Hank. I think that is why Betsey seemed to have gone off the deep end that day."

"What kind of information?" I ask.

"It seems that Hank was visiting his mom a few weeks back and stumbled across something that seemed curious. He said he had gone over to use her printer. He needed to print out some paperwork, and when he was trying to log onto his email to get it, he noticed an email already logged in. It was the email address that he had previously thought was yours. He didn't talk to his mom right away. He said she had injured her knee recently and he didn't want to accuse her of anything."

"So it was Betsey that sent him the emails?" I murmur to myself. Then to clarify to Bill, I explain, "When Hank and I broke up it was because I caught him with another woman. A few weeks ago, when Hank came home from rehab, he came by and apologized about the situation outside the salon back in March. He had been adamant in March as well as when he came by, that I had suggested he be with other women. Then he showed me his 'proof' by showing me emails between him and someone he thought was me."

"Yes, Hank did break that down for us. He said that over the next couple weeks, he would look on the computer for other things. He's found a folder that was locked, and he couldn't open it. I guess he figured out the password for it, and it had all of the photos we have in evidence and a lot more. After he found them, he confronted his mom about it, and she left the house. He called that day to report it and bring in evidence. He said he didn't know why his mom was doing it, but he knew she needed to be stopped."

"That is nuts! So she's been invading my privacy for over a year?" I say.

"He also found information for a private detective. She apparently hired someone to follow you. That's how she got many of the pictures of you out in public. We talked to the PI. He had been under the impression that he was following you to prove you were cheating. We do believe she was the one that placed the camera in your house as well as the first envelope of pictures, based on fingerprints found on those objects and various prints we found in your house."

I'm absolutely floored at all of this information. "But how was she getting in my house when I definitely set the alarm?"

"When we recovered her phone, she had an app from your security company downloaded. My guess is that she figured out the codes. You said originally that you used birthdays, right? The last time, I think it took her quite sometime to figure out the code because it was random numbers. We talked to the security company, and their failsafe is three wrong codes. Then you're locked out for twelve hours. She would do two at a time and stop. I think she had been trying to figure it out for a good month."

"So what happens now?" I say, shaking my head. "What do we do?"

"Well, she's looking at quite a few charges. We've got her on stalking and assault of you and both officers as well as quite a few others. We'll have to wait and see what the DA says." He pats my upper arm. "Don't worry, honey. I don't think you'll have to worry about her bothering you anymore. I'll let you enjoy your breakfast before you have to get to work. Doreen wanted me to also invite you and Brenden over for dinner. She's dying to see your ring." He says chuckling. "Congratulations to both of you."

I had a little time to think about the information that Bill gave me before the girls got there. I called Brenden after Bill left. He had already gotten the gist of the info from Bill this morning when they talked. He's got to work the next three nights in a row to cover shifts for the guys that covered for him while we had our little mini stay-cation. At least I now I can sleep at night, not worrying about someone breaking in.

I still can't believe it was Betsey. I mean sure, she's always been odd, overbearing, and nosy as fuck; but she was truly going to shoot me. Kill me. I still do not understand the whole story, or at least I haven't gotten the whole story from her, and I'm not sure I ever will.

Eventually the ladies start trailing into the salon. They all hug me and look at the ring. Lots of screaming and jumping happen, because we're those kind of girls.

By the end of the day, I've probably hugged nearly every client that's come in. News travels fast in a small town, so half were hugging me to congratulate me on getting engaged and the other half had heard about Betsey going crazy. So many questions were being asked that I couldn't answer, or rather, didn't think I *should* answer. I don't want anything to jeopardize the possibility of her going to jail.

We close in about thirty-five minutes, and I'm in the back office going over some supply order invoices when Sammy comes running in and slams the door behind her. "Hank is out front."

I look up at her, "Am I having déjà vu right now? Because I fucking swear you've run in here and told me that before."

She throws her head back and laughs. "I'll come out front with you this time."

I let out a big sigh. "Alright, lets get this over with." I scribble a note on a post-it and walk with Sammy up front. Sure enough, Hank is sitting in the front, flipping through…well at least it's a Men's Fitness magazine instead of Cosmo this time.

"Hank? What's up?" I get right to the point.

"Hey, Molly, can we talk for a minute?" he asks quietly.

"Sure. Just a second." I go to the desk and give Gracie the post-it note, saying if it looks like things are getting heated, please call Brenden and Bill, with their numbers. Gracie looks at me and nods. "Lets step outside, Hank."

Sammy follows us outside and stands next to me. Hank looks at Sammy and then back at me. "We don't need a chaperone, Molly. I promise I'll make it quick."

"Hank, I'd rather she stay. You might just be here to say your piece, but considering your mom nearly killed me a few days ago, I'm not quite ready to let my guard down."

"That's fair. I just came to apologize. I honestly don't know what is going on with my mom. I don't understand what she was thinking or planning to do to you. I turned over her computer with a bunch of pictures and emails I found," he says, seeming sad.

"I know. I was told that. I do appreciate your doing that," I say. I don't know how he's feeling about this situation. I'm sure he feels guilty for turning the evidence over because he loves his mom.

"I didn't know she was having you followed. After you and I broke up, even though I was raging, I'd get into these depressive states sometimes. I think she was trying to help, at first. Maybe her line of thought was to show me pictures of you on dates to help me get over you. Anyway, I just wanted to say sorry…and congratulations. I heard you got engaged." He sounds sincere.

"I did." I smile. "And, for what it's worth, I really hope your mom can get some help."

I guess he doesn't have anything else to say, so he gives me a small smile and heads down the sidewalk to his car.

"Well, that went much better this time than last time. So not a complete déjà vu," Sammy says.

"You can say that again." Sammy starts to repeat it because she's a fucking smartass. "Shut up." I shake my head.

Sammy opens the salon door and starts to walk in, when I hear, "Hey, Molly." I turn around to see who is calling me, and here comes John Palmer, hobbling up the sidewalk on a pair of crutches with a full cast on his leg. I reach out and grab Sammy's arm to pull her back.

She looks at me and then over to John. "Jeez. They're coming out of the fucking woodwork. You better run inside before Bobby Beaman comes flying down the sidewalk." Bobby Beaman was a boy in third grade who had a crush on me. He was a very sweet kid, but I didn't even like boys. I thought they all had cooties. He would leave notes, candy, and stickers on my desk nearly everyday, but he also openly picked his nose in class and ate it. Bobby Beaman was the Booger Eater. He may have been the first one we nicknamed.

"Hey, John. You do not look like you should be running around on that leg," I say, wondering why the fuck he's here.

"I'll be ok," he says.

"I wondered if you had a minute to talk." He looks over at Sammy.

"You can talk, John. I'm not going inside. I'm staying right here with my girl." Sammy says, before he can even suggest we talk alone.

"Well, I just wanted to say thank you, ya know, for saving my life. But I also wanted to apologize for a few things."

I cock my head to the side and look at him, "You do?"

"Yeah, it's the reason I was actually at your house the other night. I was stopping by to talk to you and apologize for being an asshole outside the karate studio that night. I'm sorry for what I said." He says sheepishly.

"Why did you say it?" I say putting my hands on my hips. Just remembering the way he acted has my blood starting to heat up.

"You know that saying, 'Nice guys finish last?' Well, I figured, maybe if I acted like an asshole, you'd like me. I tried to be nice and ask you out, but you shot me down. Then you started dating that asshole fireman." I'm gonna stop him before he says more that would piss me off.

"Brenden's not an asshole. He might be toward you, but that's because you hit on his girlfriend, propositioned her, and threatened to shoot our dog." My blood is definitely starting to boil. "And my dog doesn't like you, so I gotta say, I trust her judgement."

"I wouldn't have shot her, but she scares the hell out of me. Most dogs do. Dogs can smell fear. Most dogs bark and growl at me because I'm fucking terrified of them," he kind of whispers. "Do you remember in middle school when I got attacked by that Rottweiler?"

"Weren't you and Denny Miners teasing that dog?" Sammy pipes up.

"Denny was. He always did when we walked past that house. But it was fenced in and couldn't get us. Then that day, it got out and chased us. He got me, and Denny kept on running. It took over three hundred stitches to sew up my leg and arms." I had forgotten all about him getting attacked by a dog. I suppose that makes sense.

"Ok John, I accept the apology. And I'm very sorry you got shot trying to protect me. But I also need you to stop asking me out or flirting with me. I'm with Brenden, and we are engaged now." I say, holding up my hand and wiggling my ring finger.

"I understand. I'll leave you alone. I'm glad he makes you happy. See ya." He seems a bit sad, but he turns around and hobbles back over to a big SUV. I guess someone must've driven him. I don't imagine you could drive with a cast like that on your foot.

"Let's get the shop closed. I'm tired," Sammy says, turning again to open the door. "By the way, I'm not coming in until tomorrow afternoon. Alexa is covering for me though."

"Where you going?" I'm nosy.

"Jared finally agreed to go see a doctor about his migraines. They've been more frequent lately, and they're starting to affect work and even his time at home with us. At work, he was in so much pain one day during a fire, he could barely see. The captain said he had to go, or he was going to put him on leave. When they hit at home, he's out of commission. He goes to bed and sleeps it off, and I might not see him awake for another twenty-four hours. It's hard to function like that, and it screws up Mom's schedule when I'm at work." I can tell she's frustrated with Jared. He's the type that won't go to the doctor unless he's got a bone sticking out of his skin. He's stitched himself up with a sewing needle when he got a gash working on his motorcycle.

"Well, hopefully, they'll give him some meds that will help," I say.

"I hope so, or I might have to smother him with a pillow next time," she says with a smirk.

CHAPTER THIRTY

October
Brenden

*L*ooking in the mirror, I slide on my jacket. Then I straighten my tie.

"Looking good, Clarke," Jared says, sliding on his own jacket.

"Thanks, man. You look pretty sharp too," I throw over my shoulder at him.

"I always look good man. What are you talking about?" Jared laughs then slaps me on the back.

My buddy Marc walks back into the room. "I gave the box to Sammy. She gave me this one for you." Marc has been my best friend since about third grade. Molly says he's my Sammy. He and his wife came to Rockplaines to celebrate our wedding day. I felt like this day would never come. It's been the longest four months of my life. When we first started planning, Molly wanted to wait until near St. Patrick's Day to get married. I put my foot down and said she had six months, max, to plan with our moms before I just dragged her to the courthouse.

"Thanks, Marc." He walks in and hands me a little box before putting on his own jacket.

The box has a little card attached to the top that simply says:

"I can't wait to marry you and spend the rest of our lives together. Don't be late. -All my love, Molly"

I open the box to see a pocket watch. It's inscribed with our wedding date on the outside, and when I open it, I find a picture of Molly, Britney, and me. I pull it out and fiddle with it to set the correct time. Then I clip it to my vest and put it in the pocket.

"Alright, fellas, the photographer is outside. She wants you to come out and get a few pictures before the ceremony. Grandpa's already out there," Mom says, walking into the room. "Don't you all look so handsome?"

I turn around and smile at my mom. I see her eyes starting to fill with tears. She's been an emotional wreck this last week. "C'mon, Mom," I say, sliding my arm around her shoulders. "Don't cry. I know Anna did your makeup, and you'll be mad at yourself if it's ruined before the pictures."

She takes a deep breath and straightens herself up. "I know. You're right. I just can't help wishing your father was here." She always get this way when something important is happening in my life. She sobbed through my high school graduation and when I became a fireman. She used to get teary eyed at every Christmas and birthday after he died too.

"He's here, Mom," I whisper to her. "He's always with us. Now, lets go get some pictures taken."

Molly

In all the movies about weddings, you never really see how not glamourous it is putting your wedding dress on. Why did I think I wanted a photographer in here to capture pictures of me trying to cover myself while five women, including my mom and closest friends, try to cover my ass with a mountain of tulle? Wearing a thong, a garter belt, and stockings sounded like a sexy surprise for Brenden when he takes my dress off later. But when you can't wear a bra with your dress, it gets a little awkward and personal. I love my dress though. It's got a very full skirt, a sweetheart neckline, and sheer sleeves that are quarter length. They won't keep me warm, but they look fabulous.

Sammy did my hair into a beautiful, low messy bun, with a thick braid. After the ceremony, I'll take my bun down but leave the braid. Anna did my make up, and I feel so pretty.

It's the Saturday before Halloween, and we decided to have a theme wedding to some extent. We'll have some fun Halloween touches in décor and games like bobbing for apples and a costume contest. We encouraged people to dress in costume but didn't demand it. We're getting married at a local venue that has a big barn and orchard. The weather is unseasonably warm, so we'll have the ceremony outside near the apple trees and then move into the barn for the reception.

Sammy is my matron of honor, and Gracie and Anna are bridesmaids. I thought a lot about having all the girls from the salon be bridesmaids but decided not to get too crazy. Brenden has his best friend Marc, Jared, and Ben as his groomsmen. None of the other girls seemed bothered by the fact that they weren't bridesmaids, but they all came up with a group costume for the reception that they won't tell me about. Sammy, Anna, and Gracie are wearing long, black, sequined dresses. Sammy's is a little different, as she's got a little baby bump growing and wanted a roomier dress. Can you believe she waited until she was twelve weeks along to tell me? The bouquets are gorgeous, all deep red, purple, and orange flowers with a few green mums peeking out. Aubrey looks adorable in her flower girl dress, and Joey looks quite dapper in his little suspenders and bowtie. Even Britney looks adorable with the flower wreath around her neck.

"You look gorgeous, Mollikins! Marc dropped off a little present for you from Brenden." Sammy hands me a little white bag.

I pull out a note card in his handwriting with a simple "I love you" scrawled across it. I pull out a long, black velvet box, and when I flip it open, I see a charm bracelet, kind of like what we got our moms for Mother's Day. There's a little silver dog charm, charms with each of our birthstones, little shears, a Volkswagen Beetle, and a little heart with our wedding date engraved on it.

"Samsonite! Help me put this on." It's so perfect. I have to show it off to the other ladies. Before I know it, the photographer is rushing us out to get some pictures before the ceremony.

Brenden

The ceremony went so quickly that the only parts I can remember are Molly walking toward me on the arm of her sobbing father. Dennis is a big ol' softie. Molly surprised me by having Mrs. Mildred sing My Heart Will Go On by Celine Dion as she walked down the aisle. What? I love that song.

I remember sliding the ring on her finger and kissing her when the officiant told me I could. I know we both read vows to one another, but I can't remember any of that. I just remember looking at her and wiping away tears as they fell down her cheeks, but she never stopped smiling.

One thing I insisted on was having a few minutes alone with Molly after the ceremony. I just wanted to hold her, look at her, and kiss her without an audience. I wanted to enjoy my wife for a few minutes before we're rushed for more pictures and ordered around by our moms. The thing that sold me on this venue was the fact that they had rooms for each of us to get ready in. And I checked. They lock.

When we made it to the end of the aisle, I wasted no time. I turned Molly to face me, then picked her up, and put her over my shoulder. I took off running toward the building we got ready in, with whoops and hollers trailing behind us as everyone cheered and Molly giggled.

The room I was in was closest, so it was the most logical choice. I put Molly down in the center of the room and went back to the door to make sure it was locked. When I turned around, Molly is just standing there with a huge smile on her face. I make my way to her in just three steps and take her into my arms.

"I love you, Red," I whisper in her ear.

"I love you too, Blue Eyes," she whispers back.

We just stand there holding onto one another for a while until I glance up at the clock on the wall and realize we don't have too much time.

"I know someone is going to be banging on the door in a few minutes," I say walking her backward towards the couch in the room. When we reach the couch, I help Molly lower herself onto it. There's so much dress. "This dress is fucking huge. I don't want to lay on you and ruin it." I kiss her lips sweetly, then pull back.

Molly gives me a pout, "I was hoping to make out with my husband a little bit."

"Don't worry, Red. I'm still gonna kiss you." I get on my knees in front of her and start lifting the mountain of fabric.

"Brenden! We can't have sex here." She screeches at me.

"We're not going to have sex here. I'm just going to taste my wife's pussy. I'll give you my cock later tonight," I say, still trying to find the end of this fucking dress. "If I can even find your pussy. This dress is ridiculous baby."

Molly just laughs until I finally find my way under the dress.

When I'm finally able to gather the dress and pull it up and get a look at her, I'm nearly speechless. She's wearing stockings and one of those things with the little straps that hook to the stockings. I can already see a little wet spot on her tiny white panties. A garter with a fireman's ax sits up high on her thigh.

"Mmmmm. You look delicious, baby." I can't wait to take her. "Hold the dress up, Red, so I can eat your sweet little pussy."

I want to rip her tiny panties right off, but I don't want her running around without panties on. So I push them to the side. I waste no time putting my mouth on her. I fucking love the way she tastes, and knowing that she's my wife now has my cock fighting against my zipper to get to her.

Molly squirms and squeaks with every swipe of my tongue. I know she's trying not to make any noise. I slide two fingers into her tight little cunt and pump them in and out, while my tongue teases her clit.

"Brenden..." she pants out. "Shouldn't the first time I come as your wife be on your cock?"

"Fuck. You sure you want it right now, Red?"

"Yes," she says just loud enough for me to hear.

"You don't have to tell me twice." I use my left hand to undo my pants while I keep pumping the fingers on my right hand in and out of her wet heat. Finally, I get my pants open and pull my dick out. She whimpers when I pull my fingers out, but gasps when I push my cock back in, in one long stroke.

"I know I should be slow and romantic, take my time. But someone will be here soon to get us. So, try to be quiet, I don't want anyone else hearing my wife come."

She nods as I start moving in and out of her. I love being inside of her, especially when I have her taste on my tongue.

"Tonight, I'm just going to remove these tiny panties, and you're going to keep these stockings and shoes on. Right now, I'm going to fill this little pussy with my come and then put your panties back so you have my come in you for the rest of the night." I rub my thumb on her clit and she nearly bucks up off the couch.

"Brenden, I'm already so close." I know she's about to get loud. So I slide the fingers I had in her pussy into her sweet mouth and pump into her harder. Her walls tighten almost immediately, and I know the second she starts to come. Her eyes flutter closed, and her pussy squeezes me so tight. Just a few more pumps, and I fill her with my come. I lean forward and lay my head on her chest. I feel her hands rub the back of my head.

"As much as I love feeling my husband inside me, I think we should probably get ready to meet everyone for pictures."

Now it's my turn to pout. "That's fine. Let's go have fun with friends. I'm pretty much going to live inside you for the next week." I sit up and pull out of her slowly. Then I pull her panties over to prevent my come from spilling out of her.

I was right that it wouldn't be long before someone was at the door. We had just enough time to pull Molly's dress down before Sammy was shouting, "Stop doin' it and get outside for pictures!"

Molly

The reception was so much fun, and the food and cake were delicious. The majority of our guests came in costume, and we danced until my shoes were killing me. I didn't exactly wear a costume, but I put enormous fairy wings on. Brenden didn't wear a costume either, but he put an empty water gun in his pocket and kept telling everyone that he was, "Clarke. Brenden Clarke."

When we were ready to depart, we ran through a line of sparklers to the firetruck waiting for us. The guys from Station 4 dropped us off at our house. Ben is taking Britney home with him tonight and will watch her while we're away on our honeymoon.

We barely make it up to our room, and Brenden has my front pressed to the wall while he figures out how to get me out of the dress. "Don't you dare rip my dress, Brenden."

"The wedding is over, Red, what difference does it make?" he asks, still trying to unbutton the little pearl buttons. He's lucky I picked this one with only twelve buttons. Some have them all the way down the dress.

"It's important to me that you don't. I'm saving this dress. We might have a daughter someday, and she could want it." I'm sentimental like that. "If you take it off gently, I'll tell you a secret."

"Fine," he grumbles, and when he finally gets it unbuttoned low enough that I can slide my arms out, I drop the top of the dress so that it pools around my feet.

He helps me step out of the dress and is even sweet enough to pick up my dress and toss it on the leather chair in the corner. I walk over near the end of the bed and wait for him as he removes his tuxedo jacket and his shoes.

I stand before him in my panties, stockings, garter belt, and heels. His eyes run over my body as he stalks toward me, unbuttoning his shirt as he goes. "What's the secret, Red?"

I smile at him. "I didn't start a new pack of birth control. So, every time you fill me with come, there's a chance you might get me pregnant."

The smile that overtakes his face is so gorgeous, and he wastes no time filling me up.

After we make love, we fill the giant tub in our master bath and get in. It's been a really long day, but I'm not ready to sleep yet. We are leaving tomorrow afternoon to go to a beach resort in the Bahamas. I'm not sure how much of the beach we'll even see. I believe Brenden when he says his plan is to live inside me for the next week — especially if he has the chance to knock me up.

I'm leaning against Brenden, enjoying the hot water and the sound of the soft music Brenden has playing on his phone. "So, since we're married now, I feel like there's something I need to ask you, and I need you to be honest," Brenden says seriously.

"Okay…?" I answer back. I can't think of anything I haven't told him that he would need to know.

"I want to know the story of Italian Job," he says with a smile in his voice.

I lean my head back onto his chest and laugh so hard. When I'm finally able to speak, I say, "I've been waiting for this day to come. Ok, so there was this guy I went on a date with, and…." I can hear my phone ringing in the other room.

"My phone is ringing." I start to stand up.

"Fuck that. People know it's our wedding night. Finish the story, Red," he says pulling me back down into the water.

I get comfy against him and open my mouth to talk when Brenden's phone starts ringing.

"What if something's wrong?" I say, worried about any number of people and things that could have gone wrong after we left the venue.

Brenden reaches over and answers the phone. I can hear someone talking on the other end and catch a few words about a hospital. His face gets white as a ghost, and my heart drops. Every possibly horrible scenario is running through my mind. Is it Sammy with the baby? Did Ben fall again? Was there an accident that injured my parents or Celia?

"We're on our way." Brenden says. Then he hangs up the phone and sets it down on the edge of the tub.

"That was your dad. About forty-five minutes after we left the venue, Jared had a seizure and stopped breathing. Some of the other guys from the station were still there and gave him CPR and called for an ambulance. They just got to the ER. We gotta go, baby," Brenden says quietly.

It takes me a second to register what he said. Then I'm out of the tub and rushing to get clothes on. I've gotta get to Sammy.

~THE END~

..for now!

To be continued…

ACKNOWLEDGMENTS

If you made it this far, THANK YOU for reading. I have quite a few people that were in my corner while I was writing this book.

To my friend Casey, you are the Sammy to my Molly. Thank you for being my sounding board, for reading and re reading the book chapter by chapter, sometimes paragraph by edited paragraph. Thank you for being my batch.

To my friends Kelli, Serena, Sara, Megan D. and Julie, Thank you for reading and giving me your feeback. You are all wonderful ladies and I love all your faces!

To my friend Meggy, you are the best! She is a very talented editor and I really couldn't have done this without you.

Last, but certainly not least…. To my husband, Patrick aka Mr. R., you are my rock. Thank you so much for helping me, listening to me, talking through the story, listening to me read the same parts out loud over and over and over. You are wonderful and I love you so much.

ABOUT THE AUTHOR

Carla R. is a married, mom of two that loves to read a good love story. She got it in her head one day that she could write one too, and so she did. She loves to write about strong independent women and the sexy men that love them. When she's not writing, she's usually spending time with her hubby, kids and pets or binge watching The Office ...again. She's a stay at home mom with a caffeine addiction, a part-time hairstylist, and a full-time smart ass.

Follow Carla on social media

Facebook: https://www.facebook.com/authorcarlar/

Instagram: @authorcarlar

Interested in signed copies? Email at authorcarlar@gmail.com